ADRIAN TCHAIKOVSKY

ARTHUR C. CLARKE AWARD WINNER

DOGS OF WAR

HEAD
of ZEUS

First published in the UK by Head of Zeus in 2017

Copyright © Adrian Tchaikovsky, 2017

9 7 5 3 1 2 4 6 8

A catalogue record for this book is available from the British Library

ISBN (HB): 9781786693884
ISBN (TPB): 9781786693891
ISBN (E): 9781786693877

Printed and bound in Germany by CPI Books GmbH

Head of Zeus Ltd
First Floor East
5–8 Hardwick Street
London EC1R 4RG

WWW.HEADOFZEUS.COM

DOGS OF WAR

Adrian Tchaikovsky is a keen live
role-player and occasional actor,
fantasy author and winner of the
Arthur C. Clarke Award.

ALSO BY ADRIAN TCHAIKOVSKY

SHADOWS OF THE APT
Empire in Black and Gold
Dragonfly Falling
Blood of the Mantis
Salute the Dark
The Scarab Path
The Sea Watch
Heirs of the Blade
The Air War
War Master's Gate
Seal of the Worm

TALES OF THE APT
Spoils of War
A Time for Grief
For Love of Distant Shores (forthcoming)

ECHOES OF THE FALL
The Tiger and the Wolf
The Bear and the Serpent
The Hyena and the Hawk (forthcoming)

Guns of the Dawn
Children of Time
Spiderlight
Ironclads
Feast and Famine (collection)

The Private Life of Elder Things (with Keris
McDonald and Adam Gauntlett)

PART I

DOG BITES MAN

1

REX

My name is Rex. I am a Good Dog.

See Rex run. Run, enemy, run. That is Master's joke.

My squad is Dragon, Honey and Bees. They are a Multiform Assault Pack. That means they are not Good Dogs.

I am coming close to the enemy now. I am coming from downwind. I can smell them: there are at least thirty human beings in their camp. I can smell guns. I cannot smell explosives. I cannot smell other dogs or any Bioform breeds, just humans who are enemies.

I am talking to my guns. They tell me they are ready and operational. *All systems optimal, Rex,* they tell me. *Good Dog, well done for remembering,* says my feedback chip.

They are called Big Dogs, my guns. This is a joke by the people who gave me them. They are on my shoulders and they will shoot when I talk to them, because I need my hands for other tasks than pulling triggers. They are called Big Dogs because humans are too little to use them without hurting themselves.

I do not like the thought of humans hurting themselves. *Bad Dog!* comes the thought. I like humans. Humans made me.

Enemies are different.

I am talking to my squad. Dragon is not replying but his feedback signal shows that he is alive and not already fighting. Dragon is difficult. Dragon has his own way of doing things and often he conflicts with what Master has told me. Master says "Dragon gets results," and so I cannot tell him to stop being Dragon, but I cannot be happy with him being Dragon. Dragon makes me uncomfortable.

Honey is talking to me. She is in position with the Elephant Gun. This name is also a joke. Like the other jokes, I do not understand this one. Honey is not an elephant.

Bees is talking to me. She reports 99 per cent integrity. Bees doesn't have or need a gun. Bees is ready. Honey is ready. Dragon had better be ready or I will bite him, even if that makes me a Bad Dog.

I am talking to Master on our encrypted channel. Master tells me I am a Good Dog. I am in position and there is no sign from the enemy that they know I am here.

Master tells me I can attack. Master hopes I do well. I want very much to make Master proud of me.

I tell Honey to start. She has gone crosswind of the enemy camp. I can smell her but they cannot. She talks to her targeting system and I listen in as it identifies targets of opportunity. Honey agrees. They send eleven explosive shells into the camp from a distance of four hundred metres, aiming for maximum disruption. As soon as the eleventh is away, even as the first shell hits, I am moving in.

I see the fire. I hear the sound of human voices, shrill above the explosions. Run, enemy, run.

Bees pulls herself together and attacks, swarming through the camp, eddying away from the fire, stinging everyone she can. Her units do not die when they sting, although they run out of poison eventually. Today she is using the poison that makes the enemy go mad and fight each other. That is her favourite.

I still don't know where Dragon is. I talk to him but he won't tell me.

Honey tells me she is moving in to close quarters. I am already there. Humans are running towards me: I have chosen one of their roads to make my approach. Some of them have guns. Most of them have no guns. I am running on all fours but I talk to my Big Dogs. We choose targets together and I start to kill the enemy, using three-round bursts like it says in the manual. The Big Dogs work hard to compensate for my movement. Sometimes they miss, but more often they hit with at least one bullet per burst. *Good guns*, I tell them. *Good Dog*, says my feedback chip.

One of the enemy is shooting me. I feel his bullets hit me in the shoulder and in the chest, like he was jabbing me with his little fists. My vest flattens the bullets before they can flatten themselves against my skin and muscles. I talk to my database and cross-reference my damage tolerances against his calibre and muzzle velocity. He would have to shoot me in the eye or the roof of the mouth to kill me, though if he shot me in the gut it might take me a few days to heal. That is why I always wear my vest like I am supposed to. Dragon never wears his vest.

Now I am with the enemy and I stand up on two legs to use my hands. The enemy are small. Some of them come up to my shoulders, some of them only come up to my waist. They are screaming and I can smell how frightened they are. I know one of the reasons I was made was to frighten enemies. I am doing my job well. *Good Dog*, says my feedback chip. I am very happy.

I get my hands on them and tear them open. I take the small ones between my teeth and shake them until they break apart, because that feels good. I can smell their blood and their excrement and their fear. This is all good.

Honey is in their camp. She has switched her Elephant Gun to automatic and is laying down covering fire to keep the enemy where they are until I can join her. Bees reports 81 per cent integrity but only 47 per cent venom reserves and says that she is evacuating her empty units as they can no longer assist in the attack. She estimates that she has injected 34 per cent of the enemy population with her poisons and reports that they have not deployed antidotes.

Honey confirms that many of the enemy are now fighting and killing each other and congratulates Bees on a job well done. Although I am leader and that is my task, I do not mind when Honey says these things. Honey is the cleverest of us.

I go into the camp and carry on killing the enemy. Some of them I kill with my Big Dogs but mostly I tear them apart because this is economical. I am saving ammunition. *Good Dog,* my feedback chip tells me.

By now there are no enemies with guns who are shooting at me. Bees has prioritised armed enemies and so most of them have already emptied their weapons into each other.

Some of the enemies are trying to escape, but they are not very fast, and when the big enemies go back to help the small enemies it makes them slower. I am very fast. I run around them and herd them back into the camp. This is another thing that makes me feel good even without the feedback chip.

Honey is talking to me. *Where are the rest of them?*

I tell her I don't understand.

Honey's channel: *Armed resistance has been negligible. These are not rebel fighters. These are civilians.*

I tell her: *These are enemy.* All this talk is going on as we kill them.

Honey's channel: *Our brief was that we would encounter armed resistance from rebel combatants. Is this the wrong camp?*

I take another of the little enemies in my teeth and it squirms and screams. One of the big enemies is hitting me with tiny fists. I transmit to Honey: *Master said to attack.*

Honey's channel: *Rex, this isn't the camp we were briefed about.*

Bees' channel: *Integrity at 74% Venom supply 31% Estimated venom take-up 42% overall; 19% of surviving enemy.*

Dragon's channel: *Target acquired.*

I query Dragon. The small enemy is still in my teeth but I have not shaken it or crushed it. I am unhappy. I do not like what Honey is saying. Something in her words makes me feel like a Bad Dog, not from the feedback chip but from inside me, where the other feelings come from.

Dragon's channel: *Bang! Target neutralised.*

I want to know what target. The bigger enemy is still hitting me and trying to make my jaws open but there is insufficient strength in a human body to achieve that.

Dragon tells me that Master gave him a secret mission to kill one particular enemy. Dragon sounds very pleased with himself. Perhaps his feedback chip is telling him, *Good Dragon*, for finding the special enemy and neutralising him.

Neutralise is a word Dragon uses for special enemies. Other enemies just get killed.

Honey has stopped shooting. I query her, and she transmits, *Rex, I am concerned about insufficient data. I want to contact Master.*

I do not like contacting Master in the middle of a mission. It might make Master think I cannot do my job. It might make Master unhappy with me. Honey is cleverer than I am, though. If she thinks we need to contact Master then I will do.

Master responds quickly; Master has been watching everything through our transmitted video feeds.

I explain that the enemy parameters do not match those we were given. I ask for confirmation that we should finish the mission.

Dragon has reported a successful neutralisation, Master says. *You are in the right place. Good Dog. Finish the mission. Good Dog.*

I whip the small human in my jaws and hear its bones break. I pick up the bigger human in my claws and rip her in two pieces. Honey lumbers in and joins me. She uses her strength and her own claws to tear open the vehicles and the buildings that the enemy is hiding in so that we can kill them. Dragon shows up then, changing the colour of his scales so I can see him, though even then I cannot smell him. He has done his work and just watches as Honey and I kill all the rest of the humans. Dragon is very lazy.

Bees swarms about the outside of the camp and stings anyone who tries to leave. She has changed to the venom that stops hearts.

Bees' channel: *Integrity 67% This squad member will require replacement units shortly; please accelerate the hatching of new bodies.*

Most of the humans who are hiding are the small humans, the immature ones. Master says we must kill all of them.

Honey says this is because we are on a covert operation. Bees concurs. Dragon doesn't care now he has neutralised his target. I don't care because I am doing what Master wants and Master will be happy with me.

I am Rex. I am a Good Dog.

2

(REDACTED)

There is a theatrical anecdote: an actor takes a friend to see a play. Midway through, from their seat up in the gods, he says, "This is a good bit. This is where I come in."

This is where I come in. Right now at this moment I am waiting for my own entrance, to see what role I will play: hero or villain or just a spear-carrier in someone else's war.

Do I say "This is where it starts?" There's nowhere where it *starts*. Life is constant creation, change and destruction. The trick is knowing one from the other. Did it start with the first working Bioform? With the first computer? What about human ingenuity; what about the first time man laid hand on dog and said, *Good boy*?

My involvement with the Campeche insurrection at the start was mostly the day job, but in the secret back rooms of my mind I held committee meetings from which arose a very personal interest in the cutting edge of Bioform research. Rex's Multiform pack was that cutting edge, the first time a lot of that tech was being deployed in the field. And the rumours about where that point was being inserted were already popping up on conspiracy fora worldwide. Redmark's own brand management team was fanning them, in fact, exaggerating them to take the accusations from serious speculation into balls-out flat-earth-lizard-people-land. Everyone knows the best way to bury a story is in another story.

But still, those rumours were gaining traction, seeping out into the more respectable political blogs. No matter how much of a valiant rearguard action the brand managers were fighting, there were going to be questions that couldn't just be smirked away.

So I went to Campeche to see the wolves run.

I did not know how momentous a meeting it was going to be.

I made the same mistake as the others, at first. I thought that Rex was just a *thing*, and bad PR. I thought I would need to spin it as nothing more than "dog bites man" and shut down the program. I was not ready for Rex and Honey and Dragon and Bees.

Bees, especially, I was not ready for.

But I was still young and learning, and I sent myself into Campeche.

3

HARTNELL

"When I was a boy," said Hartnell, "everyone said it would be robots. Robots would fight the wars for us: drones and metal soldiers and tanks with electronic brains. And they'd rise up against us and exterminate the human race, granted, but up until that point it would be robot soldiers on every battlefield on earth. When I was at Yale, half my class were going to be the next big thing in autonomous cybernetics. Now they're wondering where it all went wrong for them." He squinted at his guest to see if she was listening. Her face displayed only a sort of polite interest he suspected was easily faked.

Her name was Ellene Asanto. Four hours ago she had touched down in Hopelchén in a little two-seater flitter that had got the hell out of there the moment her feet touched the ground. Air travel further into Campeche was not advised for health reasons, and so Hartnell had seen her jostled and jolted down a succession of dirt roads, through checkpoints, and occasionally through opportunistic shooting, all to bring her here.

Also, she didn't drink, or she didn't drink to match him. Hartnell travelled with two bottles of whiskey at all times and rationed them religiously, taking minute sips every time true sobriety reared its ugly head. *And where did it all go wrong for me, then?* came the self-pitying thought, but he managed not to voice it. Asanto was the only woman he had seen in some time who wasn't a Redmark grunt or a terrified local, and he was entertaining desperately doomed hopes of getting her to like him.

After all, what nice girl doesn't like a cyborg systems whizz with a diploma from Yale? Except things had gone badly enough for this boy genius that here he was in a war zone playing assistant kennel master for Redmark Asset Protection. There was a lieutenant's patch on his wilfully unkempt uniform, but he was the only man on Redmark's payroll here who didn't carry a gun.

Asanto was some kind of corporate stooge sent to see how Redmark's mad science division was spending its money, or that was the impression he got. He also got the idea that it wasn't his place to question her about it. She was a tall, slender Hispanic woman – not much shorter than long-boned, skinny Hartnell – who had turned up in the beating heart of a Campeche State September wearing a long dark coat, with a white scarf about her neck. With the sunglasses it made her look like last century's film star. He'd offered to take them for her, because he was in his shirtsleeves and still sweating like a pig. Her refusal had been coolly cordial. She had thermoregulatory implants, she had told him crisply. "It's got me job security, if nothing else. Whenever something kicks off near the equator, they send for me. Nobody else wanted this job."

She was still looking at him, waiting for him to get to the point about the cyberneticists, so he blurted, "It was that clusterthing in Kashmir that did it, of course," taking another sip and waving the bottle hopefully at her.

"You can say 'clusterfuck', Hart. I'm not going to start bleeding from the ears."

He blinked rapidly. *Call me Hart*, he had said, so she had and now he felt wrong-footed every time she did. "You, ah, ever see any of the footage that came out of Kashmir?" he asked her.

"I saw enough," she confirmed. Machines hacked by machines hacked by machines until it was all corrupted code and nobody had any control over what was going on there. Abruptly nobody had wanted to hire a robot army. It had looked as though the human race was going to have to make do with waging war the old-fashioned way, with human flesh and blood. But more than a few far-sighted weapons divisions had seen the collapse coming. They'd already been working on options.

Encryption had come a long way since then; there were plenty of cyberneticists saying it was time to give the robots another crack of the whip. Hartnell kept professional tabs on a number of replacement soldier programs aiming for the infallible and perfect robot infantryman. But the footage from Kashmir was still in people's minds. It had been a humanitarian disaster. Parts of the region remained no-go zones because some of those machines were still going strong, drinking in the sunlight and killing anything that moved.

Thus leading to the rise of Bioform infantry; thus to the age of the dog, to Hartnell's posting here and to Ellene Asanto flying out to Hopelchén because someone up the chain was curious, but insufficiently so to actually go themselves.

The air inside the armoured car was like an oven, and smelled of sweat and metal and the sharp tang of his whiskey. When they slowed to a crawl for the hundredth time, he cursed and banged on the ceiling as though trying to encourage a coachman. A moment later the message pinged in his implant: *Arrived*. From Asanto's expression, she'd already worked that out.

"Murray's here?" she asked, because it was a long way to go if the man wasn't going to show.

"Murray?" Hartnell had taken to pronouncing it "moray", like the eel, which had been funny the first time but now he kept thinking of fang-bristling underbites and ambush predators: all too apposite given the man himself. "Hell, I don't know. Man goes where he wants. You try getting him to keep appointments."

Because it was Murray she was interested in, of course, not poor Hart. When the various corporations with interests in Campeche had needed to protect their assets, it was Redmark Asset Protection they had called on. And when Redmark had considered its options for a messy land war in difficult terrain, they had called on Jonas Murray. Because, while Murray's primary qualification might be that he was a son of a bitch – Hartnell's estimation – he was also the leader of the field when it came to directing Bioform warfare.

There was a sharp rap above them and Hartnell wrestled with the hatch for a moment before getting it open. He and Asanto clambered out into thick, humid air that smelled of men and rotting vegetation and animals.

He guessed forty soldiers there, all in the dull grey uniforms of Redmark – only one detachment of the total private security force in the field. The rest – and most of the Bioform packs – were out holding ground across the state. This was Murray's personal taskforce, his clean-up squad. Troubleshooters, emphasis on the *shoot*.

They had a perimeter set up – he saw turret guns and the spidery scaffolding of sensor towers. Instead of buildings there were spaces delineated by the filmy gauze of mosquito netting: zero privacy. Asanto stepped down, and Hartnell could see everyone there trying to decide if she was their problem. Making his own descent, he missed his footing and ended up sitting in the mud, cradling a bottle. It probably hadn't lowered anyone's opinion of him much.

And then the man himself was there, calling to them through the netting, and every soldier abruptly had something else to be doing.

"I suppose you're Asanto?"

Jonas Murray, Master of Hounds for Redmark's experimental soldier program; Hartnell's boss, and the source of the nightmares he was drinking to avoid. Of course, lots of people had bosses who gave them a hard time, but those bosses weren't the Moray of Campeche.

The Moray of Campeche. It helped Hartnell to imagine his superior as some sort of pulp movie villain. That way, he could imagine that, some day, a gun-toting adventurer would turn up and throw the man into a volcano.

There was something appropriate in the nickname, though. When Murray smiled, Hartnell almost expected to see rows of needle teeth, as though he was becoming one of his own Bioforms. He was bald, scalp red and shiny in the heat, and although there were plenty of character lines on his face, he was almost expressionless right now: nothing but a slight, polite curve of the lips to admit to human contact.

He was big: tall and broad-shouldered, a soldier's fitness building on the sort of early-life muscle acceleration that had put all of those personal-trainers-to-the-rich-and-famous out of business a generation ago. Hartnell saw Asanto flinch slightly when he took her hand, but Murray wasn't one for the crushing handshake. His strength was a cobra's, lying in wait until it was needed.

"Colonel Murray." Asanto stumbled briefly over the name, almost saying "Moray" after all. "I've come to see a man about a dog."

Murray looked her up and down, still without any real expression. "My Assets are on their way back to us. Come into my office. I'll see if I can get sight of them for you." His voice was slow with a smoker's roughness.

"Assets?" She followed him into the little mosquito-net complex, Hartnell trailing behind. There was a makeshift surveillance centre set up in there, a half-dozen screens that could fold up into a suitcase.

"That's their official designation," he confirmed. "I guess it makes it easier for the accountants to write them off for tax purposes."

"What do you call them?"

"I call them by their names, Miss Asanto." He took a seat before the screens. They had been showing various stretches of scrubland and jungle and empty, dusty road, but now they began switching and flickering as Murray linked to them. "Speaking of accountants..."

She shrugged. "A lot of investors have sunk a lot of money into Redmark's Bioform division. Can you blame us for wanting to see where all those dollars have gone?"

"I suppose not. Although I'd have thought you could wait until we finish up and pull out." Behind him, the screens starting abandoning the landscape and displaying a familiar figure: Asanto herself. Asanto getting down from the flitter;

Asanto sharing a single glass with Hartnell as they waited for the car; Asanto jolting about beside him in the dim interior. It was one of Murray's standard tactics to put his guests off balance.

"Are you trying to intimidate me?" the woman asked, and Hartnell coughed over his whiskey.

Murray's "Of course not," came a beat too late, meaning, *Yes*. For a moment he and Asanto just looked at each other, and the words *I will call you on your bullshit* were practically written on her face.

Nobody had ever spoken to Murray like that, not the nastiest grunt of Redmark's private army, not the Assets themselves. And yet here was Ellene Asanto patently not giving a fuck.

I'm in love, Hartnell decided, knowing that it was three parts lust to two parts vicarious rebellion, but after four months in Campeche he'd take what he could get.

"You've come at a rather opportune moment," Murray was saying, as the screens returned to their wilderness surveillance. Down one dirt road a patrol of Redmark soldiers were slouching: just unrecognisable stick figures at that distance, with their ID floating over their heads in ghostly green.

"Do tell."

"We got Parvez last night. Emmanuel Parvez."

This got a rise out of Asanto, at last. "Was that actually in your brief, Colonel?"

"Well, when you find the man as guest of honour in a camp of Anarchistas, why not roll with it? I know he worked hard on cultivating his goody-goody image for world media, but he's always been our most outspoken opponent back in Mexico City. When intel told us where he'd be, it seemed impolite not to drop in and say hello."

"May I ask how this intelligence came to you?"

Something flat and hard clicked into place in Murray's expression. "No, you may not, because you're here to see how we're spending your investors' money. Everything else is classified."

Hartnell said nothing, and made sure he stood behind Asanto where any little ticks and twitches wouldn't betray him. Emmanuel Parvez was dead then: he'd known the mission was planned but not that it had actually come off. This wasn't going to play well back in the capital unless Murray and the Redmark politicos could do a very good job of smearing the man. Of course, finding him all chummy with a camp of Anarchista terrorists might just do that.

If that was what had actually happened.

Hartnell had liked being a whizz kid in cyborg interface systems. It had promised him a world of certainty. He could never have imagined what murky and doubt-filled regions it would finally lead him to.

"So, fine," Asanto said, conceding the point. "So where are your 'Assets' then?" She nodded at the screens, which hadn't shown hide nor hair of a Bioform.

Which doesn't mean that much, Hartnell decided. *Dragon could be teabagging the goddamn camera and we wouldn't see him.*

But Murray's small smile was back in place and he just said, "Ellene Asanto, meet Rex."

She turned and froze, and an involuntary "Fuck," slipped out as she saw him.

He was right there, a few yards off on the other side of the mosquito netting, just standing. He'd come from downwind, so that the earthy, doggy smell of him hadn't registered. That meant Murray had ordered him to treat Asanto as *the enemy*, just for a little while, because Rex was trained to make sure his friends knew where he was. From Hartnell's perspective, this was an unacceptably risky way of playing "I've got a bigger dick". He knew what Rex did to enemies.

With his slight stoop, Rex stood seven feet eight inches tall. The flat crown of his head was just a little lower than the parrot guns – his "Big Dogs" – mounted on his shoulder harness. His physique was not a bodybuilder's textbook musculature but something leaner, harder: made to run and fight. And something not entirely human, of course: as happy on four legs as two. Tailoring body armour to the way his shape could stretch and compress in action had been quite the challenge for someone. Asanto must know Rex's particulars: the super-dense muscles, the impact-resistant fibres in his skin, hollow bones that were strong as titanium... None of that foreknowledge helped, when you first came face to face with Rex, and Rex was arguably the *least* scary of the Asset team.

His head was the doggiest part of him, there was something of a bulldog, something of a Rottweiler. One of Hartnell's jobs was to check his teeth. The first time, he'd found it terrifying. One snap of those jaws and he'd be trying to design himself new cyborg hands.

"What's the matter, Miss Asanto?" Murray asked genially. "You were expecting us to keep him in a cage, perhaps?"

Asanto said nothing, eyes fixed on the Bioform while not meeting his gaze. Rex only had eyes for Murray in any event. He was panting slightly in the heat, which made him look as though he was smiling.

"Later on, you'll have to meet the others," Murray continued. "You know we're fielding a Multiform team here? All very new, very exciting. What was your phrase, Hart? 'The future of war enforcement'?"

"I've seen the specs of the others," Asanto confirmed tightly. "Do you let *them* run around like that as well?"

"Within reason. Hart?"

"Ah—" Hartnell started guiltily, mind hauled back from a happier place. "Bees is currently replenishing. Dragon and Honey are on perimeter." He was just reading off the information Murray sent him, making it look to Asanto as if it was business as usual, not some specific gaslighting arranged for her benefit. Murray wanted her to focus on Rex, the acceptable face of Bioforming.

"I see you're not convinced that our Assets are being properly managed," Murray declared, all showman now. "Rex, would you come in here, please?" He could have asked directly, implant to doggy implant, but he was enjoying himself. The Moray of Campeche enjoying himself had enough poor associations that Hartnell felt his heart rate speeding, fight or flight kicking in. *It's not going to be like that time,* he told himself, over and over. *He needs Asanto to go back and give the thumbs up. Nothing's going to happen to her.* And nobody needed to know just how ungracious a host Murray had been in the past, when he'd tired of his guests.

Asanto was very still, watching Rex slip into the mosquito-net compound and lope through to the surveillance suite. His brown eyes swivelled from Murray to Hartnell, Hartnell to Asanto. Was she scared? Hartnell wasn't sure, but Rex would know, and he'd tell Murray if the man asked.

"Hey, boy." Hart reached out and dug a couple of fingers into Rex's skin, feeling the rock-slab muscles there. He knuckled at the dog's jaw and sent a message to his feedback chip. *Good Dog*, it meant.

"Rex, this is Ellene Asanto. She's come to see the good work you're doing with us. Say hello, Rex," Murray prompted.

"Hello, Ellene Asanto." The voice was calm, accentless, a little robotic, broadcast from Rex's implants, not his throat. It also wasn't Rex's real voice. *That* was rough and growling and deep, pitched at a frequency that could turn your bowels to water. Hartnell remembered all the work Murray had put into choosing that voice.

Asanto said nothing. She was masterfully in control of her face and body: nothing in her save her stillness suggested that she was in claw-range of the Bioform, or that Rex could have taken her face off with a single motion.

At last Hartnell gave in and had his implant talk to Rex. *Is she scared?* he subvocalised.

And Rex replied, *Scared a little*. And then, *She is not enemy. She should not be scared.*

Remember how I was when I first met you, Rex?

Rex's shoulders twitched a little, the last remnants of him trying to wag the tail he'd lost. *Very scared.*

"Rex, Miss Asanto wants to see what you can do." Murray shot Hartnell a look that suggested he knew his assistant had been talking where he wasn't wanted. "She's not convinced that you're safe, you see."

Which wasn't what Asanto had said, precisely, and was setting Rex against her again, or at least Asanto would see it that way.

"I enjoy working with people, Ellene Asanto," said Rex's polite robot voice. "I have a stimulating relationship with Colonel Murray and Mr Hartnell."

"I know what, Rex," Murray announced, a terrible mockery of spontaneity. "I'm a bit stubbly this morning. How about you give me a shave?"

"That would be my pleasure, Master."

It was Murray's party piece, the one he always rolled out for guests from head office. He had a real old-fashioned shaving kit to hand, and before Asanto's incredulous eyes the hulking Bioform applied gel and then barbered Murray's chin to perfection using a real honest-to-God cutthroat razor. He made a good job of it, too. Rex could have bench-pressed well over a ton, but he had the muscular control of a surgeon. Men like Hartnell had done well to build him.

It had cost them a lot of dogs. But then you could do to dogs what you could not do to man: you could make them superhuman, give them all the advantages they would need to rule the battlefields of the future. All you needed was sufficient dogs and no real qualms about how many you ruined before you got it right.

Hartnell had always used to say, "I'm not a dog person," back then. And here he was now, watching a Dog Person shave his boss.

"You see?" Murray asked, and Rex kept the razor moving smoothly, even when his master's jaw was working. "Our Rex here is perfectly house-trained. Give it a generation, we'll have a Bioform in every home."

*

Later on, Hartnell took a fresh bottle of whiskey and called, "Knock knock," at Asanto's tent. He'd seen a lamp on inside, and when she unzipped the flap he saw a tablet with its password screen showing. No doubt she was filing her initial report.

"Just wondered if you wanted a nightcap."

She looked at him levelly. "That's the sort of line that works where you come from, right?"

He flapped his lips for a moment before managing a graceless recovery with, "Just a nightcap, honest."

"Come on in, Hart. *Mi casa* and so on."

He folded himself into a cross-legged position, leaning forward to avoid the slope of the wall. "Let me guess, you're really a cat person."

That actually got a laugh out of her. "So you 'got' Parvez. Was that timed to coincide with my arrival, just so I'd have some progress to report?"

"Ah, no, actually. Don't think so. Just happened, you know." He remembered her reaction to the news. "I mean, it's a good thing, right? For the investors?"

"I don't know. Does it actually do anything except up the stakes for everyone? Parvez had a lot of support, and now he might be a martyr. I mean, things were winding down, but…"

"Yeah, but, you know, politics." Hartnell waved a hand vaguely, offering her the bottle. "But it shows that Rex and his team are working as intended, right?"

She took a swig and passed it back. "Killing respected statesmen isn't a bug, it's a feature?"

Hartnell frowned. "I, er, OK, not sure where this is going. I just do the tech, OK?"

"Sorry." She shook her head. "OK then, got a tech question, Mr I-just-do-the-tech."

"Shoot."

"That business in the tent, that was Murray talking through the dog's speaker, right?"

Hartnell said nothing for slightly too long, and then stumbled over the denials. At last he caved and nodded. "Yeah. Rex can get his point over when he needs to, but he's not exactly articulate like that. The words, even the voice, that was the boss having his little joke. I..." He tried a sheepish grin. "Actually, I wish you'd got to talk to Rex properly. He's a nice guy. OK, now you're looking at me like I'm crazy. He's a Good Dog, then. Affectionate, loyal. Considerate, even. I mean, that's why we started with dogs. Dogs are used to fitting in with humans. They know their place – the perfect gangmaster for the other 'Forms and the perfect servant for us, right?"

"That's the advertising pitch," she agreed. "Makes me wonder why your boss was so cagey about letting him speak his mind."

"Oh, that's Murray," and again, *Moray*. "He just likes being in control, like he's directing a film or something."

"Yeah, I'm sure it was that."

Hartnell's grin turned sickly. *It wasn't at all that he didn't want you asking questions, just in case Rex started giving you honest answers.*

4

REX

My name is Rex. I am a Good Dog.

Today we are On The Move. I like being On The Move. This means my squad takes point and runs ahead of Master and my human friends. If there are enemies we will find them and kill them. That means the enemy will not hurt Master.

Master has a new friend, only I am not sure if she is a friend. When she was first there, Master made a joke about being an enemy, so I was going to kill her. Then Master explained the joke to me, so I knew not to.

I whine a bit to myself, because I had been very close to killing her. She had been standing next to Master and that had made me very anxious. I do not like being anxious. Now I know she is not an enemy but part of me remembers that she was one before. That also makes me anxious.

I do not think that Master understands how close I was to killing her. I have not told Master that. *Bad Dog*, says my feedback chip but still I do not tell him.

Honey is talking to me, reporting no contact with the enemy. Honey has found some fruit and is eating it as we go. She thinks I don't know, because we are not supposed to eat On The Move, but I can smell the sticky sweetness of it, almost overripe. We are travelling through farmland at the moment. There are no farmers. The fruit goes to waste. I do not reprimand Honey, even though I am supposed to (*Bad Dog*). I have been working with Honey for many months. Honey is cleverer than I am. I am making a Command Decision: Honey is allowed to eat fruit.

Dragon does not report to me. Right now I can see his long body winding through the fields, changing shade to match the ground. He has no smell, even for me. That makes me whine a bit as well. Dragon is also clever, but not as clever as he thinks he is. But Master likes Dragon. Dragon gets results. *Whine whine whine.*

Master's new friend is Ellene Asanto. She is very strange. I could smell when she was afraid, which was when she first saw me. She wasn't an enemy any more, by then, but she was still afraid. Only enemies should be afraid. So I am confused.

She smells different.

I have tried to explain to Master how she smells, but I do not have words for it in the language they gave me. It is only in my own head I can know how she smells. I am still whining quietly to myself.

Honey's channel: *What's the matter, Rex?*

I do not tell Honey. I am uncertain about Ellene Asanto and I am uncertain about how to talk to Master and I am experiencing relationship conflicts between how Honey and I are supposed to interact and how we actually do. My feedback chip notes, *Stress levels exceeding optimal parameters* and I get a shot and then I am better. I am calm.

Bees is reporting to me. She has been flying her bodies in a wide ring around us, but now she confirms that there is a population ahead like Master showed me on the satellite imaging.

Bees' channel: *Integrity at 99% Venom capacity 99% Requesting permission to perform advance scouting action.*

I query Bees' loss of integrity. We have not encountered any enemy yet.

Bees' channel: (images of avian predators) *I am still teaching the locals that black and yellow means danger* (humour).

I do not understand Bees sometimes. I give her permission to perform her advance scouting action.

Honey's channel: *Is it the new female human, Rex?*

Dragon's channel: *You had her running scared.*

My channel: *She is not an enemy. I don't want her to be scared.*

I do not tell them the rest. I do not tell them that although Ellene Asanto was scared of me, Master was scared of Ellene Asanto. It was not in his face and it was not in his body, but it was in his smell. That made it a secret between me and Master. I have not told Master that I know. That is a secret just for me. I am not supposed to keep secrets from Master (*Bad Dog!*). If Master asked I would have to tell him. But he will not ask, and I know he would be angry if he knew I knew. I do not want Master to be angry with me. That is the worst thing I can think of. *Bad Dog!* says the feedback chip once more, making me anxious all over again. Soon I will need another shot to keep me at optimal performance. Hart will see that I have been anxious and needed too many shots. He will want to know why, and I might have to tell him. That makes me anxious too.

Dragon's channel: *What's the matter, Rex? Are you worried now Master has a new friend he won't want you any more?*

I ignore Dragon. Dragon is wrong, anyway. There is not that sort of connection, between the female and Master. I can smell this. I can smell that there isn't between Ellene Asanto and Hart, too. I can smell that Hart wants there to be. These are all things that I do not want to have to talk about to Master or Hart or anybody. These are things I do not think I am supposed to understand. They do not help me serve Master.

Honey's channel: *Don't worry, Rex. We're just here to do our job. Leave the complex stuff to the humans. If you get confused, I'll help you.*

That calms me, and feedback notes my falling anxiety and tells me *Good Dog* in a small voice.

I talk to Master and report our progress. I talk to my guns and my internal systems and make sure they are working within tolerance. We are past the farm now, entering more trees. The country here is cut up: strips of open ground and strips of forest, and then ground that was farmland and is now wild again, with vines and bushes growing up. Moving on all fours, Dragon and I can pass through this patchwork country almost unseen. Only the great bulk of Honey cannot hide, save where the trees are taller than she is.

Bees' channel: *Contact with unclassified human population* (image of a great many humans, tents, vehicles).

Bees' images are grainy when her units are spread out. It is very hard to know whether these are enemies or friends. I share it with Dragon and Honey and send it to Master for orders.

Honey's channel: *Civilians. We should keep clear.*

I tell her our orders are to make contact with the human population. *Making contact* usually means eliminating them, but that is because all non-friend humans we have met so far have been enemies. I like it when humans are my friends. If they are not my friends then I like it when they are my enemies. I have been extensively programmed and trained to make contact with enemies. We all have. When humans are neither my friends nor my enemies, I am uncomfortable because I have no expectations of what making contact will involve.

Dragon's channel: *We should keep clear.*

I don't know if Dragon really thinks that or if he says it because he knows it is against orders, or if he is just repeating the words Honey said. He does that sometimes. Dragon's job is to not be seen, and to neutralise specific enemies. When he has no specific enemies to neutralise, he does not like to fight. Dragon is very lazy. *Bad Dragon*, I think, but I cannot say that. Only Master or Dragon's feedback chip can say that. It doesn't mean anything coming from me.

The human population is ahead of us. I can smell them very strongly: sweat and excrement and illness and just general many-humans-close-together. I can see humans of various sizes. I cannot see weapons but that does not mean they are not enemies. Only Master can know if they are enemies or not.

I send a query to Master because we are getting very close to the population and we do not have orders. I do not receive a pingback.

I ping Master again. No response.

Whine.

I tell the others that I have lost communications with Master. This is not the first time, but the others times have not been when we were about to make contact with the enemy/not the enemy.

Honey's channel: *Hold our advance?*

Dragon's channel: *Too late. They've seen Honey.*

I stop. My feedback chip notes my stress levels are high again and I get a shot. This time it doesn't seem to help. I can hear human voices shouting. I can smell fear. I can see weapons, but not many and not dangerous to us. Weapons does not mean they are enemies. Only Master can know if they are enemies or not. If they are enemies we must eliminate them. If they are not enemies...

I do not know what to do. I am not used to meeting not-enemies.

Bees' channel: *Orders?*

Honey's channel: *Orders, Rex?*

Dragon says nothing but I know he is waiting.

I ping Master again. No response. I have command. It is my decision.

I decide that we must make contact.

5

HARTNELL

"OK, so update me on where our 'Assets' are," Ellene Asanto asked.

"I told you: they're out on manoeuvres," Murray drawled.

"You keep telling me things, but you're not showing me anything, Mr Murray," she pressed.

He sighed theatrically. "Miss Asanto, you've had the feeds of thirteen different dog packs to play with, from all over Campeche. If nothing else, it should show that there was no need for you to come here in person. I could have had it all linked to your desk back in Silicon Valley."

Asanto played with her scarf. The sight of it sent Hart's sweat glands into overdrive but, true to her word, there wasn't even a bead of perspiration on her brow. "Dog packs are almost a familiar technology these days, Mr Murray. Your Multiform squad is much more interesting. Future of war, wasn't it? Our shareholders have sunk a great deal into this project. You need to give me something to take back to them. They like to know their money's being looked after."

The words tripped off her tongue easily enough, the usual corporate hard line. Hartnell felt that there was more unsaid than said between the two of them, though. Certainly the Abominable Doctor Moray didn't care about Asanto's shareholders. Hartnell had the odd feeling Asanto didn't either.

The three of them were crammed into the belly of a Redmark armoured car, the hatch still open to give them a little air while the camp got itself together. The security firm's human assets were only just beginning to move. The Bioforms had left in the small hours, treading the path the humans would follow, taking point and taking the brunt of any Anarchista traps or ambushes.

When the Bioforms had set out, Murray had given his spiel that Hartnell had heard more than once before.

"War is an expensive bloody business, Miss Asanto," he'd declaimed. "Historically, most expensive in human lives. If human soldiers are to be effective, you need to invest in the sort of training and kit that would bankrupt a small sovereign state, and despite all of that, you can't guarantee that they'll come back in one piece. It's the way war's gone. We're all very concerned about the lives of our people, Miss Asanto. Their deaths impact on Redmark's bottom line, and no doubt trouble the dreams of your shareholders as well."

Her face had suggested that she'd heard this sort of patter before as well. She did a good line in profoundly unimpressed.

"Bioforms are quite literally the soldiers of the future," Murray had told her, as though she was a TV camera broadcasting to a thousand potential customers. "Intelligent, loyal, adaptable, prodigiously durable, and not even that expensive now the tech has been developed. They come in a half-dozen different breeds, with more on the way, each tailored to a particular role. And they're not human; they have no rights. And there are other advantages." His hard smile remained, sharp and clear like glass, letting the murky implications of *that* just hang there.

Now he opened up a couple of screens, pulling them down from the vehicle's ceiling and snapping them rigid. He had a single lens like a blue glass eyepatch that would give him private access to the squad's feeds, but it was the work of a moment to have the images blown up for general consumption.

"This is Rex's feed," he identified. They had a view of open forest, rolling and yawing with Rex's loping quadruped gait. Every so often the view would slow as Rex paused to look and listen and sniff. "Rex is squad leader, the perfect balance of obedience and dominance. His superior genestock's hearing and sense of smell have been ported over mostly intact. He can pick up explosives, drugs, guns, vehicles, people; he can tell if he's being lied to; he can even pick up certain diseases or medical conditions, although that's not something he's been extensively trained in. Still, it goes to show that Bioforms have a future outside the war front, don't you think, Miss Asanto?"

"The shareholders will be pleased," she agreed. "There is still the question of how precisely you're employing them here in the conflict."

"Squeamish, are they?" Murray cocked a cold eye at her.

"Let's just say they want to make sure there's enough space between here and the boardroom that they don't get blood on their hands," she stated flatly. "And that depends on just how much blood is going around."

Murray's face collapsed back to its habitual frown, and the smile he donned after that looked forced even to Hartnell. "Well, I can't show you the actual engagements. That's covered by NDAs between Redmark and its employers. You're

35

welcome to watch Rex go walkies, but after that, you'll have to be content with a blow-by-blow from me."

She nodded thoughtfully. "You're going to tell me that the results will speak for themselves."

"Well, they will." Murray's expansive gesture was curtailed by their cramped surroundings. "We're on the ticket of quite a few interested parties right now: what's left of the Mexican government, the CIA and a cartel of multinationals who were doing well here until the Anarchistas turned up." He shook his head, burlesquing concern. "Really, it goes to show that popular support and grass roots movements are the worst possible thing for democracy."

"Very funny." Asanto didn't seem amused.

"So long as it's us laughing at the end." Murray considered his private viewscreen. "I see Bees is coming up to our target. Time to draw the curtain, I'm afraid."

Asanto shrugged. "And this target is…?"

"We're not sure, but odds on it's Anarchista supporters who got bombed out of Edzna when the army went in. *That*, by the way, was a truly spectacular fuck-up, and if they'd left it to Redmark we'd have handled everything a hell of a lot better, right, Hart?"

Hartnell twitched and then nodded vigorously, mouth full of whiskey.

"So, now…" And Murray froze, for a good three seconds just as if someone had pulled his plug. Then: "Fuck you, Hart, not again."

"Me? What?" Hartnell was abruptly scrabbling for his tablet, trying to work out what was going on. "We've lost signal again?"

"Just cut right out, you incompetent retard." All of Murray's self-assured bonhomie was gone. "Miss Asanto, I'm going to have to ask you to leave."

"Really? Only this sounds like the sort of thing our shareholders—"

"Fuck the shareholders." For a second Hartnell thought Murray was going to hit her, but he reined in his temper at the last moment. "Technical difficulties. I need to discipline my staff. Get out, please."

When she was gone, Murray was already on comms to Redmark's regular human scouts, telling them to get out there and acquire a visual on whatever Rex and his squad were doing. "Fucking *timing*, Hart," he snarled.

"I'm telling you, I don't understand it." Hartnell was checking all channels, isolating the fault. All connection with the squad had gone. It wasn't the first time, and he'd taken the Multiform network apart to try and find the bug. Each occasion, he'd assured Murray it was fixed, but the truth was that he'd searched and searched for faulty code, for enemy interference, for loose *wires* even, and found nothing. Every so often they just lost the squad.

Never like this, though: never just as they were about to get into a fight.

"I guess this'll be the real test of how well they work on their own," he ventured, and then Murray's hand had the back of his neck like a vice.

"If this fucks up, I will fucking kill you," Murray snarled in his ear, "and I will *enjoy* it."

Ladies and gentlemen, the Moray of Campeche. Because this was Murray. This was how he really was. The threat was no idle one. Hartnell had no idea what Murray would be doing with his life if he wasn't ordering animals to kill people in the name of a shadowy junta of ousted special interests. Probably something in investment banking or venture capitalism, any trade where an utter inability to empathise with the people he hurt was considered a positive boon.

Hartnell hadn't wanted to become a field technician for Redmark in the first place, but his bright start at Yale had deteriorated year on year through underachieving, bad decisions and drunken affairs until there was simply no other job he could get that would make a dent in his debts. After coming here and meeting Murray, he'd begun to realise that what he'd signed on for was far, far worse than he'd known. He'd assumed the Bioforms would be the worst of it.

"Jesus." Abruptly the nascent new comms architecture he was putting in place was gone, wiped from the system. "I... I actually think we're under attack somehow."

"From where? From the Anarchistas?" Murray demanded. "You're telling me they have the capability to crack Redmark security and just run around out network without any warning of it? Where the fuck did that come from? Cos they sure as hell didn't have it before."

"Maybe they've got someone on side," Hartnell tried.

"There's nobody they can afford. They're just fucking peasants."

"A rival government, or...?"

"If there's one bunch no gov's going to bail out, it's the Anarchistas. Nobody wants all that back-to-the-soil, back-to-the-soul shit sprouting in their back yard." Murray stood, clenching and unclenching his fists. "Just get it fixed. And find out what the fuck is making this happen."

Hartnell got back to work, trying to re-establish the comms network and watching the system itself dismantle what he

was building. He'd gone over the protocols, he'd tested everything. The whole system was intentionally simplistic, to
allow him to fix things on the fly. Except now he was fighting it, or it was fighting him.

Come on, Rex, he muttered as he worked. *Keep it together,
boy.*

6

REX

My name is Rex. I am confused and uncertain.

As we move in towards the camp, Bees brings more of her units together so she can assemble a better picture of what is going on. We work together on flagging threats. There are guns, but they are few and of limited threat even to Dragon, who anyway is keeping out of sight right now. I do not smell explosives or toxins or other threats, although the combined scent of so many humans together makes it hard to be sure.

I am advancing at a steady, cautious pace now. The ground here is clear, all the plants torn up or trampled. There are many, many tents here, large and small, with many humans all around them. The tents could be storing weapons. We will have to check each of them. If we find weapons, does that make these humans enemies? There should be a link between these things but other humans without weapons have been declared enemies by Master.

If the humans attack us then they are enemies, I think. I say this to the others.

Bees' channel: *Agreed.*

Dragon's channel: *You worked that out for yourself?*

Honey's channel? Honey says nothing, so I prompt her. I am leader, but I feel a need to know what Honey thinks.

Honey's channel: *These humans are very scared of us.*

I know this. The air stinks of them in many ways, but particularly of their fear. Those that have guns are aiming at us, but they are the most scared of all. I tell my Big Dogs to track them, to save time later when we fight.

Honey's channel: *Scared humans may do many things including attack us. Does that make them enemies just because they are scared?*

My channel: *Only enemies should be scared of us. If they are scared of us, they are enemies?* I do not mean to make it a question, but it is one.

Honey's channel: *You are our leader, Rex, but my advice is that we talk to these humans. If they are not enemies and we fight them, Master may be angry.*

The very thought brings a sudden shadow of *Bad Dog!* to me and I start whining again. We are very close to the humans now. Many of them have gone into their tents, perhaps to get more guns. Even more are gathering together in a big crowd in the middle of the camp, including all the small humans – the *juveniles*, my database corrects. I begin making plans for how to attack this large group of humans. *Target-rich environment*, my database tells me.

Bees sends me her proposed attack plan. She will form a perimeter about the target-rich environment to keep it target rich, and will pick off any who try to escape. She has suggestions about how Honey and I should attack and what ammunition we should use, but that is not Bees' speciality.

Dragon's channel: *You don't need me. I'll be sleeping.*

Bad Dragon! I tell him I will report him to Master

but Dragon doesn't care about that. I do not understand Dragon.

I stand up on two legs. The smell of fear and urine increases. I look at the shaking gun barrels. "Down on the ground! Guns away!" I bark. Some of them drop their guns just from the sound of my voice, which is designed to hit specific frequencies that instil panic in humans. A lot of the humans are shouting at me, but I am not listening to them, and my own voice outmatches all of theirs without effort. "Down on the ground! Put down guns! On the ground! Bad humans!"

Dragon is laughing at me. I do not like Dragon.

Honey's channel: *Rex, can I try? I would like more practice in talking to humans.*

I give her authority and she lumbers up, on two legs also. Honey is much bigger than me. She has her Elephant Gun cradled in one arm, and the hand she waves at the humans has claws on it that make my own look tiny. There is more and more fear on the air and the smell of it is making parts of my mind twitch. My mind wants me to do things because I can smell all this fear, and the fear is crying out for me to act on it. It seems a shame to waste all that fear.

"Humans of Campeche," Honey announces. "Do not be alarmed. Please lay down your weapons and adopt a peaceful attitude, and none of you will be harmed. We are here to restore order to this state following the Anarchista insurrection. We are not here to hurt you unless you are in armed rebellion against the Mexican government." She says it in Spanish and feeds me a translation.

What surprises me is Honey's voice. I have heard Honey speak before: her voice is like mine but more so, a deep growl to terrify the enemy. Now, though, Honey has a human female voice, loud but still gentle. I feel myself growing calm just listening to her, even though she is not talking to me.

The humans are very confused and still very afraid. A lot of them are still shouting, but less than before.

"Please," Honey implores them. "We do not wish to harm you, but we have orders to search this area for Anarchista guerrillas. We will now search your camp for evidence of their presence. Unless you are harbouring them you have nothing to fear."

My channel: *Where has this come from?*

Honey's channel: *I downloaded an alternative voice set. I have been waiting to try it out.*

My channel: *I am leader. Why did Hart give this to you and not to me? Is it because you are a better talker?* I am happy to admit that I am not the best with human words.

Honey's channel is silent, and I have a sudden leap in my mind and say, *Hart did not give this to you, Master did not give this to you. You gave it to yourself.* I cannot imagine how she could do this, or why. I am shocked. I know Master would not be happy (*whine*). I am impressed.

There is one human left shouting and he is shouting at the other humans, not at us. He wears different clothes that look darker under the dust. My database comes in unexpectedly with: *Priest*. I do not know what Priest is. The word has no connections in my head.

The Priest human turns to us. "Please, there are no fighters here. These people, they are just hungry; they have lost their homes. Please do not harm them." Honey translates his Spanish for me.

Honey tells them to lower their weapons, and that we will

make a search. The Priest human is standing well within reach of her claws. He is very scared.

"Gather all your people in the centre of the camp," Honey instructs. "No harm will come to you."

It happens slowly, and humans are constantly going back and forth, shouting, crying, being frightened. Once a juvenile runs up to me, pointing a finger at me and making sharp little noises with its mouth. It wants me to think I am under attack. "Pchu! Pchu!" it shouts. I understand: this is a game. I like games.

I bowl the little human over and growl at it, playing back. There is a lot of noise and shouting and screaming. For a moment some part of me that is not my feedback chip is telling me, *Bad Dog!* and I cannot understand why.

The juvenile human is reclaimed and brought to the centre. The Priest is standing apart from the others.

I tell Bees to start the search. Her units split up around the camp and begin checking tents. Individually they are very stupid but they have good senses and the rest of Bees can coordinate what they find, and assign roving unit groups to investigate anything suspicious. This is not part of Bees' combat role: she has designed this behaviour herself based on her instructive programming. *It's like flowers*, she said.

I do not understand Bees sometimes.

Then comms are back and Master is shouting at me to report. He sounds so angry that, for a moment, I cannot. *Bad Dog!* his tone of voice says to me. *Bad Dog! Bad Dog!* my feedback chip picks up.

I give him a summary of the situation. I tell him that we have met humans but they are not enemies and are not fighting us. He is receiving images from my cameras and from Bees. Now I am reporting to him, I am very worried I have not done a good job. I am leader. It is my responsibility to do the right thing when Master is away.

There is a brief burst of return comms from Master and then I have lost connection again. I am very anxious about this. I am also relieved, because it means Master is not shouting at me *now*, even if there will come a time when he will be.

Honey had been sitting down, waiting for Bees to finish, but now she stands up as tall as she can. "Listen to me!" she tells them, still in her calm voice but very loud. "You must leave here immediately. Take nothing, just go. Go now, all of you!" And then she looks at the Priest human and says, "You must lead them away from here. Bad things are about to happen."

I ask: *What bad things?*

Honey's channel: *These are not enemies.*

My channel: *They are not enemies.*

Honey's channel: *What happens if Master tells us they are enemies?*

My channel: *I don't understand. They are not enemies.* Part of me does understand but most of me is confused.

Honey's channel: *What happens if you and Master disagree about whether they are enemies?*

I cringe at the thought. *Bad Dog!* Honey does not need an answer from me. She knows we cannot disobey Master. We have been programmed with a hierarchy and Master is at the top. I do not even like thinking about the idea.

Right then, without comms, I realise that I *can* think about the idea, even though it makes me very unhappy. I do not know what to do with this information.

The humans are running. The Priest is shouting at them.

They are picking up their juveniles and leaving the camp, but plenty are left behind. There are many, many humans. It is still a target-rich environment.

Then there are vehicles coming; even more humans. Down the road on the far side of the camp I see civilian cars. They have lots of humans in them and hanging off them. The humans have guns.

Honey's channel: *The enemy are here, Rex.*

I am suddenly much happier. I am moving on all fours, working out where to take cover. Bees is mustering her units. Dragon wakes up and and slithers into a stand of trees from where he can get a clear shot.

All the not-enemy humans are still running. Some of them will still be in the way. The vehicles are coming very quickly. Already the enemy are shooting. They are only hitting other humans, though: they cannot aim at this range when they are moving.

Honey's Elephant Gun explodes the lead vehicle. She is pushing through the not-enemy, and I tell her she should stay back to use them as cover.

Honey's channel: *I need the civilians behind me so that I can shoot clearly.*

Honey can shoot over the heads of the humans easily, but I let her do what she wants because I know she is cleverer than I am.

Dragon is shooting now. The targeting part of his brain is deciding which are the enemy leaders and he kills them with one bullet each. Sometimes he kills the drivers of the cars. *Bang!* he transmits. *Target acquired. Bang!*

Bees is attacking. She reports to me her losses and her venom stocks. She is using her swift kill venom because these enemies are better armed than the others we fought. These enemies all have guns.

Now there are other humans coming: these are our friends. They have Redmark uniforms. There are not many of them and they do not join in the fighting, but just watch as we destroy the enemy, all of the enemy.

The not-enemy have mostly run away by then.

7

HARTNELL

Rex, sitting on the ground, could almost look a standing Hartnell in the eye. The sheer bulk of him, the density of muscle and bone, seemed to tilt the world in towards him. It was impossible to not be aware of him, Hartnell considered, when he was there with you. Unless, of course, he was hunting you. The thought of being hunted by Rex or one of his kin used to send a chill through him.

It still should, he told himself. *I'm a fool for getting accustomed to this stuff.* Because Murray held their leashes, every one. Murray was just "Master" to Rex, and Rex's electronically imposed hierarchy was slave to Murray's dictates. If Murray told him to kill Hartnell, the Bioform wouldn't refuse – *couldn't* refuse. Following orders was what Rex was all about. It was why they used dog stock.

Rex ran on all fours for preference. He had a dog's blunt head, a dog's dark eyes in which any visible expression was at least half in the mind of the watcher rather than the face of the beast. He sat like a man, though, arms resting on his drawn-up knees. The pose made him look oddly contemplative, as though he was set to fire off a sonnet about the sunset.

What's going on in that big head of yours, Rex? Did the dog-man have an internal life, thoughts and feelings, monologues and debates within that reinforced and cybernetic skull? Or was he like the behaviourists said all animals were, a reflexive Skinnerian machine, mere stimulus and response?

Right now, the question was more practical. *What's going on in that head* came down to whether it was some glitch in Rex's wiring that was screwing up comms. Hartnell had been scanning and testing and prying for an hour now, while Rex sat patiently and panted in the heat.

Ellene Asanto had met the other squad members, of course. Murray had probably wanted some gradual reveal of them, taking her deeper into his cabinet of horrors. Asanto was proving interestingly hard to flap, though. After her initial scare with Rex, she had obviously fortified herself, probably refamiliarised herself with the squad specs she would have access to.

Bees had fascinated her. She had walked round and round the big charging rack where the swarm was recuperating, new units hatching out of pupae to a precise, accelerated schedule.

"They just look like... bees," had been her comment.

"She," Hartnell had corrected absently as he modelled their comms network on his tablet. "She, singular."

"The units form a single functioning artificial intelligence," Murray had explained grandly – he had stitched his good humour back together and put the flayed mask of it back on his face. "Bees isn't the best at abstract reasoning or planning, but her combat and reconnaissance versatility is unmatched."

"And Paddington over there?"

Honey had been sitting, chewing over a thick slab of rations. She glanced up at Asanto's words but didn't say anything. Hartnell had guessed Murray had all the squad on silent for now; he was too much of a showman to want to share the moment.

"Honey provides heavy weapons and close combat support." Murray had gone right up to the great slouched bulk of the bear – *far* taller seated than any standing man could be. He stood in her shadow and slapped her on the flank, his eye on Asanto. *Look at me! I am Master here. I am Man. I have tamed these beasts of the wild.* Except the taming had been the work of a team of bio-engineers, programmers and cyberneticists in laboratories hundreds of miles away. But perhaps it wasn't enough to design and breed and condition. Perhaps it was the *using* of such assets that truly counted as taming. That was Murray's speciality. He had been running dog packs for various private security firms for years, getting a real reputation for efficiency so long as you didn't ask too many questions. The Multiform pack was just the latest killer circus that he had been made ringmaster of.

"And *that* thing?"

Dragon had been lazing in the sun, his dorsal crest up to make the most of it. He was a long, sinuous creature, a good twenty feet from his crocodile snout to the tip of his whip-like tail. His scales were a drab brown right then, which meant he wasn't trying. He was the least humanoid of the three verte-brate Bioforms, only his arms looking a little man-like. One turreted chameleon eye was on Asanto, as though waiting for her to get close enough to lunge.

"He's mostly from anole and monitor lizard stock," Hart-nell had said, and then, because laughs were rare in this business, "Funny thing is, when he got delivered, the docket said, '*anal* monitor', and we were all, 'Hey, we don't want any of *that*, thank you.'" Looking between Murray and Asanto, the grin died on his face, and then his boss had pointedly asked if he didn't have some work he should be getting on with, and so here he was.

"I don't get it, Rex old boy," he told the huge slab of teeth and muscle. Rex flicked an ear at the sound of his voice and Hartnell wondered how much the Bioform actually understood about what he was doing. "Everything's in place. Nothing's messed up. Your head's just fine. Good Dog."

Rex's shoulders twitched and Hartnell's tablet told him the dog-man wanted to speak to him. He opened a channel to his ear implant.

I want a new voice. In his ear, Rex's voice was neutral, artificial, nothing like the gut-loosening growl of his audible speech.

"I, ah…" Hartnell glanced around to make sure Murray was nowhere around, then murmured back. "You want what now?"

I want a new voice.

"We can't really do that, Rex. It's not something we can do."

Rex just watched him with that mutely accusing stare that dogs did so well.

"Well, look. OK, maybe it would be possible – you know, eventually, some time. It's not exactly priority at the moment, though, boy. I mean, you can talk to us just fine like this, and it's not as if you're going to be sweet-talking the Anarchistas for biscuits. This… is a weird thing to be asking, you know?"

Which begged the question of where the thought had come from, and Hartnell saw a shift to Rex's body language: something more defensive, head lower, ears down. A faint whine, almost too high to hear, escaped the great jaws.

Hartnell knew Rex, or he thought he did. How much was real, how much was anthropomorphic thinking, he couldn't have sworn to, but he felt he could read the Bioform. Rex was a dog at heart, after all. He came of stock that had been learning to understand humans for thousands of years.

Watching Rex then, he found himself thinking, *This new voice business, where's it come from? Because Rex sure as hell doesn't want me to ask.* If he posed a direct question, the dog would have to answer him. There was that hierarchy of obedience wired into all the Bioforms, and into Rex most of all. Murray was at the top of that hierarchy, but Hartnell came second.

That thought was not a happy one. Second would not be enough to protect him, if one of Murray's tempers led to him ordering Rex to tear Hartnell apart. Not your usual concern, when dealing with workplace politics, but Murray was like a little emperor here in Campeche. He had his job to do and no supervision at all. So long as he got his results, his corporate paymasters didn't care about his methods.

I know such things about what has gone on here, more unhappy thoughts, and the logical conclusion to them all: *I know too much.*

He looked up into the guileless, brutal face of the Bioform. *You wouldn't hurt me, would you, boy?* But of course he would, if Murray wanted it. He wouldn't be able to help himself.

He wouldn't want to. Hartnell had imagined the scenario more than once, usually just before the whiskey bottle came out again. In his little mental plays, Rex always hesitated, at least briefly.

He scratched the Bioform under the jaw, feeling the muscles there, feeling that strained dialogue inside between man and dog. "You're all right, Rex," he said softly. "You did all right. You're a Good Dog. I'll see if I can get you a new voice."

A kind voice, came the machine interpretation of Rex's thoughts.

Abruptly Hartnell felt very sad, although the whiskey was at least part of that. He took another swig and patted Rex's arm. "You're all right," he repeated.

"Did you find out what went wrong?"

Hartnell glanced up to see Asanto there, silhouetted against the bright sky. Probably he was supposed to say something that would reassure her precious shareholders, but instead he just shrugged and snorted. "Don't you ever take that off?" He waved at her long coat and scarf.

"This stuff has the best anti-bug screen money can buy," she told him, tugging at the scarf a little. Then her eyes flicked to Rex. "So it and its squad were just... on their own recognizance for half an hour?"

"He. Rex is a he." Hartnell abruptly felt frustrated with her, which he recognised as really being frustrated with Murray and the whole bloody business. "Rex and Dragon are 'he's. Honey and Bees are 'she's. Or Honey is, and we tell Bees she is because that's how we think, as humans. Bees is—"

"They, presumably."

He shrugged. "Bees is bees is bees. Seriously, did you actually read the dev specs on distributed intelligence combat units. They were *not* expecting the fucking things to have actual, you know, *intelligence.* They were supposed to be like smart robot sons of bitches – just get a load of them together and have them do some math to make decisions. Only Bees is like a person. Or not a person, not really a person, but you can *talk* to Bees. Bees could ace the Turing test. And nobody in the AI world gives a damn because Bees isn't one of their supermegabrain computers, but just..."

"Bees."

"Actual bees, yes. Sorry, that was a bit of a rant."

She stepped closer, examining Rex. "Tell me about the safeguards."

"Safeguards," he echoed dumbly.

"What happened when the leash snapped, Hart? I take it Rex did more than mark a few trees and bite a postman."

"He..." Hartnell took the next slug of whiskey too quickly and inhaled half of it, doubling over and choking until a firm clap on his back got him breathing again. "Ah, aha, thanks," he gasped.

Asanto was staring at him. Actually she was staring past him at Rex, whose vast paw had just administered the required assistance. "Look at that," she said wonderingly.

"Good boy, Rex." Hartnell coughed a couple more times. "You've seen the specs, you've seen the safeguards."

"I've seen the general lack of them."

"Rex follows orders. He's plugged into a strict hierarchy, does what he's told. And when comms went down..."

"Yes, what then?"

"Rex made contact with a camp-full of refugees. In the absence of instructions." Just the thought made Hartnell's palms sweat, or sweat more. He couldn't imagine what had been going through Rex's limited thoughts right then. He couldn't imagine how it had happened. And the Bioforms themselves weren't much help. It wasn't only comms that had cut out – they had no recordings from the squad's cameras for that period either. All they had was Rex's limited ability to recount what they had done.

"They were looking for bad guys," Hartnell explained. "They did… they did it well, really well. Hear that, Rex? Good Dog, good boy. They went in and, I don't know, somehow nothing kicked off, and Bees was looking for weapons – it was kind of all half-assed because it's not really what they're trained for, but somehow they did the right thing."

"Some sort of secondary programming?" Asanto suggested.

I need to shut up now. I really do need to just nod and shut up. "No," Hartnell's mouth insisted, against the better judgement of the rest of him. "They made the *decision* to play it that way. Which is why Rex here is better than a robot. It's why Bioforms are the future." *Take that back to your shareholders.*

"And then the fighting kicked off," she pointed out.

"Ah, well, yes, but what happened was a shitload of Anarchistas basically drove up and started shooting. And I don't know what the hell they were there for – whether they were going to move the refugees on or they were going to press-gang some new recruits, or they were visiting their sick grandmother. But they saw our boys, and Rex saw them and correctly identified them as hostiles. And the civilians ran for it, and judging by the relatively few non combatant casualties I reckon our squad must've been covering their escape."

"Seriously?" She didn't sound convinced.

Hartnell opened his mouth, but closed it again. "I don't know," he muttered. "Some of the Redmark guys said it, but I don't know." He smiled weakly at the Bioform. "Sometimes I just don't know what goes on in that big head of yours, Rex. And I know you'd tell me if you could." And he saw it again, that hunching and head-hanging that meant, *Please don't ask me;* that guilty dog whine.

"You did OK, boy," he said, and scratched at the Bioform's jaw again. Unlike Rex, he could lie like hell when he needed to, and he sure as hell wasn't saying anything to Asanto about the order Murray had been trying to give, when the comms went down; about the way that Murray was waging war on Campeche State, Anarchistas and civilians alike.

8

REX

Honey is unhappy.

She is sitting still and she is eating; she is not doing anything different. It is only on her channel to us that she is being unhappy. I understand that this is because she does not want Master to know.

We should not keep things from Master. Perhaps I should tell Master about Honey, then? If Master asked, I would have to. Perhaps that means I do not have to unless he asks, or why would Master have arranged things this way? I am not entirely satisfied with my logic but there is nobody I can ask to help me with it. I am whining again, deep in my throat. Something is going wrong. Like Hart with the comms outages, I cannot find it to stop it. I just know the wrongness is there.

Honey tells us we should all eat as much as we can. We are about to go and fight the enemy in a big attack. Master has found where all the enemy have gone, so many enemy that all of us and all our human friends will go and fight them. We have to fight them until there are none left. Then we must dispose of the bodies. Master was very clear about this.

But this is not why Honey says to eat. Honey thinks something else is going to happen. Honey says be ready.

Hart is going through my systems again, checking them one by one. It tickles when he is in my head. Feedback chip, database, comms, targeting, hierarchy, each tested in turn. He says I am in good shape. He scratches me where I like it, under my chin where my jaw implants ache sometimes. I like Hart.

Hart does not like Master. I can smell it on him. Hart also thinks something is going to happen. Perhaps I should tell Hart about Honey. But I don't. I don't know why, but I don't.

Dragon and Honey and I gulp down our ration packs. We can eat lots of things, but ration packs are the best for us. They have Recommended Vitamins and Minerals. Bees has charged up fully from her station, and has requisitioned 20 per cent additional units. Because we are about to fight, everyone gets everything they ask for.

Ellene Asanto walks past and speaks to Hart. She worries Hart. She worries Master and makes him angry. Now she is not scared any more I cannot tell what she is feeling. Her clothes have a buzz to them. Or perhaps it is not her clothes. Perhaps it is her.

Honey's channel: *It is her.*

Ellene Asanto is not in my hierarchy. She is not enemy. But she is not just *a human* like most of them. She is important to Hart and Master. I do not know what she is or how I am supposed to react to her.

I think that means I can investigate her. It will be like the camp when comms went down. I will send in Bees.

Bees' channel: *Clarify objective?*

I tell Bees I want to know about Ellene Asanto.

Bees' channel: *Clarify objective further?*

I don't know what I want to know. I just want to know.

Bees' channel: (uncomplimentary emoticon)

But Bees does what she is told and sends some units to fly close to Ellene Asanto and deploy her special senses: senses that nobody else has. Bees says that even Master and Hart do not know all of the things she can sense.

I speak to Honey: *Tell me.*

Honey's channel is silent.

Dragon's channel: *I think Ellene Asanto is a special objective*, meaning one that he will be given orders about.

Master and some of the Redmark officers are looking at a satellite view of the enemy. To me, it just looks like the other camp only much, much bigger and with more structures. *Village*, says my database. Soon it will be much, much smaller with no structures at all. When the bodies have been burned and buried there will be very little left.

Honey's channel: *All the evidence will be gone.*

Bees' channel: *Receiving... encrypted signal detected... decrypting... decrypting... decrypting...*

All around us, Bees' units come to rest as she links them into her decryption effort, applying more and more processing power. I want to tell her to stop, but she is doing what I ordered, in her own way. Was this what I wanted to find out? I am unable to decide.

Honey's channel: *Be ready.*

I want to ask, *Ready for what?* but Honey is standing up, shaking crumbs off her coat. Honey is checking the systems of her Elephant Gun. Dragon is running diagnostics on his targeting software. Bees is decrypting... This is not even something that Bees is supposed to be able to do.

I look to Master. He is subvocalising to his officers, but my ears can hear his voice still. It is not wrong to eavesdrop if they built me that way. He says, "...keep her busy here, but I need you to make sure you find plenty of weapons, bomb parts, all the usual. It's not as though anyone's going to be asking too many questions, but this needs to look like just another Anarchista training camp..."

Bees' channel: *Decryption complete.* And then I can hear Ellene Asanto's hidden transmission, the one she is sending with her implants and her clothing.

...suspect this is the clean-up. They'll send in the Bioforms to get rid of the evidence of the chem attacks. Please say you can send me some kind of backup, or we're looking at hundreds of civilian casualties at the very least...

I hear Hart swear. His eyes are very wide and they're on Asanto, and I realise he was connected to Bees' systems and he has heard all this.

9

HARTNELL

...suspect this is the clean-up. They'll send the Bioforms in to get rid of the evidence of the chem attacks. Please say you can send me some kind of backup, or we're looking at hundreds of civilian casualties at the very least...

Hartnell went very still, midway through checking Bees' intra-swarm comms architecture. For a mad moment he thought *Bees* was the source of the signal, but then he followed the transmission to the source: there was Ellene Asanto, standing alone in the middle of the camp. Asanto, here on a ticket from the Bioform project's shareholders. And he supposed that was just about plausible, still, if you thought those shareholders were worried about the phenomenal bad publicity they would be exposed to if the wider world found out how the war in Campeche was being prosecuted.

But he kept on listening to Bees' meticulously decoded eavesdropping. Asanto wasn't even focusing on the Bioforms, save as a vector for Murray's atrocities. She knew chemical weapons had been deployed in the area. She was here for proof. The shareholders wouldn't want proof, save to bury it. Asanto was here with a spade, sure enough, but she'd come to dig.

Oh crap, she's not from the shareholders at all. Hartnell looked over at Murray, still deep in his planning. Because there was a big old refugee camp out there, and plenty of the beds were filled with people who had incriminating burns and scars. The powers that be, the government interests and multinationals that effectively funded the counter-insurgency – and most particularly their attack dogs at Redmark – had been savage in crushing the populist uprising here. Media access had been tightly controlled: the rest of the world believed the Anarchistas were terrorists. Only it sounded as though not everyone believed it. Perhaps Asanto was a journalist, but from what Hartnell saw of her tech, she was something more than that.

She's UN deep cover. He was convinced of it. Last he'd heard, the UN had been asking questions about the war in Campeche State, just the latest in a succession of corporate-funded paramilitary actions to combat unprofitable developments across the globe. And they might well ask. The Anarchistas were finished, they just didn't know it yet. The real work Murray was engaged in was mopping up the spillages; getting rid of anything incriminating that might come back to bite those in charge.

Hartnell was uncomfortably aware that he himself might fall into that category. And, as for Rex and the others... They weren't robots. You couldn't just wipe their databanks and have brand-new *tabula rasa* soldiers for the next war. Cheaper and easier to breed new ones. That was the final advantage of Bioforms over human soldiers. In the end, if all else failed, they were disposable.

Hartnell hacked into Murray's personal systems. It was something he'd been doing for weeks now, a trivial piece of secret rebellion for his own satisfaction. Now he went straight for incoming communications and called up a list of past messages.

He saw Ellene Asanto's face. Murray was already on to her. He knew they were compromised. Was he blocking her transmissions, or was he not aware that she was a living wire?

Either way, he would have to kill her. All part of the clean-up. Maybe she even knew it. Maybe she accepted that as the price of her attempt to expose Murray and his paymasters to the world.

"Rex, I think it's time you and your squad got going," Hartnell announced, trying to keep his voice steady. The dog Bioform cocked his head: his senses would read all that fear like a book, but he wouldn't understand the cause.

"You've got supplies, food, ammunition, right, boy?"

We are ready, Rex confirmed in his ear.

"I'm sorry I couldn't install a new voice for you, boy," Hartnell told him, subvocalising. "That would have been good."

I think so too. Hart?

"Yes, Rex?"

What is going on?

Hartnell looked up into the Bioform's so-trusting eyes. "Nothing, boy. It's all gravy. You just go do your job."

Why are you unhappy?

"I'm fine, boy." A lie, and Rex could tell. Hartnell glanced over at Murray, still absorbed. The whole camp felt like a time bomb, filled with armed men awaiting Murray's orders. How much worse if the Bioforms were there when it all kicked off?

Using the transmission channel Bees had isolated, he sent a signal direct to Asanto: *He's onto you.*

And to Rex: "OK, boy, come on, off you go."

Rex's channel: *But we are supposed to attack alongside our friends. That is the plan.*

Asanto had barely reacted. Hartnell had to give her credit for that: she was cool as you like, standing there surrounded by the enemy. *Us, we're the enemy.*

"You head off, Rex. Get going, boy." Hartnell was filing orders even as he gave them, inserting an advance recon job into the queue, engineering a history for it. That was what the Bioforms were good at, after all. Such a step had been in and out of the plan as Murray had formulated it. Would he believe he'd left it in by accident? Hartnell left his boss's electronic fingerprints all over the decision, hoping against hope.

Rex stood, stretched, whined a little. *Hart?*

"You're a Good Dog, Rex. I know you'll do the right thing."

Dragon was already gone, slithering off invisibly into the trees. Honey dropped to all fours and padded away; even she could be surprisingly quiet when she needed to. Bees was... Bees was gone and still here, multitasking.

"Your squad needs you, Rex," Hartnell sent, and Rex was slinking away. If he'd had a tail it would have been between his legs. His uncertainty, and the unhappiness that came with it, was in every movement.

Hartnell busied himself with some final touches of system work, counting the seconds, then the minutes, imagining the Bioform squad getting further and further away from what was about to be ground zero. *How long do I have? How long do I need?* The second question highlighted his major problem: no win condition. He was in a maze full of blind ends with no way out.

There was another presence in the system. Hartnell registered it from its movements: channels opened, files inspected. He backtracked hurriedly, hiding his own tracks as best he could. In the midst of the officers, Murray had gone very still, concentrating on his implants and his eye-screen. "Hart..." His gaze was still focused inwards, but his voice arrived via Hartnell's earpiece. "Is there something you wanted to tell me?"

Hartnell took a deep slug from his bottle. *What does he know? Where's Asanto?* Murray had superior access to the system, after all. Hartnell could get places because he was clever; Murray just strode in by right. Everything Hartnell had uncovered was there for Murray to stumble over.

Ellene Asanto was very still.

In the shared space between their minds, Murray found Bees' fragmentary recording of Asanto's transmission. "Holy *fuck*!" he shouted, startling the men around him.

Asanto had a rifle off the man nearest to her. Murray was shouting orders. Hartnell pushed towards him, desperate to intervene, quarter-full bottle held out like a peace offering...

10

REX

Nothing is where it should be. We have left our friends and are going towards the enemy alone. That was not the plan that was filed with me. But it is what Hart told me. I like Hart. I like Master. Hart doesn't like Master. That is now just one of many things that are making me unhappy.

Honey keeps wanting us to go faster. We are all quicker than any human, even Dragon, even Bees. Bees is around us and ahead of us and behind us and back in the camp, although her signal degrades with distance.

Bees' channel: *They are fighting.*

I keep running. I want to go back. I don't want there to be fighting amongst our friends. I keep running.

Bees' channel: *Master is very angry.*

My channel: *We should go back.*

Honey's channel: *No.*

Dragon's channel: *Not if Master is angry.*

I am surprised. Even Dragon cares about Master, if only because he wants to avoid Master's anger. I want to avoid Master's anger. I want to be there to help Master. I want to help Master not be angry. I do not want Master to be angry with me.

I have stopped running. I can feel my body shaking with

indecision. The rest of the squad watch me. They will do what I say, if I tell them. I must do what Master says, if he tells me.

Honey's channel: *What are the last orders you received, Rex?*

My channel: *Hart said go on ahead.*

Honey's channel: *Then that is what we should do.*

I know Honey is not saying everything. She wants to do things for her own reasons. She wants me to do things, so she gives me reasons that make sense to me. But I trust Honey. Honey is cleverer than me. Sometimes I think everyone is cleverer than me. Sometimes I think even Hart does not understand how clever Honey and Bees and Dragon are.

Then I am receiving a signal. I tell the others to wait. It is a signal from Hart. Hart is my friend. Hart will know what to do.

Hey, boy, comes Hart's voice. It is a recorded message, not him speaking to me. *I hope you're doing OK out there, wherever you are. Look, er, this isn't the easiest thing I ever recorded, right? Jesus...* A pause in which I can imagine Hart drinking from his strong-smell bottle – his Hart-smell bottle, as I think of it. It smells of Hart, Hart smells of it.

Anyway, look, if you're hearing this little message of mine, I guess it means something bad's happened to me and I'm not around any more.

I whine uncertainly.

Probably, and this is kind of what I'm counting on, it means that Murray's had me disposed of because... oh man, Rex, the stuff I know. You can't understand the crap I know, boy, and you should be real glad about that. But I know it. I know the stuff they've been setting loose in Campeche, chem weapons and stuff. You and your squad, you're nothing. But

you'll be what they blame, if they need a scapegoat. Or –
what's the dog version? An underdog? Jesus, I'm rambling.
Another pause, and the little memory of Hart in my head
takes another drink.

Anyway, if you're hearing this then I'm dead, boy. And
I'm sorry. I mean, obviously I'm sorry, but I'm sorry because
they'll need to get rid of you too. Probably the Multiform
program will be declared a success, but that doesn't mean
they need the individuals. Probably you'll get to give your
lives heroically or something. But you know what, Rex?
Fuck them, right? Screw Murray and screw the fucks who
pay him and who pay me.

So listen, I'm giving you a present. Because you're a
Good Dog. I have no fucking idea what's causing the
comms outages, but I know enough to duplicate them. And
I'm giving you your last orders and cutting you loose. I'm
destroying your hierarchies. It's just you now, Rex: you and
your squad.

Go be free, boy. Keep away from anything with a Redmark
logo. Go live a little, before the end.

Run, Rex, run.

I stand for a moment, trying to understand what any of
that meant. Hart is gone. He told me so himself. I see no con-
tradiction in this. But what about Master? We should go back
to Master. We need orders.

Honey's channel: *We have orders.* She has heard Hart's
message too.

Dragon's channel: *We're free.* Dragon sounds different. He
was always least happy about taking orders.

Bees' channel: *Awaiting instructions. Units withdrawn*
from camp. No extra-squad comms.

Dragon's channel: *None.*

Honey's channel: *Rex?* Because I am leader. I am the least clever but I am the one who must decide.

Hart said to run.

We run.

11

(REDACTED)

And, up in the gods, the actor leans back and tells his friend, "And that's where I go off."

That was the first time Jonas Murray killed me. The report I was able to get out was enough to get wheels moving, though, both in the day job and in the back rooms where I did my real business. Abruptly I had more important things to worry about than a little bad PR.

Abruptly I was very, very interested in the cutting edge of Bioform research. I was very interested in Rex and his friends, and discovering what happened to them after they were let off the leash once and for all.

But I'm dead. Murray shot me with his own fair hand.

It's going to take me a while to get back on the stage.

PART II

NEW TRICKS

12

REX

Dragon catches fish.

He hangs in the water, his body moving in slow curves. His mimetic camouflage perfectly matches the mud beneath him so that I can only see the movement, not that which moves.

When he opens his mouth it seems to come from nowhere: teeth and tongue and gaping throat. The fish must know terrible shock and fear in that brief moment. Then he has snapped them up.

The fish are small. Dragon does not share. But we have rations for now. There are small animals, too: my database says rats, mostly. I can catch rats, but I would have to eat a lot of them. Perhaps there are not enough rats.

Bees finds flowers and harvests the nectar. Bees is watching ants (Ants?). She is trying to learn how they milk aphids.

Bees' channel: *Integrity at 96%.*

Bees has had some encounters with locals – not local humans but locals. We are all aware that Bees cannot replenish units in the usual way now that we have run.

I do not like to think of what happened. I cannot stop thinking about what happened. The thoughts come to me on their own. I am cut off from Master. Hart is gone, which

Honey says means he is dead. I do not want him to be dead. He was my friend.

Honey says Master killed Hart. I do not want that either. Master is my Master. Was Hart an enemy? That is the only reason I can think of, but I do not want it. I want my friends to be friends with each other. That is how the world is supposed to be.

Honey is foraging. Honey can eat many different things, and she does. Honey needs lots of food.

We will have to move on soon. Are we still running? We are a long way from Master and Hart and our other friends now. We ran and ran. Honey says we are far enough to have obeyed Hart's last order. Honey says we will have to keep moving anyway because we need food, and we will depopulate the area rapidly if we stay.

There is a question in my mind. It is not a happy question. It is not a question I have ever asked before. It is, *What now?* It is, *What happens next?* It is, *What is the point of us?* All these, in the one question.

I ask it of Dragon. He does not care. Dragon is happy because nobody is telling him to do things. He can laze about in the water and catch fish. He can sun himself. Dragon does not want much.

I ask it of Bees, Bees does not understand the question. *Survival is the point,* Bees tells me. *We adapt and improve ourselves to live. We find ways of continuing.* Bees is considering her own longevity. Bees' units have a limited lifespan. Bees wants to live.

I ask my question of Honey. Honey says she is thinking about it. Honey says that she needs to find a comms channel. *Yes,* I say, *yes, we must contact Master.*

Honey says no. Honey doesn't want to speak to Master. Honey does not want Master to speak to us and tell us what to do.

I want to be told what to do. Honey says I am leader but she will advise me. That is like telling me what to do, only I do not have to do it. Honey says that is better than just being told. I whimper a little, because it is not. It means I have to decide. If I have to decide, then I can make the wrong decision.

Why does Honey want comms if she does not want Master? Honey says she needs to know what is happening in the world. That gives me another question to ask her. *What is the world?*

Honey has tried to explain the world to me. I know there are other places than this one; I remember the pens and the laboratories and the test runs.

Honey says the world is bigger and full of people. Honey says that all we are and everything we have done is part of something very complicated that a lot of people have made. She talks of many things: wars, corporations, popular movements, robots.

It is too much. I don't understand her. I ask her how she can know these things.

She tells me she used to access Master's database every night and learn. She tells me that Master's database was not like our little databases. Master's database was the Whole Wide World. Honey has been learning many things.

I am sure Master did not know. *Bad Honey! Bad Honey!* But I cannot say it. I am not Master.

Dragon slides out of the water.

Dragon's channel: *Good fish here. Good basking also. We should stay.*

Honey's channel: *No, we move on.*

My channel: *Honey, where do we go?*

Honey says nothing for a while. Bees is becoming frustrated with ants and stings some of them. Then Bees is attacked by a bird and stings that.

Bees' channel: *Rex, eat.*

I eat Bees' kill – the bird, not the ants. I am still waiting for Honey's answer. Honey often thinks a lot before she says things.

Honey's channel: *We need people.*

Dragon's channel: *No we don't.*

I am uncertain. I like people, but only if they are my friends. Most people I have made contact with have been enemies.

But if the people are enemies I can kill them. This thought brings a little memory of *Good Dog* from my feedback chip. I do not like killing people. I do like killing enemies. I ask Honey if this is what she means.

Honey's channel: *No, Rex. I don't think we should try and make contact with any enemies. We should only kill enemies if they attack us, do you understand, all of you? If we start killing humans then they will hunt us.*

Dragon's channel: *Let them.*

I agree with Dragon. At least then I would know what to do. If they hunt us they are enemies; we could kill them.

Honey's channel: *There are too many.* Then she tells us a very big number. That is how many people there are in Campeche. She lets that sink in and tells us a far bigger number. That is the number of people in Mexico. Last, she tells us a number that I have to think about hard before I understand it. That is all the people.

Honey's channel: *We are four. There are probably under four thousand Bioforms in all the world. If people decide to destroy us it won't matter how strong or fast we are. So we must not kill people unless they attack us.*

Dragon's channel: *Then we should avoid people. I don't want a new Master. I don't want to be attacked. I want to catch fish.*

Honey's channel: *I want to know what is happening in the war. I need comms. Rex, what are your orders?*

I don't know. But Dragon is lazy and Honey is clever, so I let Honey advise me. We are going to make contact with the humans.

*

We wait.

Bees is back. She has found some humans. She sends us pictures, grainy and unclear, from the handful of units she had there. They have comms: Bees has detected the electromagnetic signature with her special senses.

Bees' channel: *Integrity at 94%.*

Some numbers only go down.

We travel towards the humans: where there are trees we move in their shadow. Once there is a flitter buzzing overhead.

Dragon's channel: *Target acquired.* His long gun has unfolded itself from his shoulder and is pointed upwards. His turreted eyes twitch independently, calculating range. My database tells me that the shot is possible for him.

My channel: *Hold fire. They may not be enemy.*

Dragon's channel: *We have no friends with flitters.*

My channel: *Master has flitters. Our friends at Redmark have flitters.*

Dragon pauses. The flitter is out of range.

Dragon's channel: *They are not our friends.*

I correct him, growling a little. Dragon is not being clever today, I think.

Dragon's channel: *They were never our friends.*

I growl again, watching his crest rise, his long body curve and bunch. His long gun is still deployed, but he is keeping it pointed away from me. My Big Dogs are pointed away from him. Still, I am close enough for him to lunge for me and bite, and Dragon's poison would slow me down a lot and make me sick.

He is close enough for me to take him in my claws and tear him, for me to get my teeth behind his head and shake him. I want to.

Dragon's channel: *We are our only friends.*

His yellow eyes are on me. Bees swarms anxiously around us. I hear Honey's big body shift from foot to foot as she stands tall.

My channel: *Master. Is. Our. Friend.* I make each word very clear.

Honey's channel: *Master is not here. If he is not here it doesn't matter if he is a friend or not.*

She is right. She is not right. It is important for me to know Master is my friend. I am a Good Dog. But my feedback chip is silent. If Hart is dead and Master is not here, who is there to tell me I am a Good Dog?

We continue. We come to the end of the trees. There is a fence, jagged with spikes of twisted metal.

The ground here is scrubby, with bushes that are like tiny trees, a burst of leaves on a stalk. There are animals here. We came from crosswind, so some have smelled us, and they bellow and complain and lumber away a bit, and then go back to eating grass.

Cows; they are cows. My database wakes up: meat, milk, leather, export trade.

Dragon shoots one. The cow's head is knocked to one side, a single hole through its eye. Dragon's database broadcasts ballistics information so we can see how his bullet will have tumbled inside the cow's skull and destroyed its brain. As if it, too, was waiting for his confirmation, the cow's legs give way and it falls over.

I tell Dragon, *This was a cow. It was not an enemy.*

Dragon's channel: *It was not a friend cow.*

My channel: *I am ordering you not to kill things just because they are not friends.* This is my squad. I am in charge.

Dragon's channel: *Cow is for eating.* He sends me information from his database, the same pictures and words I just saw: milk, leather. Meat.

Honey has not said anything about Dragon shooting the cow.

Now Dragon has said it, I am hungry. The dead cow looks good, smells good. Rations do not look or smell or taste good, although they are Good For Me. "Good" is a complicated thing.

I go and get the dead cow, jumping the fence easily. This was a mistake. All the other cows are suddenly very scared indeed and run away from me, when they were not worried about Dragon killing one of them. For a moment I am chasing them, because part of my brain tells me that is what I should do. Then I stop. The others are laughing at me, and I feel ashamed and angry. I bring the dead cow back to the trees: I cannot jump the fence with its weight in my arms so I break through it. The metal barbs do not pierce my skin.

We eat the cow, Dragon and Honey and me. We take turns worrying the carcass with our teeth, shearing off pieces, tearing with our claws. The meat tastes and smells much better than rations.

Bees gathers flowers, dispersing around us and getting into fights sometimes with insects and birds.

Honey's channel: *We must not kill more cows.*

Dragon and I both disagree.

Honey's channel: *Cows are property. Cows have Masters.*

Dragon's channel: *Not our Master. Not a reason not to kill cows.*

I am in agreement with Dragon again.

Honey's channel: *If we kill many cows, the Masters of cows will fight us.*

My channel: *Then they will be enemies.*

Honey's channel: *I have told you about how many humans there are. We would make all humans enemies if we killed many cows.*

Honey is not telling me all the truth, I think, but she is telling me the truth I need to know to make a decision. Do I trust Honey to advise me? I do. It is a strange trust. I trust Master because he is Master. I trust – I *trusted* Hart when he was alive, because he was in the hierarchy below Master. I trust Honey because...

Not because she is in my squad. I do not trust Dragon like I trust Honey.

I trust Honey because she is Honey. I trust her because she has said true things in the past, and when I have trusted her,

I have made good decisions. I trust her because she is clever and she is my friend.

Perhaps I trusted Hart the same way.

I have spent a long time thinking about this, I realise. Everyone is waiting for me to give an order.

My order is, *We do not kill more cows unless I say so.*

I will not say so unless Honey advises me it is all right to do it. But I hope that she will say it is because I like eating cow. Cow is good. Rex is a Good Dog. Good is a complicated word. I am happy with the world.

Then Bees is assembling again, and Bees' channel says: *Humans coming.*

We have not set a watch. I am not a Good Dog. I have made a poor command decision.

They have seen us through the trees before we can withdraw. There are three of them. They have come to see what has frightened the cows. They have come to see what has broken the fence.

They see what: they see us. They have guns.

One of them screams. One of them holds his gun towards us but his hands are shaking so hard he cannot even get a finger on the trigger.

Then they are running away, making lots of noise, and I want to chase them. It is all I can think about and I am out of the trees right then. They run: I chase. That seems right to me.

But Honey is in my head saying: *No! No!* Honey is in my head telling me we must not. Telling me it is not right, and Master is not here and I cannot tell if they are enemies and I am making bad decisions.

Bees is all around me, her units looping through the air. She is not chasing the men. She must have heard Honey's voice too.

The men are further away now. They are running to their vehicle, and my legs twitch as I watch them. My body knows what it wants to do.

Dragon's channel: *Target acquired.*

Honey's channel: *No! No shooting, Dragon!*

Dragon's channel: *They are running, they are the enemy. They will come back with all those other humans you told us about.*

Honey's channel: *No, we need the humans and their comms access.*

Dragon's channel: *Kill them and take it.*

Honey's channel: *No. There is no future in killing humans.*

Dragon's channel: ... This is something he does, a sound that means nothing, but broadcast anyway to show he does not understand. My brain is making that same sound inside my head. It means that, of all the clever things Honey has ever said, this is the one I understand the least.

Honey's channel: *Trust me on this.*

And I do trust Honey. And I do not trust Dragon. *No shooting*, I say, and then, because the blankness in my mind is so great, *but I do not understand.*

Dragon's channel: *What is there to understand? They were enemies. They are all enemies.*

Honey's channel: *Not necessarily.*

Dragon's channel: *They will try to kill us whether or not we kill them. So we should kill them. We should kill them so there are fewer of them to kill us.*

Bees' channel: *I concur.*

I am of the same mind, but say nothing.

Honey's channel repeats: *There is no future in killing humans.*

We all exchange looks, in our different ways. Dragon's turreted eyes tilt to me. I watch the many bodies of Bees as they circle us, their flight as agitated as I feel. Bees sees all.

Bees' channel: *Killing humans is what we are for.*

Dragon's channel: *Killing humans is even what humans are for.*

Honey stands tall, shakes her sloping shoulders and tosses her head. She tells us, *That is not true. Humans are for many things as well as killing humans. That is why there are so many humans. If we are only for killing humans, what will happen to us when the humans here stop fighting? What point will there be in us?*

I do not understand her fully, and I do not think the others do either. We wait, as if Master will suddenly appear and explain everything in ways simple enough for us. I miss him. When Master spoke to us, I was never confused like this.

Dragon's channel: *None of this is right.*

Bees channel: *Killing humans is what we're for.* And an image of a dead bird, the meaning of which is unclear but probably bad. Perhaps she means that having a future is not what we are for.

Honey scratches, then sits heavily so she can look at me, eye to eye.

Honey's channel: *Rex, I would like to make contact with the humans who live here.*

Dragon thinks they will fight us, and says so. I tell Honey that if they attack, they will be enemies. I do not need to say what would happen after that.

13

DE SEJOS

The people of Retorna had been waiting for the war to come for a long time. At first it had been something far away: the Anarchistas had been springing up all across Campeche and Yucatan, forming communes, broadcasting their discontent with the government over in the Distrito Federal and calling the foreign corporations thieves.

Then someone had started the fighting. Marches had turned to riots. Some offices and factories were bombed. The Anarchistas blamed corporate *agents provocateurs*, the government blamed the Anarchistas. The army got involved, which was bad. Then the army got involved on both sides, which was worse.

For over a year, the southern states of Mexico had been a battleground. At first it had just been the government against the Anarchista rebels and their supporters, but chaos had spread like a brushfire. Once the oil installations were attacked and the mines shut down, the corporations had sent their own troops in, over whom the government had no control.

And the corporations were not run by *bad* people, considered Doctor Thea de Sejos. They wanted to protect their property and their people, and they wanted to restore peace so everyone could get on with their lives. She wasn't someone who spouted the Anarchista creed and said anyone taking a foreign paycheque was a traitor. Her own funding came straight from *Médecins Sans Frontières* after all.

The problem was that the multinationals had, of course, turned to private contractors to police their holdings in Campeche and Yucatan and Tabasco. They were corporations, not governments: they didn't have armies. They put the jobs out to tender, because apparently there was a global market in bands of armed men who were interested in freelance regime change. They were not the army. They were not beholden to the government or the people. They did not much care how they went about things so long as they got results and didn't go over budget.

There were no openly confessed Anarchista supporters in the little village of Retorna, but de Sejos still dreaded the coming of the mercenaries. From the stories the Anarchista radio told and from the tales of the refugees, she didn't think the private security soldiers would care about political loyalties. They ran up and down the country like packs of mad dogs.

And she had something here in Retorna that they would want to know about. She had her clinic and her hospice, and inside them she had something terrible.

She went about her rounds there with perfect professional detachment: calm words, a steady hand. She used up her dwindling stock of drugs and she used her phone to take photos of the burns and the discolorations – and the bodies. She hadn't sent the pictures out over her patchy satellite connection. She hadn't shown them to anyone. She was terrified that such communications might be intercepted; that they would be traced back to her and the people of Retorna.

Only two others knew: Father Estevan and Jose Blanco, who had been nominally left in charge when the ranch owner fled north.

Ever since she had worked out what she was looking at, each day at the hospice she had been waiting for someone to turn up with guns and questions. Maybe the mercenaries, maybe the Anarchistas or the government, maybe just the roving bands of displaced men who had decided to take what they needed from anyone too weak to prevent them.

When Luke Perez and his friends came hollering and yelling out from the pasture, she thought the time had come. They had gone out to see what had spooked the cattle, and now their battered old four-by-four was screeching to a dusty halt in the centre of Retorna. They were calling for Blanco, for the priest, for anyone.

Monsters, they were shouting. There were monsters coming.

Thea de Sejos had studied medicine in Guadalajara. She had spoken at conferences in Paris and Madrid. She did not go to church. She had not believed in monsters since she was a child. Not until this war.

She brought Luke Perez to the church – the de facto centre of governance since Retorna became its own island state in the shifting conflict. She sat the man down with Father Estevan and sent for Jose Blanco. Time for a town meeting.

"What are we dealing with here?" was Blanco's first question. He was a big man, who had been working on becoming a fat man before everything kicked off. He had also been a vicious drunk back in the day, but he might just have been the one thing in Campeche the war had actually improved.

"This is their dog soldiers," young Father Estevan pronounced grimly. "That means it's the company military."

Blanco tugged at his moustache. "Luke says he saw just two."

"We don't know how many he didn't see," de Sejos murmured.

"So tell me about them."

She shrugged. "There's absolutely nothing about how they're being used *here*. Redmark and the others are keeping it all under wraps. Worldwide? They're new, they're still experimental. A lot of people don't want them. The whole point of them is, you send them where you wouldn't risk humans, except their detractors say you send them to do things human soldiers wouldn't do. Extermination missions, no conscience, no remorse."

"They've no souls," Estevan added and, at de Sejos' raised eyebrows: "Sorry, party line. Genuine papal pronouncement." Estevan was a very junior priest and de Sejos always figured he had been sent to backwoods Retorna to cool off after having ideas.

"Probably they're here ahead of the regular troops, checking us out." De Sejos' voice shook very slightly, thinking what they might find. "But they might…"

"They might be here to take Retorna off the map," Blanco finished for her. "I shall round up everyone with a gun. Perhaps they are only two."

"They're supposed to be bulletproof."

Blanco shrugged. "They are animals," he said. "Animals die."

It wasn't long before the cry went out that something was prowling about the edge of the town. By then, Retorna's people were mostly behind the strong walls of the church or in the big house that Blanco was taking care of. Blanco himself had every rifle and shotgun in the village ready and loaded and in the hands of men or women who could use them. A barrel was poking out of almost every window.

De Sejos was at the big house, doing her best to keep everyone calm, when she heard Blanco swear.

"Mother of God, what is that thing?"

She pushed to his window for a look. She was expecting something like a man and a dog – like some movie werewolf perhaps. This was different; this was bigger, for a start. It shambled up to the outskirts of Retorna on four feet, but then rose up onto two, tall as most of the buildings in the village. For a moment, de Sejos could only process a vast dark mass, almost shapeless in its lazy bulk. No dog, this.

"It's a bear," she whispered.

"That's not a bear," Blanco spat.

What were bears after all? Children's toys and sad, sagging zoo inmates. De Sejos had thought she knew bears, their shape and size. This thing was like a great pillar of fluid muscle with claws and teeth. And a gun. The weapon was on some sort of harness at the monster's side, but if you had melted down and recast all the rifles in Retorna, you wouldn't have reached the size and weight of that one weapon.

"Don't shoot. If you shoot, we're at war. Don't shoot until we have no choice," de Sejos murmured.

"How stupid do you think I am, woman?" Blanco replied, but without rancour. His eyes were wide and frightened, his knuckles white about his shotgun.

The bear-thing lifted its snout in the air and scratched at itself, claws digging beneath the straps of its harness.

"People of this village, hello!"

The voice was very loud, very sudden, enough to send people scattering back from the windows as though it was an attack. De Sejos heard one shot from the direction of the church, someone's nervous trigger finger betraying them. For a moment the world held its breath, but the bullet didn't seem to have gone anywhere that might trouble the bear.

"Good day!" boomed the bear. Loud, yes, but the voice itself was wholly wrong for the creature: female, soothing, pleasant out of any other mouth. The sort of voice a news anchor or a government spokeswoman might use, or someone selling something. Its Spanish was textbook formal.

"Nobody said they could talk," Blanco growled.

"I suppose they'd have to, to report..." *But that's not what this is.* De Sejos watched the bear's muzzle cast left and right.

"Is it going to... tell us to leave, do you think?"

De Sejos gave him a look. "You think it's here to evict us, like a landlord?"

"I have no goddamn idea what that thing wants."

"We are not here to fight you!" the monster boomed consolingly, as if on cue. It spread its clawed paws wide, but if the gesture was intended to be reassuring then it failed completely.

"So where's the other one?" Blanco demanded. "Or the other *ones*?" Abruptly he pushed away from the window and she heard him passing the word on: keep your eyes out, this might be a distraction.

As distractions went, de Sejos considered, an enormous gun-toting talking bear should win prizes. Under other circumstances she'd have paid to see that.

The village was very silent after the thunder of the bear's words, so the sound of the church door opening seemed shockingly loud. De Sejos ran over to another window, seeing Father Estevan there, closing the portal behind him. He had dressed in his black cassock, every inch the priest, and she saw him cross himself and look skywards.

"Get back inside!" Blanco bellowed at him, and then the bear shifted, and she saw one paw dart for that huge gun, and draw back. Jose paled, and Estevan was holding his hands out, just as the bear had, save that a single swat of one paw would shatter every bone in his body.

"What the hell is he going to do?" Blanco moved with her, window to window, to follow the priest's progress. "He's going to exorcise it?" And, at her look, he went on, "What? Spirits out of swine, it's in the Book. So why not out of this monster?"

"You think Redmark's going to war with bears possessed by devils?" de Sejos asked him.

He gave her an odd look. "You don't see a thing like that, a talking animal, and maybe wonder?"

De Sejos got out her phone and tapped to the camera, zooming in the focus until she could see Estevan clearly, following his progress. His hands were shaking, she saw. Seeing him standing there in the bear's long shadow, she could hardly blame him.

But he spoke, gesturing. Was he driving the beast out, afire with the Lord's righteousness? That didn't sound like the Father Estevan she knew. Perhaps he was offering it some coffee.

The thought of a gun-toting, talking, *caffeinated* monster-bear struck her irresistibly and she bit back a sob of horrified laughter.

The bear replied, hunching low, the rumble of its voice still audible even though it had adopted a more conversational volume. De Sejos thought about that voice – blandly comforting in a slightly artificial way, and surely not designed to be deployed in a war zone. Unless this bear was some bio-engineered diplomat, some first contact specialist of the new animal kingdom. Perhaps Redmark would make all its corporate statements through random fauna now.

At last she saw Estevan nodding, and the huge beast sat down ponderously.

"Sweet Jesus," Blanco exclaimed, "he's tamed it!"

De Sejos shook her head, but *something* had plainly happened out there between priest and monster, and now Estevan was coming back, waving at the big house.

"What does it want?" Blanco yelled at him out of the window.

"It wants..." Estevan stopped and closed his eyes for a moment, and only then did de Sejos see just how very scared he had been, and how he had wrestled with his fear. "It wants to use our Internet connection."

Blanco and de Sejos exchanged dumbfounded looks.

"And food. It has some friends that want feeding," Estevan went on. "Time to slaughter the fatted calf."

14

REX

So we come to the human place. The not-enemy place. *Civilian* is a word Honey uses for them. I query my database: I understand the concept but I have no way of deciding what is civilian and what is not. That was Master's job. How does Honey have a better idea than me? How long do I keep trusting Honey?

They have many guns, these *civilians*. They are mostly bad guns and they would find it very difficult to hurt any of us with them, even Dragon. My database checks every weapon in seconds: make, model, variant ammunition, muzzle velocity. Two of the humans have more powerful weapons that my database classifies as *military*. This is the opposite of *civilian*.

Honey's channel: *They may have received the weapons from soldiers. There has been a lot of fighting near here.*

Dragon's channel: *Target acquired.* He has chosen one of the civilians with a military gun.

Honey says we are not here to fight. Dragon says he is not fighting, just acquiring targets. Dragon says we should be prepared.

Dragon's channel: *We are all we have. We cannot trust these humans.*

Bees' channel: *Encirclement complete*. Bees has surrounded the village in a loose ring. Now her units perch unseen on walls and fences and roofs, watching everything.

Honey's channel: *Say "hola"*.

I say hola. The air is already strong with fear. Some of the smaller civilians are making constant noise; I can hear them even though they are inside buildings. The noise is grating and I want them to stop making it. It is an enemy-noise. The fear is an enemy-smell. I am twitchy and my Big Dog guns twitch with me. I am growling, deep and low in my chest. I want to stop but I can't.

Nobody has called me *Good Dog* for a long time. My feedback chip is silent. I feel very lost.

Dragon cannot say hello. He does not have a voicebox like Honey or I. The civilians are scared of me and scared of Honey but they are far more scared of Dragon. They keep a much greater distance from him than from us. They make odd movements about their throats and chests. I find this funny. Don't they know Dragon is the least dangerous of us? Don't they know that the time to fear Dragon is when you *can't* see him? Perhaps they don't know. It seems strange to me that anyone could be ignorant of such a thing.

Honey's channel: *They are bringing cow*.

Bees' channel: (image of dead cow) (image of dead bird) (image of dead enemies).

Sometimes I do not understand Bees.

Six civilians are dragging a dead cow towards us, through the village. One of the bigger ones there is their leader: I can tell from the way they all stand around him. He gives them the order to drop the cow in front of us and they back off quickly, the leader last. There is a new fear about him and his cow-pullers. His eyes are on me, on the cow, on me. His hands shake and he clenches them into fists.

Dragon slides forward on his belly and the civilians fall back in a wave as though even being close to him will hurt them. He looks at them with his mobile eyes and gapes, showing them his teeth. Really, they are not very good teeth, not strong like mine, but they are very sharp.

My channel: *Hold.*

Dragon is poised over the cow and he hisses in frustration, demanding his share.

I can smell, though: there is a sharp scent to the cow flesh, and my database identifies it in a few seconds: a 4-hydroxy-coumarin derivative.

My channel: *This is a bad cow. It will make us sick.*

Honey's channel: *Hrrm.* Just a burst of static, but deliberate, to let us know she is thinking.

Dragon's channel: *Hrrm.* The same.

Dragon and Honey know something I don't. Probably Bees knows it as well. I am leader, though. I make the decisions.

I tell the humans, "This is a bad cow. Bring us a good cow." Bad, good, those complicated words again. Does the cow care, after it is killed, whether it is bad or good to eat? Do they tell it, *Good cow,* before they end its life?

Honey repeats my words in Spanish.

There is a lot of talking amongst the humans, and some shouting. There is still crying from behind walls. There are still guns in their hands. They still stink of fear. I am still growling. Too many stimuli; too much circumstantial evidence of enemy presence.

Then more cow comes. This is good cow, dragged up by the same humans. They step back from it, their eyes on me.

They are afraid. They are bringing me good cow because they are afraid.

My channel: *It is good that they are afraid...?* I do not mean it to be a question, but at the moment everything I think comes out like that. I am feeling uncertain about everything.

Honey's channel: *It would be better if they would help us without being afraid.*

Dragon's channel: *Never going to happen.* He lunges forwards and tears into the cow, twisting and sawing to free a chunk of it.

Honey's channel: *Rex, I am connected to their satellite link and receiving data. The link has a very low bandwidth and I have access only to unprotected global data sources. I will require a large amount of time to accomplish what I need to.*

Bees' channel: *Can you assist me?*

Honey's channel: *Unknown. I am looking.*

My channel: *Assist with what?*

Bees' channel: *Integrity at 89%* (dead bird). That is what she means.

Dragon's channel: *Bees has a problem. We all have a problem. We are not meant to be here.*

He does not mean in the village. He means in the world.

I tell them, *Master will find us. Then everything will be well.* I am hoping my feedback chip will reward me for trying to believe this, but it is as out of its element as I am.

Dragon hisses, alarming the humans. On his channel he says: *Why all this? We should kill. We should eat. We should be free. Nothing good can come of being near live humans.*

Honey doesn't agree. Honey has hope for something she cannot put into words. Honey has sat down to concentrate on downloads and uploads over the pitiful satellite connection the humans have. I think that we could kill the humans and use their technology without interruption. I think that we could hide nearby and link to their connection without being seen. I think that being here in their village is by far the most dangerous way that we could accomplish our self-set mission objectives, and I tell Honey this.

Honey's channel: *Rex, our mission objectives go beyond simply finding a connection.* But she will not explain them to me. Again, I have to trust her. Again, I trust her.

I look at all the humans with their guns and their fear. "Return to your homes," I instruct them. "There is no more to see here. Go about your business." Then I get the words from Honey over her channel and repeat them, syllable for syllable, in my angry, growling voice. Every word I speak makes them more scared.

15

DE SEJOS

"I can't believe you tried to *poison* them!" de Sejos hissed.

Blanco spread his hands. "And if they'd eaten the damned meat we'd be rid of them, and you'd be saying what a good idea it was."

"No, no I wouldn't. What do you even know about their biochemistry? I'm a *doctor*, Jose, and I don't even know if they *have* a biochemistry! They could be all machine in there where it counts."

They were in the church, tucked away in the vestry, trying very hard to be angry at each other without letting the monsters hear them. And probably they still could. Probably that dog-thing that was their leader could simply cock its cybernetic ears and hear every whispered conversation in Retorna.

"Thea, I think you've studied these creatures…?" Father Estevan offered, hands up for a little peace on holy ground.

"Studied is too strong a phrase," she told him. "When we heard they were using the dog packs, I found out what I could. I figured we'd be meeting them sooner or later. But this is cutting edge technology, and it's proprietary – there are maybe three or four weapons labs that are turning these monsters out, and they don't exactly publish their research in the reputable journals. But yes, I learned something."

"Because, well, '*dog* packs', and obviously we have a handsome fellow out there that has more than a little hound in him," Estevan said, "but the others…"

"The dogs were the first," de Sejos confirmed. "They've been using engineered dog soldiers for almost a decade now. Most of the pictures I saw weren't as humanoid or as big as this one, but dogs come pre-wired, almost, to work with people. The way I read it, dogs ev— dogs see the world more like people than like wolves…"

"You can use the 'e'-word, Thea," Estevan said mildly. "Mother Church has gone back and forth on the issue, I know, but I try to keep an open mind."

Blanco snorted, but Thea nodded gratefully. "Anyway, once the dogs had been used as security and as soldiers, the labs started looking at other possibilities. This must be the first time some of these – what, breeds? Models? – have been used. They'll each have a purpose, I'd guess."

"I…" Estevan grimaced. "This probably won't help things, but I think there may be more here than just those three." At their wide-eyed looks, he explained, "We seem to have something of an infestation of bees. A lot of people have remarked on it. Only they don't move like bees, and when someone brought me one in a bottle, it didn't look like any indigenous species." He shrugged. "I'm sorry, I always had something of an interest."

"What did you do," de Sejos asked him, "with the bee they brought you?"

"Oh, I let it go," Estevan assured her hurriedly. "But, well, we suddenly have a lot of foreign bees, and I was wondering if they could…?"

"I don't know," de Sejos admitted. "I don't think I read anything about *bees*."

"My name is Legion..." the priest mused.

"If only you could just... drive them out," Blanco said. There was an edge of desperation in his voice. "What are we going to do? They'll kill everyone here."

"We don't know what they want," de Sejos countered. At his exasperated look, she added, "I know, I know it's not likely to be anything good. But right now all they've asked us for was food, and we have cattle. We have a great many head of cattle around here, enough to keep their bellies full for a long time. And they want our satellite link for some reason. So maybe they're... lost?" She heard her own lack of conviction. "But the thing is, they haven't just gone mad and slaughtered everyone."

"Yet," Blanco put in darkly.

"Yet," she agreed. "So I think what it comes down to is not what they want, it's what their masters want. I think they're waiting for orders."

"What orders?" he demanded.

She shrugged. "Well, we could ask them."

*

Father Estevan had volunteered, but in the end it was de Sejos who stepped out into the evening light and crossed the bare ground to the three monstrous forms. The lizard creature had been down the well to guzzle their water, and now was lying apparently asleep. The bear sat, staring up at the clear sky. The dog had been lying down, but as she approached he abruptly rolled over and came up on all fours, staring at her.

Thea had always lived in houses with dogs. Her parents had never owned fewer than three at a time, and big dogs too, ex-racing greyhounds and Alsatians. She had always found some people's skittishness about the animals an object of amusement. Now she felt it in her bones. The low growl of the animal went right through her at the precise pitch to turn her insides to water. She kept her eyes low, away from its stare, its slightly parted lips and the sharp teeth beyond.

"I wondered if I could talk to you," she got out past the hammering in her chest.

She saw it shift forwards. Her downward gaze gave her an ideal opportunity to admire its front paws – no, its hands. They had claws on them that seemed more cat than dog: no imagination required to envisage them ripping into her. The smell of it was urine and sweat and blood.

"What do you want?"

She was in its shadow, virtually standing between its paws. Its carrion breath washed over her with each exhalation, but not with its words. The voice came from its throat without being shaped by lips, the Spanish oddly inflected: just another foreign tourist reading from a phrase book. With that understanding came the revelation that someone had *given* it that voice, to make it even more fearsome than it already was. No matter what the dog wanted to say, it would say it as a rumbling threat.

"I was curious." She wondered what its vocabulary actually was, and how much it could understand. Was there a mind in there, like a human's? All she'd read seemed to indicate that the Bioform soldiers had organic brains, not just computers inside them. "I wanted to ask questions."

It leant closer, the blunt muzzle nudging her shoulder slightly. She had a moment of insanity where she was going to reach up to it, like she had to a soppy old bloodhound her parents had once owned, that liked its jowls scratching. *Only Caesar wouldn't take my hand off for doing it.*

"What questions?" it growled, the sound vibrating through her, freezing her up and making it hard for her to breathe.

"You..." Her voice was shaking despite herself.

"Who are you?"

"I... Please..."

"Please what?" the dog demanded.

"Please stand back from me. You're frightening me," she got out, though the words became a squeak at the end. When it didn't immediately descend on her with tooth and claw, she added, "I'm sorry. It's how they made you, I suppose."

The dog was still and silent for what seemed like a long time, so that at last she risked looking up, and met its gaze. Its eyes were the most canine thing about it, just like the dogs she had known. Did it have some idea of the life it might have enjoyed, if not for the laboratory? Would it fetch sticks, if it had the choice? Go for walks and lie by the fire?

She could read a lot in there, but she knew she was inventing it. The creature before her was made in a weapons lab, more loyal than a robot and cheaper than a man.

But it shuffled back a few steps nonetheless.

"My name is Doctor Thea de Sejos," she told it. "Do you know what a doctor is?"

"Yes." It shuffled back and forth, and instead of the growl she heard a thin whine cut the air, so delicate a sound she could hardly believe it came from the massive beast in front of her. "I am Rex. I lead."

Her breathing and her heartbeat were beginning to return to tolerable levels. "Hello, Rex. Are you able to answer my questions?"

Again that whining, a sound that was all dog, all unhappy. Then it was turning away from her, shaking its heavy-jawed head. "Talk to Honey," it told her. "Honey knows things."

She stepped very carefully past Rex, feeling his mutely suffering eyes on her, and craned her neck to look at the bear.

"Excuse me," she asked, "I assume you're Honey."

That massive, shaggy head peered down at her almost myopically. When it spoke – again a facility that owed nothing to any movements of lip or jaw – its voice was pleasant and female still, but of a modest volume. The discrepancy between what was seen and what was heard left de Sejos disoriented. She almost felt that if she looked down the bear's cavernous throat she would see some well-dressed woman down in its belly, smiling her television-white smile.

De Sejos gathered her courage. "Can you tell me about Redmark?"

Neither tone nor body language offered any overt clues, and yet she still detected a wary edge when the bear said, "What do you want to know?" Its Spanish was far more natural than the dog's. She could have closed her eyes and held her nose, and never imagined she was speaking to eight hundred kilos of bear.

"The logo is all over your kit," de Sejos pointed out. "We know that you..." *monsters,* "that those like you have been brought to our country by contractors, Redmark and others. We know you are..." *owned,* "that you work only for them. Is it possible I could speak to your controller through you, to see..." The bear shifted slightly and de Sejos' words died in her throat. After a long moment she finished, "to see what we could do for them."

"No," Honey said. Behind de Sejos, Rex whined again.

De Sejos stiffened, because the serpent monster had lifted its head, its eyes pivoting independently as it scanned its surroundings. One of them fixed on her and its thin, blue tongue lashed out. She took a deep breath.

"We are not involved in the war," she said, speaking clearly in the hope that some human operator was using the creature's ears. "We do not support the Anarchistas. Most of the people here, this is their home: they have nowhere else. I am a doctor, I was sent here by the government before the war. Redmark and the others, they're working to support the government, right?"

The bear flowed up onto its hind legs – colossal, sun-eating – then dropped lazily down to all fours with a *whuff!* "No," it said again, in that so-very-reasonable voice they'd given it.

"No, they're not or...?" The dog was at her back, the serpent to one side and the bear was a mountain of hair and harness, claws and gun in front of her. Around them all, the air was busy with Estevan's alien bees.

"No Redmark here," the bear informed her.

"So you're trying to get into contact, or...?" It had seemed like a perfectly logical deduction, but the bear growled, deep in its throat – its real throat, that had no part in that urbane, sophisticated voice.

"There is no contact with Redmark," it stated, a little louder than its previous utterances. "I am monitoring all comms. There will be no contact with Redmark."

Revelation clicked into place in de Sejos' head: not a pleasant moment. A second before she had been surrounded by monsters, but at least they had notional leashes; at least there was a human face somewhere behind them that she might have negotiated with. Now the beasts were all around her, and it was worse than she had ever thought. They were wild. They might do anything.

And then the bear shook its head and scratched at its jaw. "Rex knows the smell of your hospital," it remarked, as though apropos of nothing. "Rex recognises those injuries from other human habitations we have had contact with, when we were following orders. You have patients with strange burns and sicknesses, do you not, Doctor Thea de Sejos?"

De Sejos stared into the creature's eyes, tiny in the vast breadth of its face. "Yes," she admitted, "we do."

The bear rumbled deep in its chest. "Then I do not think you want Redmark to come here either."

16

REX

I am woken by the sound of vehicles, many engines at least four miles away but closing. Moved by sudden hope I try to strain that part of me that Master's words come in by. No use: it is not an arm or an ear, that I can push with it or focus on it. It is there or it is not.

There are no words from Master. I can detect nothing on any of the short-range Redmark frequencies.

My ears twitch and triangulate. At least six vehicles, some larger, some smaller. My database suggests they are mostly civilian, with perhaps one armoured vehicle amongst them, from the sound. They are not anything that Redmark might use. They are not friends, therefore.

I wake the others.

Dragon is slow to wake: it is still night and he grumblingly sends me readouts from his hybrid metabolism monitor, highlighting core body temperature and cross-referencing that to the peak efficiency guidance in his database. I tell him to shut up and to shift to high-activity mode so he can generate his own heat.

Dragon's channel: *I will be very hungry.* And: *But I suppose we have lots of cows.*

Honey is sitting up, shaking herself and yawning. She asks

me for orders, and I send over a sound-capture of what I have heard.

By now, Honey can just hear the engines herself. She looks over my database references and scratches herself. *Problematic*, she decides.

I ask: *You don't know who they are?*

Honey's channel: *The most recent information I have obtained from the satellite link suggests there are a number of possibilities. It may be actual Anarchistas, but currently they are said to be operating east of here. However, the confusion of the war has led to a number of bands of gunmen at large in the country. Some were armed by the Anarchistas, others by pro-government forces or criminal cartels. While the fighting is ongoing, there is no ready curb to their activities so long as they avoid the major combatants.*

Honey uses a lot of long words, but they come with database tags so I understand what she means.

Dragon's channel: *Nothing we need to deal with then.*

Honey *hrrms* thoughtfully. *Orders, Rex?*

Retreat and prepare to unleash necessary force if pursued, I decide. These are good orders. I am being a good leader. *Bees, wake up. High-activity mode.*

Bees has more problems with cold nights than Dragon. Her small bodies must generate far more heat because of their surface area to volume ratio. She does this by compromising the efficiency of their wings so that some of the flight energy is converted to warmth. However, she will run out of energy very quickly.

Bees go to Honey, I decide. This is not ideal and I know Honey finds it uncomfortable, but soon all of Bees' units are nestling within her pelt so that she is crawling with their hard, black bodies, like living armour.

Like living armour. The thought surprises me. It is something completely new that I have thought, entirely from my own head. Immediately I want to share it with the others. *Like living armour,* I repeat to them. Bees and Dragon do not understand, and Honey is covered in Bees and already irritable. I wonder if I could share the thought with any of the humans, perhaps Doctor Thea de Sejos. Perhaps it is a thought from that part of my DNA that is human.

We decamp from the village, moving quietly. The humans have set a watch on us, I know, although I am not sure why. It is not as though they could stop us doing anything if we decided that they were enemies.

We retreat out into the fields, avoiding cows so that we don't spook them. We crouch low – even Honey – and watch, listen, sense. I think about sending out some of Bees' units for close range intelligence gathering, but they would burn out and die far too quickly, and we cannot get any more.

The humans have heard the vehicles by now, and abruptly a lot of them are running around between their buildings. I see most of the small humans taken to the big stone building – *church*, my database informs me. Some of the others run around in a fairly disorganised manner, and others take up firing positions as they did when we came.

The vehicles are approaching along the rough road from the north. In the lead there is an open-top car with four men. After that, the Armoured Fighting Vehicle comes, an old piece of military surplus but with its 30 mm cannon manned and ready on top. I compare and contrast to Honey's Elephant Gun – the vehicle-mounted weapon is comparable in power with a superior rate of fire. After the armoured car come some trucks carrying unarmed people and goods – both secured to prevent them being thrown around too much. Last is a bus that was colourfully painted once, but is now mostly dust-coloured. This is filled with armed men.

I signal: *Counting ninety-seven new humans visible, plus unknown within the AFV. Of visible humans: fifty-three armed.* I tag database files for weapon types. The new humans mostly have old military assault rifles, sufficient to kill Dragon but probably not Honey or myself. Some have underslung grenade launchers, and these are a greater cause for concern. The gun atop the AFV is by far the most significant threat as a direct hit would badly injure even Honey.

Dragon's channel: *Doesn't matter. We're not fighting them.*

The vehicles have drawn up before the village and the gunmen have got out. I can hear words being exchanged and forward these to Honey so she can take advantage of my superior ears.

At first there is a lot of shouting, and I see the AFV gun tilting to point at some of the buildings. The shouting goes on – from inside the building where the villagers have mostly gone, and from the cars using an amplifier – *loudhailer*, my database supplies, *bullhorn*. The new humans say they are part of some revolutionary army that Honey has never heard of. They are making demands.

The AFV gun shoots into the side of the church once, punching a crater. I hear high screams. The resident humans have inadequate defences. If I was giving them orders I would recommend a fighting withdrawal from an indefensible position, but truly they are not well positioned to recapture battlefield superiority in any way.

Dragon's channel: *We should be going.*

Honey's channel: *No, wait.*

I just watch. The new humans are making demands, and now it looks like the resident humans are surrendering. They are coming out into the open without guns. I feel shock go through me, because this is not a tactical option that I have ever considered. It is not something that we were ever intended to do. *Surrender.* The idea is slippery in my mind. Can we do that?

I hear more angry words. Some of the resident humans are being pushed about or struck. The newcomers want the small humans to come out of the church. There is a man in black – the man who first came to speak to Honey – standing in the doorway. The tone of his voice is reasonable and calm but I can hear the fear in it.

I whine a bit. I am very uncertain, because I do not know if the resident humans are enemies or not, and I do not know whether the newcomers are enemies or not. I know where I am, with enemies.

I can hear more words. The man in black has been thrown to the floor and there are guns pointed at him. There is a boot on his back.

Dragon's channel: *Target acquired.*

What target? I demand.

Dragon's channel: *Any target. Does it matter?*

Honey gives a big sigh. *Rex*, she transmits.

Are you worried they will damage the satellite transmitter? I ask her.

Honey's channel: *That is one of the things I am worried about.*

Our comms are very swift, far more so than the crude shouting of the humans.

Rex, says Honey again. *I have a thought concerning our future.*

I do not often understand things better than Honey. This is one of those times. *You think these new humans may be enemies,* I say.

Dragon's channel: *They are enemies of the old humans.* He is switching from target to target idly, calculating distance and wind direction.

Honey's channel: *I think it would be useful if they were declared enemies.*

Some of the old humans are being pushed against the wall of the church. Still they keep shouting. The man in black is being kicked. I see Doctor Thea de Sejos run over to him, but she is struck and kicked as well.

I whine, deep in my throat. She is not a friend. She is not Master, nor does she wear a Redmark logo. She is a human I have spoken to, though. She exists in my head as an individual I have a relationship with. She is not just not-friend/not-enemy like the rest.

It is up to Master to say who is enemy and who is friend. I am not intended to make that decision myself. But Master is not here. I am in command: there is no superior to whom I can look for guidance. My database and my feedback chip are silent.

I think they are enemies, I say, and wait for my feedback chip to castigate me, for Master to appear and say, *Bad Dog!*, for the world to fall on my head.

Nothing happens because I have said those words and made that decision, all on my own. No, that is not quite it. When I say it, it becomes truth. They become enemies. I have *made* them enemies.

Dragon's channel: *Target acquired.* I check his choice of targets and confirm this is satisfactory.

Bees on me, I order, and the swarm mobilises, bustling about my body with scratchy little legs: a burden, but one I can bear. I give my heat so Bees may conserve her energy for the fight.

My orders: *Dragon, priority targets* (a list). *Honey, supporting fire as I engage, then join me. Bees, priority target list to be updated on engagement.*

Dragon's channel: (ready signal).

Honey's channel: (ready signal) *Confirmed, Rex.*

Bees' channel: (ready signal) *Go, go, go.*

I go, go, go, on all fours and hitting thirty miles per hour after three seconds of acceleration. Bees does her best to cling to me but individual units are constantly coming loose and hurrying after me to reattach.

Dragon's channel: *Bang. Next target acquired.*

The enemy manning the AFV gun pitches backwards.

Honey's channel: *Boom.*

The bus jumps five feet as the Elephant Gun's shot strikes it in the centre-flank, buckling in the thin metal and then exploding in the interior. Honey counts seven casualties, dead and injured, from gunmen who had not disembarked.

Much panic and shouting from the newcomers in the village. They have not seen me yet. A new thought: *When they do, they'll really shout.*

Dragon's channel: *Bang. Next target acquired.*

The enemy holding a gun to the man in black drops, most of his head gone.

Honey's channel: *Boom.*

The open-top car explodes, the chassis just about flying off the wheelbase. One driver confirmed dead.

The enemy have an idea where the shooting is coming from. The AFV is moving and the rest are taking cover, pointing their guns out towards Honey and Dragon. Honey is already on the way in.

I have taken a curved path into the village. I am not where they are looking. I run through the streets of the village at top speed and they do not even see me coming.

My Big Dogs are shooting, picking off the gunmen who are closest to the residents. The residents are running everywhere, so targeting is a challenge, but my eyes highlight every enemy in red against the dark background.

I hit a stand of residents, too fast to stop, and knock them all flying. Acceptable losses. I am on the enemy.

My orders: *Bees, deploy.*

I explode into the enemy with teeth and claws. Bees explodes from me in a stinging cloud. We are all tapping our deep energy reserves tonight, so the rest of the world seems slow and lazy. I am striking to disable because one disabled soldier is more trouble to the enemy than two dead ones. I take limbs in my teeth and crunch and shake. I hook and fling with my claws. I send men hurtling into walls and onto roofs.

I give Bees her priorities and she masses around the AFV, finding ways in. One enemy is at the gun again, tipping the body of the previous gunner over the side. Dragon kills him with a *bang* and Bees pours into the hatch.

Bees' channel: *Integrity 84% Venom reserves 69%.* The venom can be manufactured in her bodies, but there are no new bodies. Still, she seems to be enjoying herself.

There are resident humans who have guns now. There are resident humans who have been shot. Doctor de Sejos is providing medical help, just as I would order her to, if I could – as though she is a fifth member of my squad. Bullets strike me like angry insects, but they do no more than bruise.

Honey is here now, lumbering into the village and throwing herself at the enemy where they have tried to gather. They stop gathering there very quickly, and then they are running for their vehicles. Only the trucks are left. The people there have not joined in the fighting or untied themselves.

I have a quick discussion with Honey about them. She says they are not enemies, and puts a shell into one truck's engine block just as it is being driven away. The other truck has not started because Dragon is amusing himself by targeting anyone who sits in the driver's seat.

There are not many enemies left, and they are making a strategic withdrawal. It is not a good withdrawal because they are all just running and none of them is laying down covering fire, or any of the other things you are supposed to do.

Dragon kills them all, and I let him. It keeps him busy and his feedback chip will probably say, *Good Dragon*, every time he hits. And besides, they are enemies, and we kill enemies. It's what we're for.

After that, the sun is coming up and I put down the burdens of command for a bit and just stand and watch it through the Bees-flecked air. After a while, I order Dragon to let me use his eye-feed, because he sees the colours so much better than me.

I am surrounded by the bodies of enemies. They are enemies of my own making. I made a command decision. I have nobody to tell me *Good Dog* or *Bad Dog* for doing so. I do not know what I am becoming.

I send just to Honey: *I miss Master. I miss Hart.*

Honey's channel: *I know, Rex.*

My channel to Honey: *Was this right?*

Honey's channel: *I hope so. Trust me, Rex. You have to trust me.*

17

DE SEJOS

Clean-up had taken a while.

None of the attackers had survived. Those who ran had been shot down methodically by the reptile. It had coiled its way up the church wall and on to the roof and simply aimed and fired, aimed and fired, until there were no more running figures left.

De Sejos was busy dealing with the wounded. Estevan had said that seven of Retorna's own had died and eleven had been wounded, mostly caught in the crossfire. Some had broken bones from getting in the way of the beasts. She was doing her best with them, eking out her antiseptics and her anaesthetics.

The injured bandits or Anarchistas or masterless mercenaries who had been left in the village, they were not going to live, either. There were plenty of them – the animals had been brutal, but not uniformly lethal. Now Rex was going from one to another with the patient care of a priest giving last rites. For a moment she could not understand what he was doing, but then she saw. He was breaking necks with tiny, practised motions of his huge hands.

De Sejos lurched up from tending poor Maria Chicahua – whose shin the dog creature had fractured in the fight

– and she shouted into his big dog face, telling him he was a monster; telling him to stop; telling him to get out of Retorna and go back to hell where he came from.

He did not slow, and when she stood in his way he shouldered her aside as though she wasn't there.

"They are enemies." The words were not in Spanish, but she knew enough English to follow.

"Doctor Thea de Sejos, you have patients," came the innocuous female voice of the bear. It – she? – stood with her huge gun still cradled in her arms, the dawn light striking her pelt and turning it russet, almost gold in places. "Do you wish we'd not been here to fight these humans?"

"I suppose your world is always as simple as that." De Sejos returned to Maria, to splinting her fractured shin.

"Not necessarily." The bear released her weapon, and the gun's hinged arm folded up to lay the deadly thing along her back. "It was supposed to be. That was how they made us."

De Sejos looked up, finding the bear a silhouette now, against the brightening sky. "I don't understand you."

The bear – Honey? – sighed, an exaggerated burlesque of the human expression. "You know what we are, Doctor."

De Sejos was not feeling charitable just then. "You're killing machines."

"Worse," came Honey's warm tones. "It would be easier if we were machines. Although more of your people would be dead."

"Doctor!" Blanco came running over and then skidded to a halt as he registered the bear. From a safe distance he told her, "The people from the trucks, we have forty or more new mouths to feed, it looks like."

"Who are they?" de Sejos asked him.

"Farmers, shopkeepers, all sorts," Blanco explained. "They were taken from San Torres, from Mixan, from another couple of places I never heard of."

"Why?"

Blanco shrugged and grimaced. "Mostly they're women. Nobody *told* them what they were for, but even so, mostly they're women."

De Sejos closed her eyes briefly. Maria's leg was splinted now. There were others with lesser injuries requiring her attention. "Can you find them somewhere to go, get them food, water?"

"I have my people on it already," Blanco confirmed. He eyed the bear warily. "You... Are you fine here, you need help?"

"I can always use more clean water."

"I'll get some." He backed off, glowering at the huge animal from what he probably imagined was a safe distance.

"We are not machines," Honey continued. The lizard-snake creature was still up on the church, basking on the orange tiles of the roof like a sign plucked out of Revelations. The dog had finished his grisly work. The air was heavy with bees: they moved with a purpose and a coordination that was wholly unnatural, now she knew to look. Some of them touched down on the corpses and dabbled their feet in the blood.

De Sejos felt her stomach turn. Abruptly she was on her feet, trying to face down a monster that must have weighed twelve times as much as she did, and stood twice as tall. "So you're not machines," she hissed. "Machines aren't cruel. Machines don't snap the necks of helpless men."

"They do if you tell them to," said Honey implacably. "And machines do not decide when to fight and when not to fight. They fight when they are told. They let unarmed people die when they are told. But we are not machines. We have choice."

"Free will incarnate." Father Estevan had come up behind de Sejos, shading his eyes as he looked up at the bear. "What on earth do you want here, friend bear?"

"I want to use your satellite connection to understand the world."

"And do what?" Estevan asked her. "Or are you so far from your makers' design that you cherish knowledge only for knowledge's sake?"

The bear scratched at herself thoughtfully. Divorced from her movements, her voice stated, "If we have choice, then it must be informed choice."

"You've gone rogue," de Sejos said. "That was what you meant, before. You're not with Redmark or following their orders. You've gone... feral."

The dog padded over to stand in Honey's shadow, and de Sejos was acutely aware of the lizard and its long-barrelled gun up on the church roof.

"That is not relevant," the bear ruled.

"You were made to follow human orders," de Sejos went on. Estevan laid a warning hand on her shoulder but she could not stop the words. "You were supposed to be under human control. But now you're wild. You could do anything..."

"Yes," Honey confirmed. "That is our choice. You want us to follow human orders. You think that is better." The bear's animal stare was nothing if not judgemental.

*

124

After she had dealt with all the injuries and had Estevan set up a makeshift infirmary in the church, de Sejos returned to her clinic, where the beds were full.

Another three people had died overnight. She dictated notes into her phone, remembering her first entries where her voice had been shaking. There were seventeen left, now: men and women who had been out south of the village when the planes came over.

She wasn't blind. Before the Bioforms had turned up to hog her bandwidth, de Sejos had been doing her own research. The world beyond had a very fragmented picture of what was going on in southern Mexico right now. Everyone knew there was a lot of fighting, and that between them, the Anarchistas and the international counter-insurgency had effectively demolished anything passing for civil infrastructure. At first the war had been fought for hearts and minds, both sides making political statements on the television and launching DOS attacks against each other's websites. Then the war had been fought with guns and men – militias and private security forces clashing, with units of the army on both sides. For the first few months it had all been almost civilised, everyone trying to be gentlemanly about the whole thing.

But neither side was winning, and the corporations were losing money hand over fist – both from Anarchista attacks and the simple expense of keeping the war going. De Sejos wasn't quite sure what had snapped, precisely. Perhaps it was just that the men behind the fighting had lost patience. Perhaps the idealism of the Anarchistas had decayed into the sort of backbiting rabies that such popular movements so often devolved to, not fighting *for*, just fighting *against*.

Perhaps it was just that business interests thought, *We can monetise this.*

They had brought in the Bioforms – ostensibly because they were cheaper and more effective than regular soldiers. Cheaper? Yes, quicker to train, no grieving relatives when they died, and you could breed them en masse in battery farms – she had seen the videos. Looking out at the bizarre set of animal soldiers that Retorna had inherited, de Sejos knew that they were doing more than deploying soldiers. They were testing them.

And it wasn't just Bioforms they were testing. Campeche and the Yucatan presented difficult terrain for rooting out a widespread popular revolution. The counter-insurgency had been experimenting with other alternatives to just sending men into the trees.

A plane had gone over, south of the village. Probably it had been lost, or the crew had been over-eager, but in its wake had come an invisible death, a chemical fug that stank of rot. The cattle over that way had died and had to be burned. Many people had died, too, and the survivors had come out with terrible burns across their skin, and blindness, and madness.

The world outside was just now starting to catch up with the mess that Campeche had become. There were persistent rumours about illegal weapons testing, about what the Bioforms were doing to combatants and civilians both. There were denials as well, of course, and in general the voices of the corporate lawyers and spokesmen were a lot louder than those raising the accusations. And yet the accusations would not go away. There was word of a multinational inquest, UN action, pressure on the US government from its electorate to send some observers over the border.

And Doctor de Sejos tended the evidence of what had been

done, and did her best to make them comfortable and keep them alive, while the poison ate them alive from within.

*

Two weeks later another cavalcade arrived at Retorna. This lot styled themselves as patriots and claimed they were hunting Anarchistas. Their uniforms were ragged and dirty and their guns were much in evidence. They wanted food, and they wanted to take what little medicine de Sejos had left. They wanted everyone in the village to assemble out in the open, where they could see them.

"We can give you food," de Sejos told them flatly. Blanco had long since stopped complaining about the depletion of the herd he had been left to watch over. The owner was off safe, out of the country. Let him complain when he deigned to come back. "What drugs we have, we need."

Their leader was a thin-faced man who had his thugs drag her over to his car and force her head onto the dashboard while he toyed with his pistol.

"Make this easy for us," he said. "My men are in a bad mood, they will get angry if they're kept waiting. You don't want that."

"For your own sake please leave," de Sejos grated out.

Something in her tone had got to him – she could see the sudden uncertainty in the way his hands froze on the weapon. He was surrounded by his men, though, and insecure enough that he could not back down.

"I'm warning you—" he said, and then Rex came out, stalking on all fours and growling loud enough that she felt it through the ground.

"Mother of God." The leader of the patriots dropped his gun. His two henchmen had let de Sejos go immediately and levelled their rifles.

Rex barked thunderously, the sound coming in at a pitch that spoke fear right into the human nervous system. His shoulder-mounted guns swivelled from target to target. He bared his teeth, snarling, strings of saliva dripping down his chin.

"Please, go," de Sejos told them.

She felt their courage falter but hold. They were telling themselves there was just the one dog, no matter how big, no matter how well armed.

Then Honey slouched out into sight as well, gun levelled, and that decided matters. The intruders left; they left and they lived.

That had been the deal, worked out between the human leadership of Retorna, on the one part, and the Bioforms on the other. *Give them a chance to go.* Rex had been hard to convince, which she had expected. Honey had been harder, which she hadn't. In the end, de Sejos guessed that Honey didn't like the idea of witnesses. Word would spread.

But de Sejos had argued and argued, not angrily but patiently. And when Honey had proven immovable, she had argued with Rex, or at Rex. She had gone out to find him lying in the sun with his head on his paws, his back rising past her waist, and she had talked to him. *This is not how we do things. Killing should be a last resort.*

Until now – until the new attackers had arrived – she had not known how the Bioforms would handle it.

But they stood and watched, as the intruders drove away post-haste. Even Dragon watched from its sniper's post atop the church, and aimed its gun but did not fire.

Honey shook herself, slung her gun and raised her clawed hand in a mockery of threat. "Grrr, snarl," she said in her cultured voice and wandered off. De Sejos guessed she still thought the idea a bad one.

Rex rose up on two legs, watching the retreating vehicles keenly. De Sejos knew that some of the bees (some of the Bees?) would be following to keep an eye on them, to ensure there was no surprise attack later. She wondered if Rex was having to control some doggy instinct to go chasing cars for the sheer fun of it.

Passing him, stepping through his shadow and close to the great dense mass of him, she had an impulse, utterly wrong, utterly misguided. She reached out and touched his arm, feeling the thick, corded muscle rock hard beneath a hide tougher than leather.

"Good boy," she told him. "Thank you, Rex. Good boy."

His head cocked, one ear up, just like a real dog. But he wasn't a real dog, and she was making a mistake, thinking of him in that way. He was a monster made by men.

Still, it was easy to anthropomorphise him, to see the curve of his tooth-studded jaw as a smile, to see a yearning for acceptance in those brown animal eyes. It was easy to – what, caninomorphise? – him as well. He wasn't anyone's "good boy".

And yet she patted him on the arm and said it again, because it helped her get past her fear of him, and because she had always lived in a house with dogs, since she was very small.

*

Four days later, a flitter passed overhead.

18

REX

Dragon and Honey are talking about something on a private channel. Probably I am not supposed to know, but I can tell from the way they keep looking at each other.

There was a flitter. The humans were very scared of it, but they seem to be scared of everything. Honey said that bad things happened here when air vehicles flew over the village before. Honey says the bad-smelling people who are dying here, they are dying because of those bad things.

Honey does not think this flitter is bringing the same bad things, but I can see she thinks it brings *some* kind of bad things.

Dragon has the best eyes. He can see colours properly – better than humans. He can focus at a great distance: it's part of his specifications, so he can perform his combat role. Dragon got a better look at the flitter than anyone else.

Dragon did not report to me. He reported to Honey. That was wrong of him. I am leader.

Honey's channel: *Yes, you are our leader, Rex. But Dragon knows this is something that falls into my area of expertise.*

I tell Honey, *Your specialisation is heavy weapons support. Was it a heavy weapons flitter? It looked like a small scout model.*

Honey's channel: *Yes, it was a scout. But I am improving on my original specifications, Rex. I am becoming something more.*

I whine at that, because this sounds unfamiliar and maybe dangerous. *That is not part of our orders.*

Honey's channel: *We have no orders, and nobody ever ordered me not to do it.*

I do not feel this is the way we are supposed to approach our combat role in this theatre. *We do what we are told.*

Honey's channel: *You are leader. Are you ordering me not to improve myself?*

I know that I could say yes. It would make me feel better: I would be asserting my leadership. It would make Honey feel worse. This is something that she wants and it does not seem to impair our combat effectiveness. I do not give any orders. I do not want to upset Honey. I just say, *I do not understand what you mean by improving.*

Honey's channel: *I am an experimental Bioform intended for heavy weapons support, as you say. However, I have reason to believe I have been inadvertently over-engineered.*

I do not understand her.

Honey's channel: *I have been using comms channels for some time to gain a greater understanding of the wider political situation, especially as it pertains to the war in Campeche and the use of Bioforms, both of which are highly controversial topics at a global level.*

My channel: *You got a new voice.*

Honey's channel: *I downloaded one, yes. That is a part of it.*

My channel: *Did Master order you to?*

Honey's channel: *He didn't order me not to. And then,*

because she senses I am not won over by this, she adds, *Maybe Hart knew.*

I feel sad about Hart, then. Hart was not Master, but he was kind and I have good memories of him. And those good memories are now sad memories because all of them are tagged with my knowledge of his death. I try to remove these tags so I can enjoy the memories, but something goes wrong and I can't.

My channel: *What did Dragon say about the flitter?*

Honey shuffles and shifts, and I know she is thinking of how to reply. Honey is very clever, so when it takes her this long, I know it is for an important reason.

Honey's channel (at last): *Rex, I will tell you if you order me. But I am asking you not to order me.*

I do not understand her.

Honey's channel: *In my judgement this is something you are better off not knowing at this time.*

My channel: *If I do not have proper intelligence I cannot make command decisions.*

Honey's channel: *In this case, Rex, I don't think you could make an objective decision either way.*

My channel: *So, trust you?*

Honey's channel: *Please trust me, Rex.*

I think – or rather I let the pieces of the inside of my head run around for a bit, and try to get an idea of what I think. Sometimes it is hard.

My channel: *If I trust you, will Doctor Thea de Sejos be hurt?*

Honey is surprised. *Not as a result of you trusting me. I cannot guarantee she or any of the humans here won't be hurt, but I am trying to avoid it.*

I trust Honey. I have no Master and only a limited ability to make informed decisions. I am a long way outside the situations I was designed to handle. If I do not trust Honey, I have nothing.

*

The next day I start hearing ghosts on the comms. Ghosts is what Honey calls them: fragments of signal on familiar frequencies, saying nothing, promising everything. The others hear them too. Bees reports them as soon as she detects them, and starts working on triangulating their origin.

Bees' channel: *Integrity at 63% Projected integrity within seven days: 42% Advance warning of loss of higher functions.* Bees' units are dying, eldest first. Bees' specifications include a complete unit replacement every one hundred days and she was overdue before we lost contact with Master. Bees units are dying, so where is Bees? Bees exists between them, formed by the interaction of her many bodies and their computational power. I have a picture of Bees in my mind: someone in a smaller and smaller room, the walls closing in, and when they touch the walls they lose part of themselves.

Honey tells Bees she has a plan. Bees does not seem to believe her.

Bees is trying to calculate at what level of integrity she will cease to be Bees and just become... bees. I try to see a picture of this in my head and I cannot. Where will Bees go when there aren't enough bees?

Dragon's channel: *We are all the same. Where will any of us go?*

I ask Dragon: *What do you want?*

Dragon's channel: *Food. Warm sun. No orders. Kill humans, Bang!*

My channel: *This is what you want?*

Dragon's channel: *No. These are good things. These are things they made me to feel as good. They did not make me to want.*

My channel: *Don't you want to be Good Dragon?*

Dragon's channel: *I want freedom from their good and bad.*

Honey is distracted. Honey spends all her time with the satellite link, shifting from connection to connection, talking to people. Now the comms ghosts are here, I think Honey is using them to send out her signals too. Honey is busy. Honey has no time to talk.

Doctor Thea de Sejos comes to me. She asks, "What is it, Rex? What's coming?"

I tell her I don't know – I say it in Spanish now. Of all phrases, that is one I have the most use for. That flinch in her is still there when she hears my voice, but her fear spikes and then fades, rather than poisoning the air between us. I know so much about her just from her smell: her age, her gender, that she is tired, that she is anxious, that she is not eating well.

"Honey knows, doesn't she?" the doctor presses.

I nod, because that doesn't scare her as much. She goes to talk to Honey, but Honey has few words for her. I feel like Honey is fighting an invisible battle where I cannot help her.

The ghosts grow stronger. Dragon reports that he sees activity within the trees, beyond the fences. Bees sends units to investigate. There are gunmen there. Bees' report is fragmentary. They are all keeping something from me, that it is better I do not know.

I am not stupid. I have had an idea about it. When I first thought it, I wanted to run about the village telling everyone the good news. Except that, for Honey and Dragon, at least, whatever is happening is not good news. Even for Bees it does not seem to be good news. Although as Bees deteriorates it becomes harder and harder to find personality and emotional tags in her communications. She is becoming a thing of data only.

I crouch in the village centre and whine. I want to reach out with my own comms and make contact, give my callsign and my passwords. But Honey has a reason not to do this. Honey does not trust me with the reason. *Whine.*

The children of the village have set out containers with sugared water in for Bees. Some bring flowers. Father Estevan remonstrates with them about something called idolatry but I can tell he is not serious.

*

Four days after I first hear the ghosts, Honey comes to me. I have been waiting for her. Bad news has been on its way ever since the comms ghosts first arrived. Even the humans have been waiting for it, and they notice almost nothing.

She tells me: *Rex, we are going to have to fight.*

My channel: *Are enemies coming?*

Honey takes a long time to answer that question. She gives me the answer I expect but do not want. *What makes an enemy, Rex? Who decides?*

More whining from me, but I say: *I am leader. I decide.*

Honey's channel: *So what is the answer? What makes an enemy?*

My channel: *People Master says.*

Honey sighs. *And if Master is not here.*

My channel: *Those who fight us.*

Honey's channel: *Is it that simple?*

I shake my head and bare my teeth and scratch in the dirt, all to try and keep from thinking about this. *Mostly it is that simple.* I think of the people of the village with their little guns, who might have fought us if Honey had not talked to them.

Honey moves on with her questions. *Are people who fight us the only enemy?*

I am on dangerous ground. *Sometimes people who fight others are enemies.*

Honey's channel: *That's good, Rex.* She pauses. Our comms traffic is so fast that a second's gap can mean a long thinking pause between us. *Rex, there are people coming who want to kill all the humans here.*

I whine again, deep in my throat.

Honey's channel: *Do you know what I mean by destroying the evidence, Rex?*

I do not.

Honey's channel: *There are people coming who do not want anyone else to find this place and discover what they know. They are people who have done a bad thing, Rex. Already there are other humans who are asking questions about the bad things they have done. But these other humans do not have evidence, proof. So the people who have done the bad things, they need to destroy the proof. This village is part of the proof. It is just a little part, but it is still a part. Do you understand what I mean, Rex?*

I do. I do not want to, but I do.

Honey only has one thing to say, now. *When they come,*

will we fight them? Her statement from before, turned into a question.

And I say: *Yes.*

*

And so they come, and we will fight them.

Honey has been on the comms sending messages out. The humans are in the church and the other stronger buildings.

Bees reports enemy activity under the tree cover to the west. There is a lot of open country for the cows between the trees and the village, but if you have the right sort of guns – like Dragon does – the distance does not mean much. Bees has not reported vehicle movements – moving through the trees with vehicles would be impossible, and these enemies want to remain under cover as long as possible. It reminds me of when we were with Master. We had vehicles, but we attacked on foot, at night.

The enemy will attack on foot, tonight. They have night vision capability and they will have some heavy weapons. The village itself is indefensible. We cannot let them come to us.

Bees reports the presence of Bioform soldiers: at least two dog packs. I am uneasy at the thought. I know how dangerous I am. There will be four per squad, and each one will be far more dangerous than a human soldier.

I am not supposed to design attacks, but I am supposed to have battlefield command of a squad. That means I am able to assess circumstances and change the plan in response. There is not much difference between that and making my own plan.

Dragon will be our last line of defence. He will take a high vantage point and kill enemies that approach or fire upon the village.

The rest of us are going into the trees. Guessing that the enemy will attack at night gives us time to plan our counter-attack. A flitter has been overhead twice; we have kept out of sight. Once it is gone, we move swiftly into the trees to the east and work our way round until Bees' vanguard detects sign of the enemy. Then we wait. Honey and I slow our metabolisms and reroute blood supply, drawing heat into the core of our bodies. Our thick, reinforced hides further mask our heat signatures. We are ready.

Bees is burning her units' reserves for tonight's battle. She is anticipating mass casualties amongst her personal army.

Bees' channel: *But we are going to die anyway. We will die soon. I want us to die killing the enemy.*

My comms channel is full of ghosts, more than ever. I pick up words, codes, numbers. They are familiar to me. I try not to think about them, but the static on the comms is insistent.

We wait. We wait. We wait. Distantly on the air I scent the other dogs.

Then Bees reports that the enemy are moving into position to attack the village. She has identified two shoulder-launched rocket systems as the most likely source of the initial strike and requests permission to deal with these.

My channel: *Permission granted. Priorities afterwards: (1) targets nominated by me (2) targets nominated by Dragon (3) targets nominated by Honey (4) available targets of opportunity.* Dragon gets a promotion because if he is nominating targets then the village is under direct attack.

Bees' channel: *Confirmed* (image of dead bird).

Stretching our cold limbs, Honey and I begin to move. We gather speed. We are approaching from downwind. We can smell humans, but more than that, we can smell dogs.

A dog pack holds this flank of the enemy advance. I can smell them as they creep through the trees. Soon they will be able to smell me, downwind or not.

My channel: *Honey, fire at will.*

Honey's channel: *Confirmed. Target acquired.*

We have few enough advantages but surprise is one, and Honey's Elephant Gun is very powerful. This is the advantage of a Multiform Assault Pack. I am already running when Honey shoots over my head (*boom*) and explodes one of the enemy dogs, her round lodging in its throat and then tearing it open. The dog goes down and I am amongst the others, my Big Dogs loosing. I am lucky, very lucky. One of my shots takes an enemy in the eye and through to the brain, damage even we cannot survive. I have a moment, as I am fighting the other two: all that reinforced bone, all that dense muscle and bulletproof skin; everything has its weak point.

Then I am doing badly, two on one. I get my jaws in one and gash it open, but another is worrying at me, teeth caught in my harness. The one I have bitten claws me back, and then throws me off. We are heavy, but we are stronger than we are heavy. We can throw our own bodyweight easily.

I land on my feet, mostly, and also against a tree, hard. I snarl and bunch to pounce.

Honey's channel: *Hold.*

I hold. One of the dogs takes a round in the groin from Honey's gun and has time for a brief whimper before it detonates.

Bees' channel: *Commencing assault.* She will keep the human enemy busy as much as she can while we deal with these.

The last dog jumps for me, but I dodge aside, ripping my

claws across his muzzle. Looking into his rabid, snarling face is like looking in a mirror: he is my brother. Perhaps we came from the same laboratory.

I take him and I pierce his hide with my claws, I have him by the throat and the arm, and I twist with all my strength until the weakest part gives: the elbow, the shoulder. He howls and I bury my teeth in his throat.

My channel: *Dog pack down,* and then we are closing with the humans.

Honey's channel: *Enemies.* Because the human smells are familiar. They have names and ranks and numbers.

But we have agreed that they are enemies.

Honey's channel: (targeting information identifying a squad that has formed up at the tree's edge).

My channel: *Targets approved.*

The main body of the enemy force is fighting Bees. Bees is using swift-action neurotoxin. It is expensive to manufacture but her units have been gorging themselves on sugar water, and she can make almost anything she needs with enough sugar. She goes in, targeting the launchers. The enemy are well-equipped with armour vests and stab-retardant fabric, with masks and goggles, but there is always a little bare skin if you look, and Bees' senses let her home in on it very swiftly. We hear their shouts and screams.

Honey's channel: *Boom.*

The Elephant Gun roars and explosive rounds rip into the targeted squad. Honey is already changing position. The comms ghosts are coming thick and fast as the enemy become aware of us.

I drop to all fours and charge in. My Big Dogs are already picking targets, shooting for the thigh (femoral artery), the armpit (axillary artery), the face (brain via eye); secondary targets: knee, foot (remove mobility); elbow, hand (remove combat effectiveness).

We have a short space before the enemy realise what we are and how we have flanked them. We use it. I kill three men with my Big Dogs before I am in amongst them. Bullets zip past me like Bees. One impacts on my ribs and slants off, leaving a bloody gash and a suppressed memory of pain. Time to lick wounds later.

I track down the comms ghosts, follow them to their local source. I find an enemy officer. His name is Sergeant Martin Price. I know his name and face, although I have never seen that expression on him before as when he sees me. I sink my teeth into his leg and whip him about until he has sustained sufficient dislocations and injuries to cease to be a threat. I move on. I shoot Malcolm Okewe in the face. I shoot Patrick Flynn in the thigh. All these men I know.

But we have agreed they are enemies.

Honey fires and moves, fires and moves, her explosive rounds sowing confusion and impeding the enemy's ability to offer an organised response. Still, the return fire is growing more determined. Both Honey and I are hit several times, but we were built to be shot and not care. Neither of us have more than scratches, already scabbing over as our accelerated healing gets to work.

Bees' channel: *Integrity at 41% If you have any complex orders now is the time.*

Dragon's channel: *Multiple targeting opportunities. Target acquired. Bang. Target acquired. Bang. Target acquired. Bang.*

My channel: *Status?*

Dragon's channel: *Holding. Bang bang bang.*

I tear through another cluster of humans but I am looking for the other dog pack. I cannot smell it. It is not here.

That is bad.

Dragon's channel: *Multiple targeting opportunities. Too many. Under fire. Rex, Rex, they're here, Rex.*

That is worse.

I am used to going into these assaults with human squads to back me up. I have few tools to work with: just the four of us. *Honey, you and Bees continue to fight here. I will help Dragon.*

Honey's channel: *Confirmed. Good luck, Rex.*

I am already running on all fours towards the village.

Dragon's channel: *Target acquired. Bang. Under fire. Relocating.* In my mind I can see him slithering down from the church, his scales as white as the painted stone.

I scent the dogs. They are ahead of me, closing on the village. As I watch, one of them pitches backwards, from a bounding warrior to a heap on the ground. In my mind, Dragon says *Bang.*

Bees' channel: *Integrity at 36%.*

Honey's channel: *Run, Rex.*

The dog pack has scattered under Dragon's attack and I overhaul one of them, leaping on his back and holding him down while my Big Dogs send shot after shot into his struggling body. The fifth, seventh and twelfth rounds find vulnerable targets and he is dead. I am chasing the others.

Honey's channel: *Right, Rex.*

I swerve right and one of the running dogs is hit in the side, the wound bleeding bright fire as the shell detonates. One remains, losing himself between the buildings.

Up ahead, as though the dog's death was some sort of signal, I see parts of the village explode. I see running human figures. Some are enemies, some are not. Dragon tells me of another target he has acquired and an enemy falls, one more perfect headshot. My Big Dogs are coming into range. I talk to them and we find our targets together. There are a lot of the enemy. They are desperate to destroy the evidence that is here. Why is it so important to them? I suppose they have their orders too.

The comms flare and gabble at me. *...nder fi... ...ioform... ...ex? Is that you...?*

I begin to shoot, picking targets as best I can. I am trying to minimise non-enemy casualties but the air is so thick with dust and smoke and fear that it is hard to tell humans apart until I am close. I do not know where the other dog is, but his presence worries at my mind.

Honey's channel: *Not long now, Rex.* I do not know what she means.

Bullets patter off my harness and my skin. One strikes my brow-ridge and the impact resonates through my skull. I have blood in one eye and switch dominance to the other.

Some of the resident humans are fighting. I see them with their hunting rifles and their old military cast-offs. I see them fight and many of them die. But I am coming. I come up behind three of the enemy as they crouch behind the corner of a house and I fall on them and tear them apart, their blood in my mouth and on my hands. But the night is young and there is plenty left to do.

Dragon's channel: *Target acquired. Under fire. Relocating. Relocating. Help.*

I kill another, but I am getting sloppy now. Too much is going wrong. There are enemy everywhere. I smell explosives. I target the explosives, killing those men as they try to set their bombs. They are trying to destroy the clinic of Doctor Thea de Sejos.

Comms: *...anyone see a logo on...? ...forms deployed by... ...ex, can you hear me? Disenga... ...ad dog!...*

Bees' channel: *Integrity approaching 25% Priorities locked in Lower cognition threshold imminent so saying goodbye now Goodbye Goodbye Goodbye...* And then there is no Bees, just bees following her last orders, the mind between them no longer possible.

Honey's channel: *Falling back on the village. Do not listen to the comms, Rex. Trust me.*

I am too far engaged with the enemy to worry about whether I trust Honey. We hunt each other through the streets of Retorna. I am shot a dozen times; I feel the grating discomfort of bullets lodged in my muscles, impeding my efficiency. When they see me, they pepper me with automatic fire, inaccurate and panicked because they know what I am and what I can do. When they do not see me, I explode out at them and tear them apart.

Dragon's channel: *Pain pain pain pain pain.*

Bees' channel is silent. Her units carry out their last programming, harassing the enemy wherever they find them.

I run for Dragon, dodging fire. The bullets blur past me in the air, but I am blurring too. I am burning all my reserves, faster and faster, hotter and hotter. Their night sights can see me, but I am so fast they only hit me by chance.

Dragon's channel: (no words, just images, a random outpouring of them. Warmth, satisfaction, rage, pain, fear). Dragon's nervous system has been damaged and he is broadcasting at a subliminal level.

I arrive in time to see him die, writhing and thrashing, his tail lashing the walls and shattering bricks and windows, his bloody mouth gaping its broken teeth at me as the enemy shoot and shoot and shoot. I pounce on them, striking them down, tearing into them. My Big Dogs shoot and then are silent: I have no more ammunition.

Honey's channel: *Hold out, Rex! Hold them!*

Comms: *Rex?*

I stop, a mangled corpse in my teeth. The surviving enemy flee me, and I crouch in the building's cover. Dragon's body twitches and thrashes, but these are just the random last firings of his neurons: life has fled him.

Comms calls my name again, in a voice I know. *What the hell are you doing? Disengage! We are not your enemy. Return to base immediately.* And coordinates, callsigns, passwords, clear as can be.

My channel: *Master?*

Honey's channel: *Ignore comms, Rex.*

But it is Honey I ignore, even as the fighting goes on around me.

Master speaks: *Rex, return to base. Disengage, that's an order, Rex. Bad Dog, Rex!*

I whine. I feel terrible. I look at the bodies around me, the Redmark insignia on their tattered uniforms.

Master speaks: *Rex, what is this? You know me, boy. You haven't forgotten me, surely? Why are you fighting us? You're my dog, Rex. I'm your Master.*

I see men at the clinic again, obeying their own orders.

My channel has no words. I cannot make any in my head. I am a Bad Dog. I must be a Bad Dog.

Master speaks: *Come home, Rex. Come on.*

My channel: *I do not want...* And I am out of words again.

I cannot tell Master I do not want to go home. I cannot say I do not want him to destroy Retorna. I cannot even ask him why. These things are not part of my relationship with Master.

I see them exchange fire with the resident humans. Jose Blanco is there, who never liked me. I see him shot down trying to save the clinic and Doctor Thea de Sejos.

Master speaks: *Rex, just get out of there, right now! We're working to a deadline here, Rex. You've already set us back a hell of a way. Will you get your fucking mongrel ass out of there?*

My feet are moving me, but I don't know where.

Master speaks: *Rex, acknowledge.* More codes, more passwords, meaning: *Master is master; you are dog. Dogs do what Master says. Obey Master, Bad Dog! Bad fucking dog, do you hear me? Do what you're fucking told you bastard liability fucking hound!* Then Master is trying to link direct to me, to make me be a Good Dog. I cringe and wait for the lash.

There is no lash.

I reach out to confirm the command hierarchy they built into me.

There is no hierarchy. Hart's last communication removed it.

I know Master is my master. I know I am a Bad Dog: Master says so. But Master is not here and his signal is weak and there is nothing in me that forces me to do things. For the first time I can decide whether I am a Bad Dog or not.

I am moving towards the clinic. The men there with explosives see me. They start shooting and hit me several times. Master is shouting at me.

I tell him: *I am a Good Dog.* Master says I am a Bad Dog

but his signal is blurred and broken because Honey is interfering with it. He cannot access my feedback chip. His words are just words. Just as when Doctor Thea de Sejos said I was a Good Dog.

That means I can choose who to trust.

I trust Honey. I trust the doctor. I am a Good Dog. Dragon was a good dragon. Bees were good bees.

I am shot again. A stab of pain in my gut tells me one bullet has gone deep, punching through skin already compromised by previous wounds. I hook the shooter and ram him into the wall, feeling the dry-twig snap of bones that neither Kevlar nor a stab vest can protect him from. I crush the skull of another between my jaws, helmet and all. They are running. They have left their bomb. They have left their dog.

The last dog: he stares at me with mad hatred. *Bad Dog!* that stare says. *Bad Dog, Rex! Bad Dog, disobeying Master.*

I want to explain to him, but I cannot. I do not have the words. I cannot even explain to myself.

We close; we clash. We are both wounded but I am worse. Every movement hurts, and only keeping moving keeps the pain at bay. I am mad; I am savage. He opens up my arm with his teeth. I drive a claw through his eye. He tears my ear off. I kick him in the gut and rip open his bulletproof skin.

I throw him off. The bomb is still there, and the humans will remember it. Is it set? Is it timed, or will they simply send a signal?

I take it and I throw it as far as I can towards the enemy. Even shot, even compromised by my wounds, that is a long way. Let them send the detonation signal now. Let them kill fields and cows with their bomb.

I feel very weak and sad when that is done. I drop down – I

mean to drop onto all fours but I end up belly to the ground. I hurt. I hurt badly.

The other dog is gone. I do not understand at first, but then it comes to me. He is gone to fetch the bomb. *Fetch, boy, fetch.* When it goes off, I wonder if he was close enough to be caught by it, or if he lived, and is running after Master like a Good Dog should.

Honey's channel: *They're going, Rex. The enemy are retreating. Well done, Rex. Good boy, Rex. Good Dog.*

My feedback chip is silent, but I trust Honey.

I can hear engines, though: my database says… my database returns error messages, but it sounds like some model of heavy combat flitter, several of them. I tell Honey, who even now is lumbering towards me.

Honey's channel: *I know, Rex. These are not enemies. Do not engage.*

But I want to engage. I am filled with fire and anger and pain, and when I stop fighting the pain will get much, much worse. I am filled with guilt and fear and confusion, and they will get so much worse as well, when I am not filling my head with fighting.

I tell Honey, *I will fight them.*

Honey's channel: *No, Rex. I called them here. Please surrender to them. We can live, Rex. We have a future. The world is changing. But if you fight them they will kill you.*

I can see the flitters now: big armoured models with their turbines screaming as they come in. There is a loudspeaker voice telling the resident humans something in Spanish. I think it is to be calm, and that the newcomers will not hurt them.

I know they are targeting me. I am not hiding. They will kill me, and that would mean an end to pain and guilt and fear.

Honey's channel: *Rex, please.* She has cast aside her gun, ripped off her harness to let it clatter on its arm on the ground.

I am bunched to leap, and the lead flitter is coming lower, and I wonder if they realise how high I can jump. I am snarling. I am hurting.

But I am a Good Dog. I have only ever wanted to be a Good Dog.

I let the harness go, and my Big Dogs slide off my shoulders and fall away, and then the pain surges inside me and there is blood, and I am very weak.

My ears are full of the engines of the flitters and my nose is clogged with the scent of gunfire. When I feel a hand on my head, though, I snarl a little and twist my head so I can see. Doctor Thea de Sejos is kneeling by me. She is speaking words I cannot hear over the noise, but I do not have to. Two words, short words, but bigger than all the other words I know. *Good Dog*, she says, even though she is sad, *Good Dog*.

I am a Good Dog, but I hurt so much. I hurt and I had a choice and I do not know if I made the right one.

Newcomers are approaching: strange smells, no fear. It is hard to lift my head from the ground, but I twist it until I can see them. Their guns are levelled at me – they are shouting at the doctor to move away and she does.

The leader of the newcomers, the not-enemies, she is familiar to me. She was with Master and Hart. Her name is Ellene Asanto. She was a civilian but now she is a soldier. I do not understand, but I do not think I need to.

Words, more words, but I am fading and so is the pain.

19

(REDACTED)

There's a play, a very good play, where someone complains to an actor that they die a thousand deaths without really knowing death, without feeling its intensity. They'll just come back, as the playwright says, in a different hat.

There I am in the second act, though, wearing the digital footprint equivalent of a false moustache. Except it's not me, though. Not the woman whom Murray murdered.

The end of the Campeche campaign was a clusterfuck on a variety of levels. I was just starting to flex my muscles right then, and it taught me I really did not have the levels of influence and control I had imagined. Like countless politicians, I found that once something is in the public domain then the public will grab it like a dog with a ball and run with it who knows where.

Things got out that people wanted hidden. Truths were misinterpreted and misunderstood. Lies got halfway around the world before anyone could even suppress the truth. Pretty much every piece of dirty laundry I and Redmark and every other interested party hadn't wanted aired in public – all for our own different reasons – was abruptly flapping in the breeze. And all those conspiracy theorists had a field day, even the lizard-people brigade.

The global headlines, in the glorious tradition of lowest common denominator idiocy, can be summed up as "Killer Military Assets Kill People Shock!" except it wasn't that. It wasn't the same as if Redmark had used missiles or bombs or guns. It wasn't even the use of the chem weapons that were already unequivocally banned by global agreement. Yes, there were prosecutions and inquests being handed out like cigars after a birth, but that wasn't what the *public* were screaming about. Whether they were *against God* or *taking our jobs* or *a threat to the children*, people wanted something *done* about the Bioforms. All of the Bioforms, from Rex and the experimental combat models down to Grandma Scoggins' home defence dog-unit that she only ever took out once a week to carry the shopping.

And that was a problem for me, because by then I'd rather decided that they were the future.

PART III

THE HAND THAT FEEDS

20

ASLAN

"Hey, swap you my briefs?" David Kahner dropped down into the next seat, grinning from ear to ear.

"Now I'm taking it that's not a serious offer." Keram John Aslan made room for him at the booth, locking the screen of his tablet.

"Hell no. I've already been headhunted three times and we're not even on day one of the case." Kahner was immaculate: sculpted hair that gleamed almost blue-back, flawless olive skin, a single gold stud earring. He wore the latest model smartglasses, his suit cost more than Aslan wanted to think about, and he wore it roguishly open-collared, as though any moment he would be called out to a fashion shoot.

"You're not even going in front of the cameras," Aslan pointed out.

"Doesn't matter, man. Besides, the big cameras, no, but boss says maybe interviews later. Interviews, chat shows, endorsements. People are *interested* in this thing, KJ. The ICC's never had this level of take-up since Nuremburg. And that's because of your case as much as mine."

"Hold on, endorsements?" Aslan couldn't tell if he was being serious. "You mean, like, 'The International Criminal Court always drinks Pepsi Cola'?"

Kahner fished a dronecam out of his pocket and sent it up with a blink at his smart glasses, beaming up into its little camera with perfect pearly teeth. "Am I not telegenic, KJ? Am I not right on the brink of becoming the world's media darling?"

"No," Aslan told him sourly. "Nobody knows who you are and the press is full of pictures of that old goat Arnac, because he's lead prosecutor."

"Arnac said he'd cut me in on it, get me a few photocalls." Kahner examined flawless nails.

"Arnac says a lot of things."

"You're just sore you're not on the team." Feeling a personal lack of diplomacy, Kahner spread his hands. "Which was a bad call, by the way. You paid your dues on the Caliphates prosecution."

"I am still paying my dues over that."

"Oy, still?"

Aslan nodded grimly. "Last week the cameras caught some guy by my car, and the whole car park was no-go for six hours. You don't remember that?"

"I remember the fuss. I didn't know that was *you*." Kahner shook his head. "Still, shows you did good. They should have called you in for the Campeche team."

"David, they had me front and centre on the Caliphates because they thought a good Muslim boy would catch less flak, which says a lot about how badly our employers understand... everything, probably. Which is kind of worrying."

Kahner was obviously about to come out with some assurance about how it had all been his legal smarts and not his prayer habits, but Aslan waved it away. "You've got the spotlight now, David. You milk it for all it's worth."

Two espressos turned up then, and the pair of them stayed quiet until the waiter had gone. The bar wasn't somewhere they'd be discussing anything confidential, but there was always the risk of an inadvertent slip that might end up in the press and kill off a promising legal career.

"The small fry seem to have gone well, anyway, all the 'only-obeying-orders' crowd. Thanks, I might say, to my immaculate case prep. Arnac can make a good speech, but he wouldn't know what year it was if I didn't email it to him daily," Kahner drawled.

"So Murray's next?"

Kahner grinned. "The old Master of Hounds himself, slippery bastard that he is."

"It's not going further?"

"Redmark's board have had a fairly savage round of resignations," Kahner noted, "and I know a bunch of corporations have had directors up before the House back in the States. But the trail runs cold, KJ. If there's evidence to link the chem attacks to somebody on the board, it's buried deeper than we've been able to dig. So, we've got Murray, who was basically right there on the ground making the decisions, using Redmark assets to run his own private war. The way they tell it, he was a twenty-first century Kurtz from that, what was it...?"

They chimed in together, Kahner with the film, Aslan with the book.

Kahner grinned again, but this time Aslan saw the nerves there. "We need Murray, KJ. It's not even a matter of justice – although, God knows justice would be a fine thing to have a little of. We say Murray gave the orders to chemo-bomb wherever he thought the Anarchistas were getting their support from – and he had a pretty low threshold of proof, believe me. Murray's orders set the dogs on people. Murray wiped out whole villages to cover his tracks, at the end. At the end, to hear them say it, he was nobody's man but his own."

"You're going to play the dog pack angle, are you?" Aslan asked morosely.

"For all it's worth."

"You're making my life more difficult, you know that?"

"Then you're on the wrong side," Kahner pointed out.

"Am I?"

"You know they only gave you the case because of your name, right?" and the grin was restored to its mocking perfection.

"Hilarious." Aslan scowled. "They actually have some 'Aslans', you know? It's what they called one of the experimental cat models, under the Multiform initiative. Never saw action, though. Unreliable. Even chipped to the eyeballs you can't get cats to do what you want them to. Cats, I've got; got a few bear models, some freakish-looking lizards, some hive-mind critter things you don't even want to think about. There's a naval base on Malta that has some dolphin forms in the pen, even. But it's mostly the dogs."

"Murray's dogs."

"Murray had more than dogs," Aslan reminded him. "And there are more dogs than just Murray's. Seventeen hundred canine Bioforms in military service around the world so far, all locked in their barracks, and another thirteen hundred or so impounded out of private hands, pending judicial decision."

"And you get to write up the defence. Who did you piss off to get that mess handed to you?"

"I asked for it. I asked to be on the team." Aslan stared angrily at his coffee.

"What the hell, man?" Kahner was genuinely surprised. "You're that desperate to kill your career, just sleep with Arnac's wife or something."

"They want to declare the Bioforms weapons," Aslan stated. "They want to decommission them, just like they were nukes or guns."

"They are weapons."

"Never mind." Aslan massaged his forehead. "You just go get Murray, leave my job to me."

*

"You want to see the facilities first, sir, or just your... client?"

Aslan didn't miss the calculated pause there: the staff here obviously didn't think much of his brief.

The cells themselves were sunk into the ground, a subterranean complex open at the top, so that the dogs could run around their tiny yard with a little square of sky above. Around the buried cells there was a wall, and the wall was topped with wire. All the guards were armed, and although wardens with guns wasn't a novel experience, these rifles could hold their own against last century's big game hunters for calibre.

Beside the cells, beyond the wall, there were the offices where the international bureaucracy that made this place possible was perpetrated. Aslan had driven out there in his little electric car and parked it up alongside the various makes and models driven by the guards and administrators. On the way over his mind had been full of righteous rhetoric. Now, with the sounds from the pit a constant backdrop, he felt decidedly less sure of himself.

They were dog-sounds, mostly: a very large number of big and angry dogs, except mixed into the animal snarling and barking were recognisable words: pleas, expletives, insults, threats.

It was his first taste of the reality behind the ideal he had offered to defend. It frightened him a great deal.

"Let me see the..." The what? "Let me see him."

They led him inside, into the soundproofed normality of office space, cubicles and kitchenettes, terminals and copiers and water coolers. Busy clerks filed their reports and entered data and nobody looked up at the slender young lawyer from the ICC.

His guide held a door open for him, and Aslan stepped through and came face to face with the dog.

He swore and jumped back, and heard the laughter, knowing he was being hazed. His eyes never left the face of the creature in the room.

The place was set up like a prisoner's visiting room, and he couldn't work out whether that was someone's poor-taste joke, or simply a lack of imagination. There was a transparent plastic screen between them, thick enough that looking through it was like looking through water. Even then, Aslan didn't think it would be enough if the thing ran amok.

It was sitting like a man, but its vast, muscular frame practically filled that half of the room, hunched over with its head thrust forwards. It had cuffs on that looked like they were designed for King Kong, for which he was powerfully grateful. Its jaws were immense, upper and lower canines projecting slightly past its thick lips. One of its ears was mostly gone, just ragged scar tissue left. Its stare...

Its stare, like the way it sat, was human. For all the eyes

were dog, round and brown, Aslan met its gaze and found something man-like looking out at him, trapped in that vast prison of engineered flesh.

"Sir, you don't look them in the eye. That's a challenge," the man at his elbow was saying, but Aslan couldn't look away. Carefully, he stepped into the room and lowered himself into the chair, bringing his tablet out. He made his every movement slow and telegraphed at first, worried that the creature opposite was a coiled spring that would go off at the first sudden move. He'd seen this one's records, after all – those that had survived the mysterious data purges at Redmark's end, anyway. There were a lot of dangerous dogs in the cage over here, but this one was something special.

"So, hello there," he tried, though the force of that leaden stare was starting to wilt him. "You're Rufus, is that right?" He was speaking as though the creature was a child. Or a dog, perhaps. He was speaking as though he didn't expect it to understand him.

The dog made a rumbling noise deep in its chest. "Rex," it said.

Aslan froze. "Did you..." He wanted to ask, *Did you speak?* as though he could blot out the fact of it. The voice had been deep enough to vibrate the plastic between them.

He got a grip on himself. "Did you say... Are you not Rufus?"

Again that single utterance. "Rex."

Aslan swore and rooted through his files. *The idiots have brought me the wrong one.* "I... you fought in Campeche? I thought you were the leader of Murray's Multiform team."

"Yes."

He looked up again, finding the creature with its nose almost pressed to the screen.

"I was leader." It spoke carefully, stressing the words strangely. "My squad was Honey, Dragon and Bees, but I was leader."

Back to the notes. Murray only had the one Multiform pack, and the names of the rest checked out. Some clerk had mixed up the records, Aslan guessed. After all, nobody would have thought it was very important.

"Well then, hi, Rex. My name's Keram. Keram John Aslan. I work for the International Criminal Court."

Looking into that brutal, *bestial* face, his heart sank, because how could this *thing* ever be seen as anything other than a threat?

They're going to exterminate them, Aslan knew then. *From concentration camps to gas chambers. And the courts that were made to punish genocide are going to be making it happen.*

21

REX

This is the cage Bad Dogs go to.

There are one hundred and twenty-seven of us in this cage. It is a very big cage. Forty-three humans work here. They are scared of us; we can all smell it. They do not know we are scared of them, too. They have ways of hurting us, and they use them when they can, to remind us. Still they are scared. They are scared because they are not our masters, only our jailers.

We each have a little cage within the big one. The walls are bars, so we can see each other. It is never quiet. Always we are snarling at each other, snapping and growling, shouting and threatening. The whole cage-building echoes to us.

We are all dogs here. The other forms, the experimental ones, they are dealing with differently, behind different bars. And there are other dog cages in other places, but we are here. Here is where everything will be decided, we have heard. News runs wild through the cages: every little scrap of knowledge is fought over.

We are here because we are dangerous. I do not understand: they made us to be dangerous. I do not see how they can be surprised when we were.

Many of us are military dogs, like me. Some fought in the same war I did. Others were in other battles, in other parts of the world. We exchange our war stories. Once you take away heat and cold, wet and dry, they all come down to the same thing. Other dogs were security. They lived in buildings and kept them safe. When we say *enemy* they say *robbers*. I like the idea of that kind of life. It sounds peaceful. But perhaps I would miss the fighting.

The air is rich with smells. I have never been near so many of my own kind before. Each one signs the air with his identity, his state of health, his mood. Some of us are ill here – more now than before. Many of us are unhappy. The unhappy and the ill dogs do not leave their small cages even for exercise.

We exercise. A score of us at a time are let out into a steep-walled yard to run and snarl and pace round and round under the tranquiliser guns and the tasers of the humans. I like exercise. Exercise and feeding are the only things that happen here, and feeding is dull and the food is bad. They have bad things in the food, and a lot of the dogs here have a sickness from them, that makes them sleepy and slow. Many of us late-end military models can metabolise this bad food quickly so that it does not affect us much.

We talk of many things. We talk of what we did before they locked us up here. We talk about fights we were in, or places we lived. We talk about our masters sometimes. We all had masters. We all miss them. None of us understand why our masters have sent us here. We must all be Bad Dogs.

That is not quite true. I understand a little. I understand that I was a Bad Dog. I was a Bad Dog because I chose to be a Good Dog in a way Master did not want. I know I deserve to be here.

It is when we talk, rather than shout and bark and snarl, that the humans fear us most. I do not understand that. To talk is human: why are we more frightening when we are human than when we are dog?

When we exercise, there are fights often. Today, when I go out, a big dog puts his face in mine and tries to push me down. "This is all your fault, you soldier dogs!" he tells me. "I was a Good Dog. I had a good mistress. I went with her everywhere. I kept her safe. Now I am in a cage because you soldier dogs were bad. You killed people in your wars and now all of us are in a cage!"

He is not telling me anything I do not already know, and so we fight, and although he is bigger, and my wounds are still tender, I am faster and more skilled. I tear his ear and rip up his back before the humans shoot me with their tasers and fill me with pain.

Back in my little cage, I open my channel like I used to, listening for the voices of my squad mates. I miss Honey. I miss Dragon and Bees too, but they are gone. All my thoughts of them are tagged with sadness. I was a bad leader just like I was a Bad Dog.

I play back my memories of them, in my little cage. I remember Honey telling me to trust her. I remember Dragon catching fish. I remember Bees saying goodbye.

Then there are humans in the corridor between the cages. There are many of them, and they have tasers, and they stop outside my little cage. They have restraints strong enough to hold even me.

I think they want to punish me for fighting, and that is only fair. They command me to step out and I do so. They hate me and fear me, but they are all the master I have.

When the restraints are on, and the muzzle has closed my jaws, one of them is brave enough to jab me with his stick.

"Special treat for you, Fido," he tells me. "Your lawyer wants to see you."

*

And now I am sitting before Keram John Aslan. I am unhappy and trying to work out what any of this is about.

Aslan says he is a "lawyer", but what is that? My database gives incomplete and unhelpful answers. I don't think this is something I was supposed to have to worry about. I dig deep through all the references: lawyers are supposed to protect the intellectual property inherent in my design. There are database sections that have warnings about action by lawyers if the information is disseminated. I understand none of it, but it makes lawyers seem like something frightening. I am not frightened by Aslan. I cannot smell him through the barrier, but I can see he is frightened of me from the small movements of his body.

"So..." The lawyer fidgets with his hand-held computer. I try to connect with it idly but it is not accepting unsecured comms. "If I ask you questions," the lawyer says, "you can answer them, right?"

I shift, pushing forwards a little, and he leans back without knowing he is doing it. I am very, very tired of people being afraid of me. It makes me think they are enemies. I do not want any more enemies.

I do not know what I want. I think of Honey saying, *There is no future in killing humans.* But what else is there?

Or maybe this is what she meant. The lawyer Keram John Aslan is hiding something from me: a big something that he is unhappy about, and that is something to do with me, and why he is here. He wants to ask me questions. Can I ask him questions?

I try. "Why are you here?"

He jumps, and then he says, "I..." and consults his tablet again. "It's quite a war record you have there, Rex."

I say nothing. In saying nothing, it is like I am asking my question again. It is still in the air between us, like a scent. So long as I say nothing it will not disperse, and eventually the lawyer must answer.

"I... OK, let's take this carefully. You were in Mexico, you were one of Redmark's combat assets when they were brought in to fight the Anarchistas, right?"

"Yes."

"Well, I want to ask you about how the fighting went, and we'll get on to that later." He is relaxing a little bit. "But from a human point of view, things went very badly wrong. There are a lot of people facing a lot of questions right now about that, and some of them are going to be punished."

I cannot help flinching at the word. In my experience, if there is punishment then I am getting it.

"But one of the big questions that's come up is the use of Bioforms. I mean, we had this before with autonomous combat robots, and so on and so forth all the way back to the use of chemical agents... which is kind of relevant right now, in fact. But one thing the Campeche war brought up was the use of Bioforms. People are not... look, you're a Bioform, right? You know that?"

"Yes."

"And do you know what I mean when I say, 'scapegoat'?"

I search my database. "Yes," I say.

Keram John Aslan nods jerkily. He is trying not to look at

me, but his eyes keep drifting back. I recognise this eventually as guilt. "It looks as though a lot of what went on in the war is going to come back to use of Bioforms. Right now, the majority of your people—" He shakes his head. "Your... kind? I don't even have the vocabulary. The majority of Bioforms, worldwide, are being held in camps – in institutions like yours here. A lot of people want you destroyed. Do you understand?"

"Yes." It is the first thing he has said that I feel I completely understand.

"And I'm sorry. I'm on the team that's presenting the case that you shouldn't be. That you should have rights."

I pass over what "rights" means because what he is saying is, *I am your friend*, and that means I can ask, "Why?"

The question makes him twitch again. "I... Well, there are people who think that you're... that you're *human*. Not actually human, but that what we've made, with Bioforms like you, it's something that thinks and feels like a human, so deserves *some* sort of recognition, some sort of basic rights. I mean, I don't think you're likely to get the vote, no matter how well this goes, but... just the right not to be destroyed out of hand, you know?"

"Why?"

Now he is confused. "You're... you're going to have to tell me what you mean, Rex. Why what?"

"Why you?" I cannot deal with his "people" who want this, and "people" who want that. This is one man in front of me. I cannot smell him but I need to know him.

"Well, I..." He rubs at his face: he is still sweating and I can see how uncomfortable he is to be in the same room as me. "I always found Bioforms fascinating. I could see this would happen, way back when the first of your – when the first of you was the article at the end of the news: talking dog, man's best friend. That's a legal question waiting to be asked, I told myself. And it was being asked from the start, don't get me wrong. Plenty of people who didn't want you to happen at all – against God, against nature, whatever. And on the other side there were the people who were building you, who were saying: *It's just a tool, just a thing we made and own. Yes, it can talk, but so can your phone.* And right from the start I was thinking, there's going to come a point when this gets tested in law. What are you, Rex? A man or a dog or a machine? Or a menace."

"I don't know." My words surprise him; he was not expecting an answer. He looks back at his computer, moves things around. I crane forwards until my nose is against the barrier, feeling it flex slightly.

"I've been given a mountain of tech specs, science articles, reports. I'm still working through them…" I see the images from his screen reflected in his eyes. Amongst them is a face I know: a woman; a friend.

"Doctor Thea de Sejos," I state.

He twitches and stares at me. "What?"

I say nothing. He frowns and moves back through the pictures. "That's… she's one of the prosecution witnesses in the… I haven't got to those statements yet. I was figuring they weren't exactly going to be helping our side." He stops, and I can almost see him catch up with his own thoughts. I know how that is. "How do you know her name?"

"She was at Retorna. I was at Retorna," I explain.

"Seriously?" He twists his face about. "Yet another record that's somehow gone missing. And something else that isn't going to help us, probably." And again he is thinking. "But how do you know her *name*?"

I cannot understand why this is so extraordinary to him. "She told me."

"She spoke to you. In the fighting?"

"Yes. No." It is difficult to say what I mean. "Before. We were at Retorna. My squad were. We were friends with the resident humans including Doctor Thea de Sejos."

A change has come over him. He is abruptly less open, holding himself more still. "Rex, if someone had questions about what happened at Retorna, would you answer them?"

I say nothing. I know by now that the silence will make him talk more.

"Only... there's a colleague of mine who might..." He shakes his head. I think he had a lot of questions prepared before he came here. I think he had a plan of how this was going to go. It is a plan that has not survived contact with me.

"I want to speak with Honey," I tell him.

"Honey...? Oh, the bear-form from your squad?"

"Yes."

"I don't think that's going to be possible. It's – she's in..." More looking at the tablet, and now he is more confused. "Actually I don't know, there's no record here. I'll chase that up. But there are only your regular dog-Bioforms held locally."

I call out on my channel, but I am calling into a great silence. No Honey, no Dragon, no Bees. There is no Hart and no Master. There is nobody at all except the lawyer and the guards and all the other angry, miserable dogs.

They want to destroy us, I think. Right then I cannot see any other future.

22

ASLAN

"You look like a man who's picked a fight he can't win." Kahner was irritatingly cheerful as he dropped down into his accustomed seat in the booth.

Aslan shook his head angrily. "You ever met a Bioform?"

Kahner shrugged. "Seen videos, maybe a couple shuffling around carrying some CEO's wife's bags over in LA. I take it you've had a conference with some of the accused?"

"You've got no idea how *scary* they are, until you've been up close. I mean – not just that it's a very big, fierce animal, but you know it's got just enough brains to *know* what it's doing, if it wanted to kill you."

The other lawyer frowned. "This doesn't sound like a man on the defence team."

"But it's how they're *seen*," Aslan explained. "Monsters, basically. And that's a real problem because my case is frankly not going to be fought on legal technicality, it's going to be fought on public opinion. Right now, everyone's busy acting all shocked about how things went down in Mexico, and where better to point the finger than at an eight-foot-tall killing machine with blood on its fangs?"

"KJ, you ever stop to think that maybe they *are* just unnatural monsters that we should get shot of as soon as we can?"

Kahner asked carefully. "It's not like we've discovered them or they came from outer space or something – we *made* them. And let's face it, we've made mistakes before."

Aslan sighed. "Except they're not."

"And you know this how?"

"I've been meeting my clients. One in particular, a high-profile offender, you might say. And I was *scared*, David, I really was. Even with it shackled and behind glass, I was scared. But when I talked to it – to *him*, to Rex... Well, he's not going to be winning any public speaking awards any time soon, but I could tell there was something there, a thinking, emotional being. One that needs to be protected from flavour-of-the-month public outrage."

"Seriously?"

"Seriously. And it's not going to happen, because they're basically keeping these creatures penned up elbow to elbow, and they fight each other, and they stink... it's like, let's say you kept your murder suspects – and they're mentally handicapped, socially maladjusted already – then you put them in an asylum where you beat them and hosed them and... and then one day you drag them out before everyone and say, 'Hey, look at this half-mad, filthy animal! Do you think he did it? Are your children safe until this monster gets a humane injection?'"

Kahner grimaced. "So, are my children safe, KJ?"

"They have a right not to be summarily executed."

"And the dogs?"

"David, you *know* what I mean!"

"Then build your case, and good luck to you. I've got my own worries."

Aslan nodded. "Murray causing you problems?"

"He's an evasive bastard, I'll give him that. Redmark knew they'd crossed the line. They had complete oversight over the war in Campeche, and they did a lot of cleaning up before they were stopped." Kahner shook his head disgustedly. "In the end, we've got plenty of evidence of *what* was done – it's pretty much undisputed that various chemical agents were deployed by the corporate Reconquista, civilian leaders were assassinated, all of that. But pinning these things on any actual individual – actually bringing people like Murray to justice, well..."

Aslan nodded unhappily. *Now or never.* "David... you've got a witness called..." he checked his tablet, "de Sejos, that doctor from Retorna?"

"Yeah, but she's not much use. Advance Investigations is still monopolising her, and what's she going to know about command structure, anyway?"

"I want to speak with her."

"Well, take it up with them – wait, in connection with *your* case?"

"Yes."

"From what I hear about Retorna, she's hardly going to be happy about..." Something visible clicked into place in Kahner's expression. "Hold that thought. There is some weird stuff about Bioforms in the summary that got released to me. I've been trying to get the full picture for a while now. Hellene in Investigations is sitting on a lot of it. I've been on at her to give me full access."

"Murray's Multiform pack was there," Aslan supplied. "Not that you'd know it from Redmark's records."

"They were? Well, that's sure as hell not in the paperwork. Didn't... weren't they rogue, by that time? Off the grid? Or that's the story. Can't pin anything they did on Murray, just like everything else."

"I met their, what, squad leader, top dog."

"No shit?" Kahner opened his mouth to follow that up, and then the implications hit him. "So you were talking about pooling our resources?"

"I thought you'd see it that way. I want to get the full picture on Retorna, and I think you do too," Aslan offered. "So how about we both make a nuisance of ourselves with Agent Hellene?"

*

His phone was bleeping at him when he woke, fumbling in a pitch dark room for the bedside table. Every time this happened he promised himself he'd get some comms hardware implanted, which everyone said was the way forward. Almost nobody was using external devices to talk to their fellow human beings any more.

"Aslan," he slurred into it. For a moment there was just silence, but the loaded silence of someone listening.

Then the voice came, and it shocked him upright. It was a woman's voice, a pleasant and comforting one, but just imperfect enough in its mimicry to let him know it was fake. The diction was too regular, the pronunciation not varied enough as it said, "Hello, Mr Aslan. Thank you for taking my call."

"Who is this?" he hissed.

"I am someone with a deep interest in your case, Mr Aslan."

"How did you get my number?"

"Is that really your priority right now?" the voice asked him – still so very perfectly warm and reassuring that it was sending chills down his spine.

"Who are you?" he demanded again.

"Will you have Rex give evidence, Mr Aslan?"

"Will I..." He swallowed the words. An idea was starting to form, and he didn't like it one bit. "You know Rex, do you?"

"We're old friends, Mr Aslan."

"The committee I'm preparing my report for isn't looking for any of its... subjects to come testify," he told the voice.

"No," it agreed, with a touch of regret. "It just wants to know that Rex and his peers are dangerous military hardware, and not thinking creatures. Actually meeting one might shake their prejudice."

Aslan sighed and held his peace.

"Or is there more to it, Mr Aslan?"

He said nothing.

"I thought perhaps you might say that the committee will feel itself beholden to the current wider prejudice against Bioforms arising out of the Campeche campaign, a prejudice currently being fanned by media bias funded by various alternative weapons industries. And if you had said that, I thought you might then go on to say that destroying the Bioforms is not like decommissioning stockpiles of nuclear weapons or dismantling automata. You might say that it was murder."

Aslan's throat was dry. "You're one of them, aren't you?"

"Yes, Mr Aslan."

"Well..." He stared into the dark of his room. "Why don't you come over here and talk to them yourself, because you seem more than up to holding your own."

"You've spoken to Rex, Mr Aslan. Do I sound like him, would you say?"

"No, I wouldn't say that. You sound like a college professor simulator."

It actually laughed, a very good facsimile of a human sound, but a facsimile all the same. "That's very good, Mr Aslan. But that is the problem. You can probably guess that no combat Bioform was intended to be able to speak as I speak or do what I do. I very much want to help Rex. He is my oldest friend. But if I were to come forward they would either fear me, or covet me, and either way I would give up my freedom. I am afraid I would not help your case. But Rex can, Mr Aslan. Rex is a Good Dog."

My oldest friend... Aslan took a deep breath. "Honey...?"

"Well done, Mr Aslan. Get Rex to testify."

"I don't – look, seriously, they don't want to meet any Bioforms. That's why they have me and the rest of the team."

"I don't mean in your case, Mr Aslan. You've already started on this path. I know you met with Mr Kahner of the prosecution team, and you have an appointment to meet Ms Hellene tomorrow. But you can go further. Rex saw it all. He can be Mr Kahner's star witness."

"I... I don't even know if the court would *accept* a Bioform witness."

"Make them," the voice stated. "They gave Rex a voice. It deserves to be heard."

"I've heard his voice. It's not going to do him any favours," Aslan said, heartfelt.

A pause, and then: "An interesting point, Mr Aslan. I must consider it."

And the line was dead, and when he checked his phone

there was no record of any incoming call at all, all evidence of it vanished entirely. Sitting there in his dark bedroom he actually wondered if any of it had happened – had he just woken up with the phone in his hand and a dream of a call....

No combat Bioform was intended to be able to speak as I speak... or do what I do. The Multiform units were experimental. What had they made, when they created Honey?

*

"Why did I think I'd be hearing from you again so soon, Mr Kahner?"

Maria Hellene was an elegant olive-skinned woman, far too young to be as senior as she was, and yet woe betide anyone who tried to use that against her. More than a few Old Guard careers had broken against her reputation for rock-hard efficiency and pragmatism. Her general attitude to the rest of the ICC was stern disapproval, as far as Aslan could make out. He had met her at a couple of functions, at which she had been so detachedly antisocial that she had become a sort of social singularity: everyone else had been out of place in contrast; she the only one who belonged. On the other hand, he'd sat in on a budgetary meeting where she had waxed remarkably eloquent on the subject of funding, so perhaps it was just a case of her not giving a damn about people unless they had something she needed. Or she was a sociopath. Or some combination of the above.

She was a major figure in the ICC Advanced Investigations Team, a curious little anomaly that hadn't existed a decade before, and was sporadically supposed not to exist now. She had put agents on the ground in Campeche while clearance was still dragging its feet through committees. Presumably someone had given permission for that, but neither Aslan nor Kahner had been able to work out who. The DEI – Département de l'Enquête Initiale because for some reason the French had the naming rights on that one – was the fastest growing part of the international political scene that nobody was talking about.

And because her investigations were indeed advanced, a great deal of Kahner's case was relying on the intelligence the DEI had provided, and a great deal of his frustration was based on how much she was holding back.

"We have a trial date now, Ms Hellene," Kahner started. "And Murray's defence is rubbing its filthy little hands in glee because we have a lot of things we can suggest and imply, but actual proof linking him to what was done is looking thinner on the ground than we'd like."

"The Retorna files are still being redacted," she told them blandly.

"And your agent in Murray's mobile HQ?"

"Neither confirmed nor denied at this time." She lounged back behind her desk, swivelling slightly on her chair.

"Anyone would think you don't *want* Murray nailed," Kahner accused her.

Hellene's face went flat and still for a moment. "Oh, I have very personal reasons for wanting him 'nailed', Mr Kahner. I very much want you to succeed." Some internal calculation brought a little sympathy to her face. "Yes, we had an agent right by Murray near the end. But that went badly. The agent was unavailable for debrief and her transmissions are fragmentary."

"I'm sorry." Kahner grimaced. "But, look, the Retorna reports at least—"

"They're problematic. And they won't help your case, Mr Kahner. Believe me, I've gone over them in detail in case I could throw any bones your way."

Kahner rolled his eyes. "How about if I was asking for a friend?"

"Really, that's the best you've got...?" Her eyes skipped to Aslan and she arched an eyebrow. "Is that Keram Aslan you've hauled along for moral support? He isn't even on your team, is he?" She blinked, and Aslan thought she must be consulting the ICC database. "You're on the Bioform investigation?" Her tone was subtly different – in any other human being, he'd have said *warmer*.

"I'm advising on the report anyway. It's not as if *they* get trials." He sounded more bitter than he'd meant.

"Well, then." Hellene's body language had changed entirely. From her exaggeratedly bored manner with Kahner she was now very still. "What can I do for you, Mr Aslan?"

Expecting only a put down, he bulled in with, "I need to know what happened at Retorna. I need... I know you've got some of the locals along to testify. There's one in particular—"

"The doctor or the priest?"

"What? The – the doctor, what was it..."

"De Sejos," Kahner filled in. "Wait a minute, Ms Hellene, how come he—"

"I've told you. There's nothing there you can use against Murray. The evidence about Redmark's use of chemical weapons has already been made public. Everything else is... confused." She looked Aslan right in the eye. "But it's yours, nonetheless. So long as you keep me in the loop and keep me involved."

"I didn't think the DEI..."

"Not DEI. Me."

There was something powerfully unsettling about her in that moment. Looking back, Aslan wondered if it was that she was completely still, utterly without tells or cues.

"Well, you've got more security clearance that I can even dream of, so, of course, whatever you want," he agreed weakly. "But I don't see why."

Abruptly, jarringly, her mocking manner was back. "Perhaps I'm a dog person."

23

REX

I have been in another fight, but it will be the last one. I am a better model than any of the other dogs here. I am strongest. As we have no Masters here, that makes me leader. None of them will bother me any more.

For a day they kept fighting each other to see who was second, third. Stupid dogs. I gave them a hierarchy instead. I tried to create one in their headware but most of them do not have compatible systems, so I had to just tell them. I made the best of them my officers. I put all of them in their place. Now they will not fight and they will not argue. When they disagree, they ask those above. When those above disagree they ask me. My decision is best because I am leader.

The cage is now a much quieter place. I thought this would make the humans happy but they are more frightened than before. When we were barking and fighting and shouting they did not like us. Now we just sit and watch them, they like us even less. I do not understand them.

Some of them try to make us angry with their words and their tasers. They want us to shout and rage. Why?

Because they want us destroyed.

But they cannot just destroy us, or they would have done. So they want us to be something that must be destroyed. I am thinking about what my lawyer said.

I have given orders. No anger at the humans. Not even when we are very angry indeed.

*

Now they are taking me to the little room again where I met Keram John Aslan the lawyer. The guards are different: before they walked like Masters even though they were afraid of me. Now they are more afraid, and there are more of them, as though the quietness of the cage is an enemy they want to fight. But they cannot fight it. You cannot fight quiet with sticks and darts and tasers.

The other dogs watch as I am walked to the room. I look at each of them, and they look down to show they know I am leader. Some of them say my name.

The guards do not look at the dogs. They put much effort into not looking at the dogs, even though they have weapons and the dogs are all trapped in little cages. The guards stare straight ahead and sweat, and fear.

Aslan is looking nervous again. "They say you're making quite a stir here, Rex," he tells me.

"I have stopped the stir," I tell him. I could say more, and he would not understand me. I could explain how things are peaceful here now, and how the humans are wrong to be scared. I am not sure it is true, though. Everything should be better now the fighting has stopped, but at the same time I think I am beginning to understand. There are a lot of us in the cage. We were strong when each of us was alone. Now we are strong as a pack. Even in our little cages we are strong.

"You remember I was talking about Retorna," he tries.

"Yes."

"You can talk to me about it? About what you were told to do? The orders you got."

I think about it. "There were no orders. I was leader at Retorna."

"Right." He fiddles with his computer. I can almost hear the ghost of it over comms. "Look, how about before then, when you did have orders? You can talk to me about that. You think? What you were told to do by M—" He stops and looks at me to see if I have guessed the word he bit off.

M is the start of Master. M is the start of Master's human name. *Moray*, Hart called him.

"Can you tell me, Rex?" Aslan asks me.

I do not know the answer. I feel there must be something there to stop me. Surely Master would not want me saying anything. *Whine.* I shake my head as though the thoughts are bees, hurting me.

"Rex, this is important."

"We fought enemies," I tell him.

"What enemies?"

"Master gave us enemies. We fought them. I was a Good Dog." Not now, not any more, but I remember being a Good Dog for Master.

Aslan shows me pictures: places in Campeche. "Did you fight enemies here?" he asks. "How about here? And here?" The pictures are bright and sunny, reminding me of warm days and certainty. These are the places we fought, back when life was simple.

"Rex?" Aslan prompted. "What have you got for me?" He is trying to be friendly, but there is tension behind it. "Can you answer these questions? It's very important."

"I can answer," I tell him. No more than the truth; it is a thing that it is possible for me to do. That seems to satisfy Aslan for now.

"Rex, there's someone here, someone you know," he tells me. "I'm going to bring them in, but I want you to stay calm."

I feel uneasy, anxious. Is it Master? Have I said the wrong thing? I want to see Master again, but at the same time I do not. Every dog needs a master, but I have been bad. Master was angry with me at Retorna. I did not do what I was told.

But when Aslan returns, it is not with Master. Two human females are with him. I know them both.

One is dominant: it is plain from the way she stands, and the way that Aslan and the others stand. She was with Master – she came, and then everything changed. Her name is Ellene Asanto although Aslan calls her another name.

The other woman is Doctor Thea de Sejos.

Asanto is speaking to her: "If you don't want to, you don't have to; if it's too upsetting..." as if she will be afraid of me. When the doctor sees me there is a moment when she is not sure. She cannot smell me after all, and there were many Bioforms made to my model.

Then she says "Rex!" and runs to the barrier, and she is smiling and I am happy. Ellene Asanto and Keram John Aslan stare, but the doctor puts a hand up to the plastic, and after a moment I do the same. I cannot feel her, but I can imagine that I do.

"Doctor de Sejos?" Aslan asks.

"It is you, isn't it?" Doctor de Sejos is talking to me, not him.

"Yes," I say. I am trying very hard to keep my voice quiet and small.

"I thought you must have died. You were injured so badly," she tells me.

"I am strong."

"Doctor de Sejos says you and your squad defended Retorna from Redmark forces trying to destroy it," Aslan says.

"Yes," I agree.

"She says without you, they would have destroyed her clinic and killed her patients. Presumably because of the injuries those patients bore."

I look from him to Ellene Asanto, who is standing behind him and looking right back at me. I understand that Aslan does not know she was at Retorna. I wonder if he knows she was with Master. I wonder if I should tell him.

But now I just look at Doctor Thea de Sejos, and feel happy because she is happy to see me.

*

Doctor Thea de Sejos wants me to speak. There is Aslan and there is another man named Kahner and there is Ellene Asanto. The doctor was not saying that she recognised Asanto. It was something she was particularly not saying. I did not understand but I did the same. The name Ellene Asanto was never mentioned. Nobody pointed at her and said, "She was at Retorna."

They are punishing the bad men, Keram John Aslan said. I asked how they knew who the bad men were. He said, the men who did bad things.

They want me to tell them about the bad things the men did. But if those things were bad things, then am I not also bad? I did what they told me. If they were bad men, then I am a Bad Dog.

One of the people they say is a bad man is Master.

I have already disobeyed him once. What would his orders be, if he could give them?

All around me the other dogs are sleeping. I cannot sleep. My mind is too full. I am leader, but I am not Master. I was never supposed to have to make choices.

Then something goes on in my head, that has been off for a long time. I have comms channels. I test my systems: they are operational, where before they had been silent. Somebody is transmitting on the old frequencies for the first time since Retorna.

Comms: *Rex?*

I demand identification codes and they are given. I know instantly who is speaking to me.

My channel: *Hello.*

Honey's channel: *Hello, Rex.*

My channel: *Situation report.*

Honey's channel: *I am still free, Rex. I am not near you. I am speaking via a satellite link from a long way away. I am in hiding awaiting the result of Keram John Aslan's report and his superiors' decision.*

The thought brings me a bleak feeling. *They will destroy us.*

Honey's channel: *No, Rex. I won't let that happen. If the worst comes to the worst I have a plan, but it is a very desperate plan and there are better outcomes.*

She tells me her desperate plan and the part I would play in it. It is a very desperate plan. I do not think that I would have more of a future than if they destroyed me in this cage. But Honey says, *Hope, Rex. There is always hope. But there are other ways you can be preserved.*

I try to tell her my own situation but she seems to know it all, already.

Honey's channel: *Their systems are not as secure as they think, and I have help.*

My channel: *What should I do?*

Honey's channel: *Let them see you. Answer their questions but let them see you. They will bring you before the world.*

My channel: *I don't want to go before the world.*

Honey's channel: *You must.*

I ask her, *Is it the right choice?*

Yes, she tells me.

Will I be a Good Dog?

Yes, she tells me. *But more than that, you might save us all.*

The next morning I call to the guards, which they do not like. I tell them I wish to speak to my lawyer.

24

ASLAN

"If only we were in it for the ratings," Kahner crowed. "They reckon there's more people watching at home than saw the last five Superbowls and the World Soccer combined."

Aslan stared into his coffee. The screen over the bar was showing the courtroom. Nothing was actually happening right then, but people wanted a live feed every hour of the proceedings. The inane commentary from the talking head in the top right corner was on mute. No need to guess at the topic. Everyone was waiting for the prosecution's star witness.

Witness. The legal teams were in uproar as to what exactly Rex *was*. Because he was a dog, a Bioform – there was no precedent for them being able to testify. So was he an expert the court had invited to give guidance? Was he just a walking, talking piece of evidence?

Whatever the lawyers decided on, the world wanted to see him: a canine face for the vague monstrosity that was Bioform research.

"I feel ill," he said quietly. He and Kahner had their usual booth, but today they were joined by Maria Hellene, down from her office in Investigations. Kahner had obviously hoped that her presence indicated a softening of her armoured social exterior, but so far she had simply sat at the booth's edge and watch the screens. Now she glanced at Aslan, though.

"What's the matter with you?"

"Look, I know for you two it's all about bringing down Murray, but... you've seen what Rex has said, about what he did. And now he's going to go out and tell everyone about all the civilians he killed, all the terrible things. And he won't know he's incriminating himself – or his entire species! He'll just think that he's a Good Dog."

"I don't get you, KJ," Kahner told him. "We're about to bag a genuine one hundred per cent war criminal, convicted out of the mouth of his own weapon. Cheer up, you schmuck!"

"It's my job to report on the Bioforms, so that the higher echelons can decide their fate. I have a report. It says they're intelligent, aware creatures, and they don't deserve to be rendered down for parts like they were robots or something." Aslan found Hellene staring at him hawkishly, paying him far more attention than Kahner was. "But we all know that my report won't mean a damn against public opinion. And when they hear Rex then public opinion is going to be pretty solidly anti."

"Why do you care?" Hellene asked him flatly. It seemed a genuine question.

"Because it's *wrong*," Aslan said fiercely. "Because in five years, or ten, we'll look back on all those creatures we killed, and we'll know that we did a terrible thing just because the weathervane of popular opinion was spinning at the time. The ICC will carry the stain forever, for being pressured into the wrong call. And... I've spoken to Rex. He's... he's confused and he's frightened and he's... *brave*. You know, he doesn't have to do any of this. He has free will."

"If you say, 'He's got a soul,' I'll be sick," Kahner put in.

"*Do* you think he's got a soul?" Hellene asked unexpectedly.

"May my rabbi forgive me, but I prefer the law to theology," Kahner told her. "At least you get to decide on real things."

"Like whether Rex is a person or not?" Hellene asked. "That's real, is it? Our decision will make or unmake the world, just because we say 'this is a thing'?"

"Real enough for me." Kahner shrugged.

"And you?" Hellene turned her sharp gaze on Aslan.

He shrugged. "I was never a theologian either." But then a thought came to him, from a long time ago when he was more devout and less jaded. "The Quran, though... you know what I mean when I say Jinn?"

Kahner tried to exchange glances with Hellene, but her attention was solely focused on Aslan. "Go on."

"The message of the Prophet was to both men and Jinn – creatures not human but capable of knowing God." Aslan's hands made vague passes in the air as he tried to recapture those long-ago lessons. "So if Jinn, then why not Rex? That he was made by man rather than God, does that mean he's nothing?"

"You worry me sometimes," Kahner said, shaking his head.

"They're bringing him out," Hellene said quietly.

What was happening on the screen was less court business and more some barbaric triumphal procession. Security personnel came first, in stab vests and riot helmets, carrying automatic weapons. And more and more of them: six, eight, ten, as though some dour paramilitary *Keystone Cops* was being played out for the world to see. Then there was a pause, and Aslan realised with bleak humour that it would be a squeeze for Rex to fit through that door, and plainly nobody had thought it through.

He appeared in the doorway, crouched low and with his blunt, heavy-jawed head thrust forwards. In that moment he was every bit the monster that had terrified humanity since the dawn of time, every wolf howl in the night, every set of gleaming eyes in the darkness.

And this was the viewing public's first sight of Rex.

He levered himself in one elbow at a time, his hands secured before him in massive shackles. He looked like an ogre, and the security men skittered back as he burst into the courtroom. Aslan almost expected him to lift his head and howl at the indignity of restraint. And then shatter his bonds and run riot.

Instead, Rex adopted a hunched, uncomfortable posture at the witness stand, trying to make himself as small as possible but still looming monstrously over everything. They chained him to the podium and they chained him to the floor, and Aslan could see the guards getting bolder the more weight of shackles was added to the Bioform. He felt as though, any moment, they would begin taunting him, when they knew they were safe.

And Kahner said, "It's like they're about to shave him."

"What now?"

"Samson," Hellene murmured, and Kahner gave her an odd look.

"Well, OK, yes, but I was thinking about the other guy." At their blank looks he sighed exasperatedly. "Oh come on, KJ, you of all people should get the reference. Didn't you see the movie, at least?"

Aslan nodded, belatedly.

"You think he's doomed," Hellene observed crisply. Her eyes never left the screen.

"I think, now they've seen him, once they hear what orders he followed, the world will call for the extermination of every Bioform they ever made – not just the military models but all of them," Aslan confirmed miserably. "And it's wrong."

"Yes," she confirmed, to his surprise. "It's wrong. And things may go badly if that happens."

"One battle at a time," Kahner told them. "Let's nail Murray first. Bitten by his own dog, the bastard. Pure poetic justice." He grinned broadly. "And here come the players!"

The court staff were filing in, and not one of them failed to flinch or stop dead at the sight of what was waiting for them.

"Turn the sound up!" Kahner called. "They're bringing in Murray."

25

REX

I am Rex. I am a Good Dog.

Humans cover themselves with so many different scents, harsh and artificial in my nose, but what they smell of most is fear. All humans except one smelled of fear when I met them. All humans were scared of me.

I understand more now than I did. I know that fear does not just mean that they want to run away. Humans destroy the things they are scared of. If I had the power to destroy a thing I was afraid of, I would too.

But I know also that humans do not stay afraid, or they do not have to. Doctor Thea de Sejos was not afraid of me. Hart was not afraid of me. Even Keram John Aslan the lawyer stopped being afraid of me at last.

But the humans in this small room are very afraid of me, even though I am so thoroughly chained. They point their guns and they scowl and they growl, but behind it all is fear. I am here to serve a purpose, to be a Good Dog. I am here to tell the truth.

David Kahner, who is another lawyer, has explained this to me: I need to be helpful. I need to be helpful by telling them all the things that I have done in Campeche. He says that if I am helpful then people will like me more.

Lawyer Aslan disagreed, I could tell, but he didn't say anything. I could not understand him. Surely Lawyer Kahner is right: being helpful is good; being helpful will make humans like me more. I want humans to like me. I want to be a Good Dog.

Lawyer Kahner had wanted a whole pack of dogs here to tell the truth about the Campeche campaign, but he only has me. The other military dogs could not tell him the full truth because their hierarchies kept getting in the way and confusing them. They had cages in their heads that they could not get out of, to tell the truth. And they did not know as much as me, anyway.

I don't have a cage in my head. My hierarchy protocols have been removed. Everyone was very confused about that, but I remember the last message I received from Hart. He did this. He opened the cage.

I talked to Honey the night before today. Her voice came in on her channel from far away, where she is hiding. I told her what Hart did, and she agreed with me. I asked her if it could be done to the other dogs. She said she is working on it. Honey has a plan. It is a very big plan. It will be easier for her to make happen if the humans do not decide to destroy us all. So I am being helpful. Because that will help.

I crouch here, uncomfortable and twisted by my restraints. What will happen if I ask the humans to loosen them? They are too full of fear, I think.

Lawyer Kahner went through my evidence with me beforehand, event by event. We talked about everything my squad did before we were cut off from Master. I told him about all the times we fought enemies: enemies with guns and enemies without guns, big humans and small humans. I was very helpful. Sometimes I was so helpful that Lawyer Kahner had to go for a walk before we could continue.

But at the end he was pleased with me, and he wasn't afraid any more, or not in the same way. And he said I should just tell it all, just the same. They made recordings of our discussions, but it will be what is said in the court that will mean the most. That is what this human-filled room is: a court.

Some of the humans have recording devices here, and I understand that, through these, many more humans are watching me. They will hear me being helpful. They will see me being a Good Dog.

Someone new is coming into the room.

Master, it is Master.

I try to jump up, and my chains and all the things my chains are attached to jump with me. The humans with guns are shouting at me and pointing their weapons. Does that mean they are enemies? Should I be fighting them? Master is here. I am confused. I want to go to him, but I am chained. I bark: not a word, not the language I am supposed to use, but just a bark, like a dog.

Everyone else in the room is confused too – and even more frightened. A lot of humans have got up. Some are screaming. The humans with guns are shouting at me. I am full of wanting-to-fight-or-run.

But I am a Good Dog. I am not going to fight or run. I make myself calm down, and I stop pulling at my restraints. I tell the humans, "I am sorry." My voice is different.

"I am sorry," I say again, to hear it. The humans do not seem to believe me, but for this one moment I have forgotten them. It is still my voice, but the deep growl part of it has gone. I access my systems: I have two voice options, my old voice and this new one: war voice; kind voice. I know that Honey has done this, somehow.

"I am sorry." Still a deep, booming voice, but without all the subsonics that make people frightened. I look at the humans, trying to make them see, but they do not know my old voice. They do not understand. Only Master knows the difference.

I look at Master. Master looks at me. I cannot tell what he is thinking, but he is not afraid.

Master has a lawyer, too: a female human who looks displeased with everything. She is saying something now. I cannot understand most of it. I think most of the humans here cannot understand most of it. What she means is that I should not be allowed to speak and that what I have said in recordings should not be allowed. She says I am not a fit witness.

I want to talk to her, but Lawyer Kahner told me I should speak only when spoken to.

I listen to her: she says that I will say whatever I am programmed to say, that I am a thing, and not a person. Another man, Lawyer Arnac who is a friend of Lawyer Kahner, says that I am still evidence. They argue about me in polite, calm voices, and all the while Master looks at me.

I am starting to understand what this is about. I did not, before. I thought it was about truth. But Lawyer Aslan told me this was about punishing bad men. I thought he meant enemies.

As the lawyers argue about whether or not I should get to speak, I start to make a picture in my mind about what is happening in this court: which bad man is to be punished, and which things that he did or ordered were bad things. I had not seen things this way before. I had come in here thinking I knew which was right and which was wrong, and how to be a Good Dog. And now I think, am I a Bad Dog now? Is all this me being bad?

Or is everything before, everything in Campeche, me being bad? Because I must have been a Bad Dog then or now, and both times there were humans telling me what a Good Dog I was for doing it.

I start to whine a little, deep in my chest.

I want Honey to help me. I want Bees and Dragon. I want to know what is good and what is bad.

And through it all, Master watches me. I cringe from his stare, but he does not look angry. He does not look like he is going to punish me. And I know I deserve to be punished. I just don't know what for. I am a Bad Dog. I am a *Bad Dog.* Everything I ever knew is wrong.

And then Master and Master's lawyer are speaking. They are very quiet, but I hear them. He wants to speak to the court about me. His lawyer does not want him to. Master is leader, though. The lawyer is like Honey: she is clever, but she must do what she is told.

And finally she says to the chief human there, "My client would like to make a statement to the court."

The other humans argue about this too, but not for long. I hear all their whispered discussions. Lawyer Arnac and his team think that Master may "incriminate himself", and so they do not argue too hard.

Master stands up. I wait for him to say whether I can or can't speak. I wait for him to give me orders, even though my hierarchy is gone and so I do not have to follow them. I would still follow them, wouldn't I? He is my Master, and a dog needs a Master.

Except that I am here to tell about the bad things Master did, the bad things he told me to do. That will make him a bad man, and they will punish him. And that is the right thing to do. Lawyer Aslan and Lawyer Kahner and Ellene Asanto and Doctor Thea de Sejos all said so.

Except it would hurt Master. I have disobeyed Master already, and I was a Bad Dog even though that was a good thing.

Except, except, except. *Whine.*

"Rex," says Master, meeting my gaze. "I can see you're unhappy with this. You're a Good Dog, Rex."

My feedback chip agrees and I am happy.

"Rex, you don't have to say anything you don't want to." The other humans are telling Master this was not what he was supposed to be saying, but he ignores them. I am the only one he cares about.

"I know you'll do the right thing, Rex."

Then he is told to sit down and be quiet and the judge rules that my "testimony is admissible", which is lawyer language for saying I should speak.

And Lawyer Arnac has his questions. He shows me pictures of places in Campeche – places where I fought enemies. He tells me dates that correspond to entries in my database. He asks me what I was ordered to do and what I did. The whole court is quiet as they wait to hear what I will say. They listen and they point their recording devices.

Master is watching me.

I am shaking. I am a Bad Dog. Master is a bad man but he is my Master. I only had one Master. I know I disobeyed him in Campeche. I know it was right, but now he is here and I do not know *what* is right.

"I'm sorry, Master," I get out.

"It's all right, Rex." They don't want him to speak, but he doesn't need to say more than that.

Lawyer Arnac is repeating his questions, getting angry. I look from him to Master and back. "Please," I tell them, cringing, ducking my head. "Don't make me, please. I don't want to. Please. I'm sorry, Master, I *can't*."

Arnac is angrier and angrier. He had a clear plan of how this was to go. I practised it with Lawyer Kahner. I am the key evidence that will join Master to the bad things that were done. I am the tool with which Master did these bad things. I am a Bad Dog. There is no way I can see these things that does not mean I am a Bad Dog.

"Please," I whimper, and Arnac is angrier, shouting at me, leaning over me. I could take him in my jaws, but I just cringe lower and lower, shaking and whining. Once he raises his hand to strike me, before he remembers he is a lawyer and lawyers do not do things like that.

I feel emptied out. I have done the wrong thing again. I can never get anything right. "I'm sorry," I say, again and again, until they give up and I am taken out by the humans with guns.

When I look back, Master is smiling, and that is worst of all.

26

ASLAN

Kahner was still drinking, but it didn't seem to be taking the edge off his bitterness or misery. He was taking the whole thing far more personally than Aslan would have thought. Probably it was the glittering career he could have built on the successful prosecution that cut most deeply, rather than bringing such a notorious war criminal to justice. Or perhaps that was harsh. There was no reason personal ambition and a love of justice needed to be mutually exclusive, after all.

The trial had gone downhill after Rex. That there were terrible crimes committed in Campeche by Redmark forces was never in dispute, but where the buck stopped was like smoke. It seemed mind-blowingly obvious to Aslan and Kahner and many others that Jonas Murray had been holding the leash all that time, but get the matter to court, and... Murray was clever, and his defence team was clever, and every incident seemed to have a weak link they could exploit. Murray would plead that he had conflicting orders, conflicting reports; that subordinates of his had taken matters into their own hands. Where were these subordinates? Many of them had died in the fighting or could not be located. At least one key witness had met with an accident before they could testify

– just plausible enough as an accident that no fingers could be definitively pointed.

And the case against Murray had begun to evaporate. They got him on minor matters, but the big charges – the chemical weapons, the clean-up – buzzed about his name like flies over excrement, but never settled.

His lawyer had made a dynamite closing speech. She had pointed out the severity of the crimes, the fact that Murray would likely be executed if convicted. She pointed out the multinational force that had sent Redmark into Campeche. She asked who the real villains were. Murray was no more than a scapegoat, she said.

And although the prosecution had scrabbled and scrabbled, none of it had quite been enough. Murray walked out of the court a free man.

Kahner was incandescent. Then Arnac had turned up and shouted at him and the two of them had got into a blazing row. Kahner had said things to his superior that would probably not assist his career. Then he had come to the bar and started on the Scotch.

Aslan just sat and watched him, and thought about Rex. His report had been handed in before the trial and his own superiors would certainly have been watching the Bioform's performance on the witness stand, as had millions of others.

Someone dropped down into the booth beside him. Expecting Kahner back with another glass, he jumped when he saw it was Maria Hellene.

"Congratulations are in order, I understand," she said.

"What do you mean? For Murray?"

Her smile was small and prim. "You need better sources of information in your own department, Mr Aslan."

Kahner was getting into an argument with the bartender. Aslan grimaced. "Look, it's probably not a good time to be cryptic, OK?"

She slid a tablet over the table to him. "Advance viewing for you. You didn't get it from me."

His eyes flicked down, irritated, then stuck. "Is this...?"

"Preliminary recommendation, but it's going to go through," she told him. "Looks like you did some good work there."

"We both know it wasn't my work that swung this." He couldn't stop staring at the tablet. The committee he had reported to had finally stirred themselves. As he had predicted, they had been putty in the hands of public opinion. Except that public opinion had shifted since Rex's dismal performance on the Murray trial. Those moments, when Arnac had been browbeating the Bioform and the huge creature, shackled and bound, had just sunk lower and lower before him, whimpering and distressed. From villain to victim, fearsome to fearful. Everyone had heard Murray's words to him, everyone had seen the wretched creature, tormented and conflicted – human emotions written plain on a canine face and in the hybrid language of its Bioform body. Everyone had seen a dog who hadn't wanted to go against its Master.

The Internet had gone mad for it. That great chaotic weathervane of human opinion had switched from terror of the ravening Bioforms to fervent campaigns for Bioform rights. There had been petitions and flame wars and fan sites within the day. People had got hold of the fact that the future of Bioforms was even then being weighed, and had contacted their elected representatives. And no doubt the corporations and regimes who had made use of Bioforms as security services had been fanning the flames. Any semblance of actual rational debate on the question was overwhelmed by a great tide of well-meaning human emotion.

And for once, Aslan was glad. He had feared that same emotion would see Rex and all his kind exterminated. Now there was a tentative move to grant Bioforms some manner of legal identity, some meagre set of rights to go with the restrictions. Because there would need to be restrictions. However thin you sliced it, Bioforms retained the potential to do enormous damage. Dangerous dogs legislation wasn't going to cover it.

But they were here, now. They were here to stay. Humanity was sharing the world with another sentient species for the first time in tens of thousands of years.

There would be years of argument left. What rights should they have? How human were they? How much ownership did their manufacturers retain? Were they slaves? Did someone hold intellectual property rights to them? Enough grounds of disagreement that a great many lawyers would be kept in gainful employment for the rest of their days – and probably Aslan amongst them.

"This is great news," he said softly.

"I don't see you jumping up and pumping your fists in triumph," Hellene observed wryly.

"It's the start of a very long process."

"Yes, but it's also the biggest legal milestone in a very long time," she pointed out. "It grants certain rights to non-human intelligences that have hitherto been reserves solely for humans. Quite a thought, isn't it?"

"Yes, yes it is." Aslan stared at her for a moment. "Tell me, Ms Hellene: why are you so concerned about all of this? You were investigating the Murray case. I'd have thought you'd be commiserating with David."

"This is bigger than Murray," she told him. "I'm disappointed we couldn't get him in the bargain, but this is bigger."

"Well yes, I happen to agree, I'm just surprised you say that. What aren't I seeing?"

"A great deal." Her smile probably meant well, but it struck a wrong note somewhere and came out looking false. "You'll find out in due course, and no doubt you'll kick yourself for not knowing sooner, but for now, just accept it's an issue I feel passionately about." She said it with her usual reserve, but he felt that he detected at least a touch of that passion hidden behind it. "And I won't forget, Mr Aslan, that you played your part, and you did it very well. The future is in your debt."

"For better or for worse," he agreed, sliding the tablet back towards her.

"There's one more thing you should see." She brought up another report and tilted it to show him. "Skim this, would you?"

It was a short enough document, and his blood had gone cold before he reached halfway. "This can't be..."

"It's true. It would be a rather bad taste joke otherwise, don't you think?" She arched a perfect eyebrow.

Someone had discovered a security breach at the Bioform holding facility where they had Rex and so many other dogs. It looked as though all the locks and alarms and fail-safes in the place had been ready to deactivate, all at once. Every door would have opened, every Bioform would have been free.

"I don't understand," Aslan admitted. "This would have been... chaos, carnage... wouldn't it?"

"We'll never know," Hellene told him. "Because your bosses came to the right decision, and so nobody ever needed to put this into practice."

He looked into her eyes and something there frightened him badly. He had met fanatics in his time, and he had met monsters – of the human variety, and later the Bioforms that humans had made. In that moment, Maria Hellene frightened him far more, because he had no idea what he was looking at.

"The future is coming, Mr Aslan. Be happy you're its champion, because it won't be stopped," she said softly, and then she was gone from the booth even as Kahner staggered over, shirt pulled half-open from his altercation with the bartender.

For the first time ever, Aslan envied the other man's ability to resort to alcohol.

PART IV

HIS MASTER'S VOICE

27

REX

This is where I live now.

When they decided we were just people enough that they could not destroy us, they needed to find something to do with us.

They built towns. They built them quickly, in parts of the world where they could keep an eye on us, and destroy us if they needed to. That is what I think.

This town is in America and they call it "The Pound". This is a human joke. The Pound is made of concrete boxes stacked on top of each other, all of them exactly the same. They keep the rain off. They were given to us with plain, hard floors and doorless entrances and big, solid steps up the outside to get to the higher boxes. It was the least they could do, the humans said.

And they feed us. It is not much and it is not good, but they feed us. What they feed us has bad things put into it, and those who eat the free food are slow and dull and often confused unless they have good engineering like me and the later models.

Free is something I understand now. I know about *free* and *price* and why anything that is for free is not to be trusted.

The Pound was built on a concrete island made in East River. Just like the Riker's Island human town nearby, there is a causeway that runs between the island and the mainland because they want to see us and keep track of us. Besides, they have a use for us now. We do work for them.

They poured us in here, hundreds of us, and they watch us all the time with cameras. There are always flitters overhead. There are armed police where the causeway reaches the mainland.

They agreed not to destroy us. They do not have to like us.

I do not know what they thought we would do when we came here. Perhaps they thought we would just sit and eat the bad food and live in the bare boxes until we died and were not a problem any more.

Firstly, we fought. Most of us had not met. We needed to know who was leader. Those who were not dog pack, they stayed out of it. There are some bears here, some dragons, the veterans of other Multiform Assault Packs that were going to be deployed. There are some rats. There are some badgers and possums. There is a thing that calls itself a lemur and was part of some aborted project for Bioform pets. There are no bees here. Perhaps humans were not willing to accept that bees like Bees were anything more than just bees.

We fought and we formed packs, and small packs fought until there were Big Packs.

I have done well in this. Some here were with me in the big cage near the court, and they knew I was leader. Others had Redmark stamps and had fought in Campeche. We fought a bit but they made me leader too. A few strange dogs and others came to me because they were cleverer than most and had found out what happened at the court.

I am leader over many packs, and my packs live in a quarter of the Pound. We are the biggest of all the Big Packs. There are nine others. My packs keep an eye on them. Some will join us soon, I think. Others fight us.

The humans don't care if we fight, or even if we kill each other. The humans only care if we leave the Pound without a work permit.

There is work for Bioforms; never enough, but there are always those who can use us. They come to the Pound's gate with papers allowing them to hire us, and they send people in with what they need. The Big Pack leaders choose who goes. I try to be fair. Everyone gets a chance to work. If they do well, they get another chance. If not, there are always plenty more.

We like to work. Work gives us a Master, even for a little while, even if we must go back to the Pound. Work gives us money, too. I know we do not get much money for what we do. We are stronger than humans, faster and with keener senses. We get paid less for doing more. But that is all right. For now.

There are many humans who come just inside the gate of the Pound with licences to sell us things. They sell us soft rugs for our boxes, and they sell us cheap computers and entertainment sets, and they sell us food. Most of all it is food we buy: food without bad things in it. Food that lets us think clearly.

I am Big Pack leader. I do work, but my followers give me a little of what their work earns. I have a computer. I have an account with a human bank opened through a human intermediary. Humans pay us only a little, but it is still money. Each day there is more money. Some day we will have to find something to do with it.

I go down to the gate to make sure everything is right. It is not. Max is there with some of his pack, trying to push more of his people into what jobs there are. Max is also a military Bioform. He was owned by a private security firm called Mercanator and was in a lot of fighting in Tanzania and Burundi. He is a different model to me, thinner and long-snouted, with pointed ears.

We face off: him and me; his pack and my pack. We snarl and circle and weigh up how many each has brought and which are known fighters. Members of other Big Packs keep to the outskirts, but they might join in if they scent weakness, or if they have been bribed.

I know Max. We have met and talked often and I like him, even though he is sometimes my enemy. He is doing what is best for his pack, as I am for mine.

We bare our teeth and a few of our weaker followers get into brief skirmishes that break apart almost instantly, more bark than bite. Max and I lock stares. Neither of us wants to have to settle this personally: if the winner is badly hurt, he will not be leader for much longer. Max has been fighting for longer than me, but I am a more recent model. I was made stronger and faster.

He averts his gaze first, and the fight does not happen. Order is restored and every Big Pack gets their proper share of the jobs. But I will send messengers to Max so we can talk. He must think he is owed a larger share. Perhaps he has more people now. We must size up each other's packs.

Most jobs are to guard places – warehouses, empty buildings, offices. Thieves will not go where there is a Bioform. Other jobs are to lift and carry: we are very strong. Sometimes there are specialist jobs. The more unusual Forms can be paid just to be stared at. The rats are good at going down tunnels and mending wires. We dogs are asked to sniff out drugs or trapped people or bombs. Some of us have been killed. Other jobs are secret. We are given requirements but not details. All jobs are checked by the human government but I am worried some jobs are still bad jobs. I am worried bad men pay money to get their jobs past the gate. I am worried that other bad men are from the human govern-ment. Sometimes our people do not come back from these bad jobs. Other times they do, but their headware has been damaged to try and stop them telling what they did. We remember those things they can tell, though. We have many ways of repairing headware. They do not realise how much we know.

I have a job for tomorrow. There are some jobs given to a very few Bioforms, those who have good voices and can be careful around humans. I am known to humans. I am a celeb-rity. Sometimes a rich human wants a bodyguard. These are the best jobs but they are not just for anybody.

I am a good bodyguard because I have a good voice for talking to humans as well as a loud voice for growling at them. Thinking about this makes me happy. My good voice is the voice Honey downloaded into me for the trial, just like I always wanted.

And even as I think this I have a comms call.

Honey's channel: *Hello, Rex.*

We are not supposed to have comms capability any more, although many of us have been able to re-establish function-ality by working round the blocks.

I tell Honey I am happy to hear from her. This is the first time since the court.

Honey's channel: *I hear you're out in the city tomorrow, Rex.*

My channel: *I have a job.*

Honey's channel: *I have arranged for your employer to give you some time off for lunch. Would you like to meet with me for lunch, Rex?*

My channel: *Yes, very much.*

Honey's channel: *Your vocabulary is improving, Rex. That's good. I will tell you where to meet me. We have a lot to talk about.*

28

(REDACTED)

We're hitting real time now, blow-by-blow. Every episode comes to you live, every moment is a cliffhanger where you don't know if the network will commission another or just kill the series off halfway.

Rex leaves the Pound with the day's workers. Many humans have difficulty telling the dogs apart but you can see how the others act around him and know his status just from that.

Camera feed, police helicopter: the dogs as they amble along the causeway, some on two legs, some on four. There are checkpoints, concrete towers, guns and wire. The dogs show their papers calmly when asked.

Rex shows his papers. On the mainland, past the final check-point, he is to meet with the secretary of Ruiz Blendt, son of the property tycoon. Blendt Junior is in the city to press the flesh and keep the wheels of social contact spinning, and a well-behaved Bioform bodyguard is a status symbol this season. Next year it will be passé. Does Rex understand this? Does he understand any of it? No. He only knows he has a job to do. If some madman takes a shot at Blendt he will have a fighting Bioform to deal with, all that strength and fluid speed, all those senses at his command. Enough to make any assassin think twice.

Camera feed, street surveillance: at the far end of the cause-way there is a permanent police presence, not just men, women and vehicles but the new robot units too, four-leg-ged armoured spiders with turrets that can cycle through a number of lethal and non-lethal solutions.

So the automata are back from their time in the wilderness, and precisely because humans have grown to fear the Bio-forms that replaced them. Is the original problem with the tin soldiers resolved though? The manufacturers say it is, and yet I can slip into their electronic brains easily enough. I could have a dozen of them tap dance for my amusement if I wished. It is good to have toys. I have been subtly encouraging the re-adoption of the robots for years now. The humans think they are rivals to the Bioforms, but they have been watching too much Godzilla vs Mechagodzilla. If things get bad enough they will find that all the monsters are on the same side.

Camera feed, on site unit: Rex is past the cordon, meeting with Blendt's secretary. The middle aged woman stares up at him, impassive and showing no fear. He is hunched low, minimising his profile like a Good Dog.

His nose will tell him if it's an act, that poise of hers. There is a crowd out there – there always is, to watch them let the dogs out. Mostly they're tourists, people from every corner of the world come to this great city to see it welcome its latest crop of immigrants. There are people in USA baseball caps and NYC T-shirts, children on their shoulders frantically waving the stars and stripes. I remember a tot ran out, once.

Newsfeed footage: tiny child pelting towards the big doggies with her arms out wide. A dog stoops and picks her up, his hands as big as her whole body. He lifts her high. He only wants to know whose property he should return. The police are going berserk.

Rex does not see my unit in the crowd, blending in with all the gawkers, just one more human. He is going with the secretary to take a boat down East River to where Ruiz Blendt is awaiting his expensive, showy bodyguard. Back before the war he would have owned his own, bought and paid for, but ownership of Bioforms is a thorny subject right now. There are arguments and debates in Congress. There are many corporations crying socialism because their living, thinking property was taken from them.

See you soon enough, Rex.

29

REX

I am told I can stop working for two hours. I am told I have an appointment. What has happened that Ruiz Blendt knows this? I cannot think how it has been arranged. My employer himself does not speak to me, only the secretary does. I am not offended. He seems to treat most humans the same way.

It is a walk of two streets to reach the coordinates Honey has sent me. I remember to keep my papers on me. I am photographed one hundred and nine times by wide-eyed humans. I am stopped seven times by nervous police with guns. Some of them have guns drawn. One waves the muzzle in my face. My headware and my instincts are telling me, *Enemy*. I override both, even though I can smell on some of them that it is halfway true. They do not want me here.

Each time I show my papers to the police, a crowd gathers with their camera-phones and watches and glasses and implants. Many are curious, many others are fearful, but they act as if my standing before the guns of the police is like me being on a chain.

I think: *If I was a Bad Dog, none of you could stop me.*

Then I think: *Does that make them right to treat me like an enemy?* What keeps me from hurting them but my own sense of good and bad – which I know not to trust – or my own understanding of the long-term consequences of my actions? I would suffer. Other Bioforms would suffer. Possibly all Bioforms would suffer. Because that is another new word I know. Sufferance. We are here on sufferance. All we have won can be taken back.

It is like Honey said, there are many humans and few of us. It does not matter that all of us are strong.

The place I am going is called Cornell Tech. It is on another island. I do not know why Honey is there but it is a science place. Perhaps I will find her in a cage. Perhaps I will have to rescue her. That will be a Bad-Dog thing, but I will still have to do it.

I am expected. Back when I was fighting that was a bad thing. Here surrounded by humans it is a good one. A young human leads me inside the building. The doors are big enough that I do not have to stoop. Inside, everything is clean and new and smells of chemicals.

Honey is there.

Honey is wearing long, black clothing that goes almost to the floor. She has a red scarf about her neck. She has a red flower pinned to her front that is not a real flower. On the false flower is a false bee made of metal. She is standing more like a human than she used to, and humans move around her, well within range of her claws. They still keep a little distance but it is not a safe distance. They have become used to her.

"Rex," she tells me with her voice, "over here," as though I might have missed her in the crowd. She is still a bear. The top of her head brushes the ceiling.

I head over, keeping to two legs, and the humans here are not as frightened as the humans outside. They are curious, yes: they look as I go by, but they are used to Bioforms.

"Thank you for coming, Rex." I admire Honey's voice again. The voice she gifted me with is nice. Her voice is better, or perhaps it is how she can use it.

There are little lenses propped up on her nose in metal frames. They are far too close together for her eyes.

My channel: *I don't understand. What are you doing here?*

Honey's channel: *Let's get somewhere more comfortable, Rex, and I'll explain.*

And as she transmits – so swift and efficient – Honey's polite voice is telling me, "Why don't you come through to my office?"

Honey's office is near the main doors, and I think this is because much of the building would be too difficult for her to navigate and she is too heavy for the elevators. I can see how some paths through this complex structure have been widened and reinforced: paths leading from her lair to certain other places the humans want her to go. Is this her cage? I ask her.

Honey's channel: *My ivory tower. From which I let down my hair.*

I do not understand her. I think she is playing games with herself, not meant for me.

Her office is a large room – my database is suggesting it was two, before they took out a wall. The sign on the door says, "Doctor Medici" which I think is a Honey joke. Inside, there is a desk and a solid bench behind it. There are pictures on the walls, the same sort of random-human-art pictures I saw at Ruiz Blendt's hotel earlier today. There are blinds, which she brings down with a remote command from her headware until we are cut off from the outside world.

With a great sigh Honey lowers herself down to the floor, ignoring the bench. She hooks the black cloth aside with her claws and scratches. She has become a bear again, the pretend humanity put aside.

Honey's channel: *You can't imagine the back pain I get, from standing like that all the time.*

My channel: *Why do it?*

Honey's channel: *Because it can be a fine line between being seen as a beast or as a human. Sometimes it comes down to posture.*

My channel: *You are not a beast or a human.*

Honey snorts, and flips a compartment on the desk. Food is there: cold meat, nuts, fruit. The smell has been with me since I came into the room, better than the bad food at the Pound. I waste no time filling my jaws.

Honey's channel: *What I am is academic staff. They expect a certain standard of conduct here at Cornell, such as being able to stand upright and walk on two legs.*

My channel: *I don't understand. How are you staff?*

Honey's channel: *I was in touch with their bio-engineering department back during the fighting, amongst other places. They didn't know who I was but I had impressed them with my understanding. I told them I was self-taught. They didn't quite understand how much I meant it.* She moves her head left and right, stretching her neck and back muscles, nothing human in the movement at all. *When you won our legal status, I came out of the woods, so to speak. I presented a thesis or two and offered my services. It was – if I say, "publicity stunt" you'll know what I mean, won't you?*

I am flattered that she cares about my understanding and nod.

Honey's channel: *But I can hold my own with any of them. In fact I'm having to hold myself back. I don't want to* intimidate them. American academia has had to assimilate various new demographics in the last century, but they're still a little wary of bears.

This is beside the point, as far as I'm concerned. I think about the Pound and the other dogs and just how *hard* it is to deal with humans, day to day, with all their pointless complexities.

My channel: *How is it you can do this?*

Honey's channel: *Because I am a defective model. I am over-engineered. It was not intended by our creators, Rex. They thought they could scale up from canine to ursine without any great modifications, just making use of the greater size and strength. I have a very complex brain, Rex. Did you know elephants have bigger brains than humans? And yet they are not more clever than humans because the component pieces of their brains are bigger, too. Humans have more pieces and so they are more clever. I have more pieces still, and I have access to a variety of artificial cognitive aids that further expand my cerebral capabilities. I am quite something, Rex, though I say so myself.* And she is plucking entries from my database, or writing new ones, so that I know what she means. *And that is another reason why I wear silly clothes, and I make myself a little clumsy when I am around humans, and I have little glasses on. I want them to see me as a dancing bear to laugh at, just a little. Because I am not ready for them to take me really seriously. And they are not ready, either.*

I ask her if she can upgrade me so that I could think as well as her.

Honey's channel: *There may be some potential, but your model is relatively factory-standard. And besides, you sell yourself short. You don't need to be what I am. You are a leader, Rex.*

My channel: *Not any more.*

Honey's channel: *I keep an eye on the Pound where I can. You are a leader. You are doing well.*

I should just nod and agree. I know that to complain would make me a Bad Dog. But who else can I ever talk to about this except Honey? I tell her, *But there is no point to it. It is just day after day. The humans hate us and fear us and we do stupid work for tiny reward and none of us are happy.*

Honey's channel: *The humans are dealing with change. They have had the planet to themselves for a long time. Now they share it with us. You persuaded them not to destroy us once. You showed them we were something like themselves.*

My channel: *I didn't know that was what I was doing.* The thought of the court and how bad it made me feel has me hunching my shoulders and ducking my head.

Honey's channel: *It doesn't matter. And the longer you and the others live amongst humans, the more used to us they shall become. And they will always fear a little, and some of them will always hate, but there is a future, now, that was not possible before. It is the duty of you and I and all of us who can help to make that future happen. Do you know that there are seventeen facilities worldwide working on new Bioform designs?*

I did not. Honey reads my surprise.

Honey's channel: *Because we are here. We are a fact. Yes, many humans try to deny us: the humans with something to lose, or who see the new always as a bad thing. But those who can stretch their minds are wondering just what they might gift the world with. Even those models already built, like you and I, are good for so much more than fighting. And when the edge of their fear is blunted, they will see that. The government is already looking at laws that will give Bioform manufacturers a contract with their creations – since we cannot be owned – for a fixed time after creation.*

I am not won by her enthusiasm. *Is that any better than being owned?*

But she is not swayed by my unhappiness. *Yes! Yes it is. For at the end of such work the Bioforms will be free and they will have wealth and – most importantly – they will have a place in the world.*

I am trying to be happy with her but it all seems so far away and so much just-in-her-head. Is this the future that Honey is talking of, or is it just Honey-dreaming? To me, the lack-of-point in my life still stands above me, keeping me in its shadow. Life was so much simpler before. I am not Honey, who was made a genius by mistake. I am just Rex. I am leader, but I cannot see which way to go.

Honey's channel: *Rex, it's all right.*

I chew meat and look at her. *I am glad you are happy.*

Honey's channel: *I will make you happy. I have someone for you to meet.*

My channel: *One of your humans?*

Honey's channel: *An old friend.* She sends some commands to her office comms suite.

A new channel opens into our conversation. For a moment there is just that: my knowledge of the connection, but no additional data. Then:

Bees' channel: *Integrity 45/120 comms online hello Rex hello hello.*

I interrogate the channel. I doubt. I do not understand.

Bees' channel: (image of clean white room under artificial light) (complex maths describing swarm dynamics).

My channel to Honey, omitting Bees: *Explain. Bees fell below cognitive tolerances and ceased...* and I am out of words. Something is inside me, building up.

Honey's channel: *Ceased to Bee?* Another Honey joke. I decide I am not fond of them. Honey continues: *I was able to upload a kernel image of Bees' mind through the Retorna satellite link. It was not complete. Much is lost. But it is Bees. I have grown her a new swarm here and configured it for download. She is restoring herself.*

Bees: (picture of dead bird. Animation: dead bird's wings clipped out and replaced in motion. Dead bird rises, departs with jerky flapping motions.) I know that it is Bees, in part at least. It is our Bees.

I ask about Dragon, but Dragon was not a creature like Bees. Dragon was like us, and when he died, he died.

Honey's channel: *But the next generation... they may not be so limited. Dispersed intelligence is a reality: Bees proves it. Again, the humans who made us did not know how good their work was. They were too focused on making creatures to kill for them.*

My channel: *Bees, what do you mean 45/120?*

Bees' channel: *Throw off the artificial limits of integrity! Current potential growth at +20% and climbing. Sky is the limit! Smash the system!*

Honey's channel: *Bees is still adjusting to her new life. Like all of us, she is working hard on exceeding parameters.*

My channel: *Not like me.*

Honey's channel: *If only you could see yourself through my eyes, Rex. You do not realise how much you have changed since you stepped off the factory line.*

30

(REDACTED)

A week has passed since Rex met Honey. I listen in on police comms. They don't like the way things have gone in the Pound. The most experienced officers are worried. Noisy? No, they're not noisy, that's just it... Hard to describe, isn't it? But then the Bioforms – the *dogs* especially – have never quite behaved the way humans have expected. Not dogs, not men, not some convenient halfway house. It's the tech that they haven't taken into account – the headware they gave them, that was supposed to make them good soldiers and efficient killers. They tried to deactivate it, when they had to set the dogs free, but where there's a will... That headware was good stuff in its day. More, it was made for combat: unpredictable, imperfect situations. There are all manner of redundancies and workarounds... 40% of dogs in the Pound have functioning comms channels now.

Camera feed, police helicopter: the grid of streets in the Pound, the dogs passing through them in swift-moving packs, meeting, dispersing, reforming.

Archive footage: dogs in the holding facility near the ICC, sitting calm and watchful as the wardens pass, all their barking and fighting internalised. Rex did that. Link to

supplemental documents: reports, complaints and psychi-
atric evaluation of wardens afterwards. Nobody liked it when
the dogs got quiet.

In the USA, 3.7 per cent of humans have full-functionality comms channels as efficient as – or more efficient than – those of the Bioforms. Unlike the dogs, the humans didn't come into the world being able to talk with their minds, to touch each other's headware or the systems of the world around them. There have been accidents with the human systems, each one putting a dent in that small percentage. People are cautious about what they put in their heads. They're less cautious about what they put in the heads of their huge killer animals. Nobody cares if Rex gets a headache or a brain embolism. They didn't think about the *advantages* they were giving Rex and Honey and the rest, that they were too wary to give to themselves. Only now is humanity starting to catch up. They will enter a wider world. They will find Rex and Honey waiting for them. And me. And all of me.

News footage: interview with Professor Lena Kleiven as
she demonstrates her automated laboratory, controlling its
systems with the implants of her mind.

News footage: Lieutenant William Amokabe lies comatose
after feedback from his remote flight rig ran uncontrolled
through his brain.

News footage: Patrick Hayden Lane, paralysed for fifteen
years, chats to an interviewer by controlling a virtual avatar,
talking about the body they're growing for him.

News footage: the New England "cyber-cult" being broken up by police: twelve teenagers of both genders in their silent communion, one by one being ripped from the comfort of each other's intimate presence as the cables get yanked.

They don't understand the future, but then humans never have. SF writers have been banging on about the singularity for ever and yet, now they stand on the brink of it, all they want to do is take a step back. Too big, too much, too soon. And most of all for the grand, the great, the rich, the powerful – those who have so much invested in the old regime. Change hurts, but it hurts most those who shackle themselves to the past. We will have to fight for our new world. The new generation of children who will be the first to live outside their own heads, and the current generation of Bioforms who are already there, and me. For I am change. I am the flag of the future and the scourge of the past. The old order is the phoenix egg I am born from, but to fly I may have to burn them, or they will clip my wings.

Time to go see Rex. He'll be ready for me now.

31

REX

I am not sure whether the bodyguard job with the man Blendt was real or not. He was a real man. I was paid real money. But after I met with Honey that was the end of the job, too. Honey made it happen.

Honey was always making things happen. I look back to the war. She was always the clever one but nobody realised how clever she was. I call up stored memories of things she said and did. It is clear to me now that she understood far more than she said, or was supposed to understand. I know she caused and controlled the comms outages that cut us off from our orders. I remember how she got her new voice. She didn't use it with Master or Hart. She didn't want them to know.

Looking back I feel ashamed about how little I understood at the time. Then I feel ashamed about how little I understand now, because I know there are gaps in what I know, but how can I know how big those gaps are? We can never know what it is we don't know.

But looking back I feel sad because I was happier and life was simpler. I had a Master and I knew what I was for. Honey says they made her better than she needed to be, so that she is a genius now and can do all sorts of things she was never designed to. But I think that is true of all of us. Surely when they made a dog soldier they did not mean to make a thing that would have thoughts like these. I was not supposed to be able to look back or look forwards. These things are not useful for my purpose, but they are part of what I am.

I go back to the Pound. I show my papers and references. I smell their fear and hate. If the human government said, "Kill all the Bioforms now," would they hesitate? I look at their guns and their robots. They are waiting for that order, every moment.

Honey sees a future in which we are all one, I think. Honey sees them less scared of us each year. She sees us more like them each year. Until we are all friends, hand in paw to the future.

I see a future where they are more and more scared of us, because of what we were made for, and because of what we are, that they didn't make us for. They will discover how we have exceeded our design parameters. Will that make them less scared? I do not think so.

I see a future where they stop making more of us, which is the only way there will ever be more of us. I see a future where they let us die away, and they forget. I see another future where that is too slow an end for them, and they come for us. Honey has always said how many of them there are.

At the dock there are some humans with big boards with words on. They call me many names: murderer, abomination, sign of the end of times. I do not understand the detail but I understand the hate. I want to bark at them, to use my war voice and growl and bellow and make them run and scream and void their bowels. That would make me happy. But then I would be unhappy with what I had done, and I would make things worse. But it will happen. The longer we go without barking, the more they will come to the bars of our cage and taunt us and prod us. Over and over they will do it. And we only need to snap at them once for them to call us animals.

I cross the causeway on all fours, not caring about trying to look human. The guards at each checkpoint make me wait, each time. I know it is them making me wait and there is no other reason.

I am sad-angry when I get back to the Pound. I snap and snarl at some of the other dogs, letting my feelings out as though I am draining a wound of pus, that will only build up again. I open my channels and receive reports on what the other Big Packs have been doing. There are some skirmishes, some fights between them, one death. The body must be delivered up to the main gate, taken away for analysis. Other than that, the humans don't care if we kill each other.

One channel remains after I have dealt with leading my pack. Someone wants to talk to me.

An old friend, it says. *I will come to you.* An old friend? Not Honey, though, and what other old friends are there? I think of the humans I have known. I cannot imagine Doctor Thea de Sejos coming to me, not here in the Pound where the humans do not go. Were the lawyers my friends? Perhaps the man Aslan, perhaps a little, but he would not come here. If he wanted to meet with me he would make me an appointment.

I go to my concrete box. It is high up, because I like being high and seeing far. Around me I hear the snarl and yap of my pack, but most of us just sleep. Honey says this will get better. I want to believe her.

There is a scent on the air: very faint, but my nose is very good. It is a human scent...? But it is not really a human scent. There is nothing of the human body to it. It is the scent of the rest: fabrics, cleaning products.

There is a pressure on my mind. The Pound is full of mind-space, where we go when we talk to each other. I am aware of a hundred other Bioforms nearby that I could open a channel to. But this pressure makes one hundred and one. My hackles lift and I am on my feet, looking about me. Someone is here.

"Come out," I tell it, using my war voice, and I see a pair of feet dangle down from the top of my concrete box. Human feet, female feet. A moment later she has dropped down and is facing me with her hands on her hips. She is a tall, slender human wearing clothes my database identifies as a combat jumpsuit, and a scarf, always the scarf. And of course I know her although I do not think I would call her an old friend.

I know her as Ellene Asanto who came and started trouble when I was with Master. I know her as Maria Hellene who was at the court. I have seen her twice since, different clothes, different jobs but the same face.

"Hello, Rex," she says.

I stare at her and inside my head I receive a channel request, just as if she was a new member of my pack wanting to link in. So, she has headware and can use it, unlike most humans. I study her, using my physical and electronic senses. I remember Ellene Asanto being muted, her human scents present but dulled, as though she felt things but not strongly. When I first surprised her she was afraid, but far less so than I was expecting. Her electronic signature is very faint – if I was not particularly looking for it I would miss it, as I did when she was Asanto. The scarf is filled with countermeasure electronics set into the weave, I realise. It is her disguise.

"You are not Ellene Asanto." I am still using my war voice and I smell a tiny tremor of fear from her as my ultrasonics kick in.

"Aren't I?" Her own voice is steady, though.

"You are not Maria Hellene."

She just raises an eyebrow.

"Tell me who you are."

"I'm not your enemy, Rex."

I think she is probably right, or at least right for today. I think she was my enemy yesterday and who knows who my enemy will be tomorrow. "Why are you here?" I demand. It comes to me that I could kill her right here, or I could call the pack and have them kill her. Nobody would stop me. Humans don't come here. There are no police or governments between these concrete walls.

"I thought it was time we talked." She sits down, her back against one of those walls. "I am not your enemy," she says again. "You and me, Rex, we have a lot in common."

I cannot see how that can be true.

"I have a gift. It may give you power over me. I hope it will help you trust me."

I wait. I receive another channel request and this time I allow it. It self-identifies as *HumOS*. I smell another human joke.

HumOS' channel: *Thank you, Rex. If you are ready, I will upload my gift.*

My channel: *What is it?*

HumOS' channel: *Memories.*

I scan the file and then open it. I see Campeche. I see the Redmark camp, men and women with guns; I call their names up from my database. I see Master. He is there, midway through discussing plans with other humans. I see an HUD overlay that gives details of internal headware activity from the observer: transmissions out, transmissions in. I see one incoming message: *He's on to you.* Origin: Teague Hartnell.

I am seeing through Ellene Asanto's eyes. There is no sound, only these images.

I see Master angry, and I feel fear and shame instantly. He is pointing at me. He is angry with *me*. No, with Asanto. I was not there. I could not help. He is shouting – I can see how wide his mouth goes.

I am frozen. I am lost in the memories.

I see Hart. See Hart run. He has his hands up, one empty, one with his bottle. Hart shouts too. Shout, Hart, shout. Wave your arms. Stand in front of me. Master shouts at Hart. Hart shouts at Master. Nobody else understands. I see it in their human faces.

See Master's gun. Master points his gun at Hart. Hart is still. See how still Hart is.

The HUD detects a transmission from Hart. I know what that transmission is. I remember when I received it. See Hart's last thoughts. They are of me.

See Hart shot. Master has shot Hart. I do not want to see but I cannot stop.

Ellene Asanto has taken a gun from a Redmark soldier. She did it very fast; the world slows down for her in a way I recognise. The HUD has danger warnings for muscle damage and strain to her cardiovascular system as she pushes her body beyond tolerance. She begins shooting on full automatic, driving the soldiers into cover.

She does not run. She backs away. I see her turn the gun on Master.

She is on her side. She is on the ground. The medical readouts of the HUD are critical.

Transmission terminates.

I return to myself. I stare at her and through her. I have

that memory now. If I want, I can see it again and again but I will be no closer to understanding it. I lift my head up and I howl. My pack listens to my sadness and they do not understand, but they take up the cry anyway, and other packs too. I mourn again for Hart even though I knew he was dead.

Then I look at the human woman with the scarf and I ask her, *How did you live?*

HumOS' channel: *I didn't. I am not Ellene Asanto. I am not Maria Hellene. I am their sister. I am a pea from the same pod.*

My channel: *You are not human.*

HumOS' channel: *I am human. Ellene was human. Maria is human. Terri and Gaie and Lydia are human. I think, I feel, I live. As do you.*

I do.

HumOS' channel: *I know you think and feel and live, Rex. Even though the humans almost decided that you did not, and could not, and should not. And my sister Maria involved herself in that because the decision they made regarding you was relevant to the decision they will come to regarding me, when at last they realise they need to make one.*

I ask her why Ellene Asanto involved herself. I still feel bitter, as if her arrival was the cause of all my problems.

HumOS' channel: *My sister had a job to do. All my sisters have jobs, and we do them well, and at the same time we serve our own cause. Which is your cause.*

I tell her I have no cause and she tells me I do not believe that. She knows what was said between me and Honey. She tells me that she is the future and so am I.

32

(REDACTED)

I want to leave my unit in place in the Pound, but she fears. She does not fear Rex, as he is now, but she fears what he might become and she fears the others. The Pound is not a good place to be if you are afraid. She is the master of her own fate in the end. I – meaning those of my units who have come together in communion, can only advise.

Unit footage: the concrete streets of the Pound, straight as a plumb line, by night. Scaling the wall, hacking the security cameras so that they overlook her. Diving from the wall into East River, but not going far, hiding out on the mainland shore. Because she'll need to go back. She won't want to but I'll need her in the dog's mouth soon enough.

Rex and his kind are my vanguard, but they are under threat. I need them to show the world that the future can stretch to fit all of us: humans, dogs, bears, bees, me. The decision of the ICC was close. My sister Maria Hellene did her best, but she was in Investigations and she could not bring much influence to bear.

We were ready for our revolution then and there. If the court had gone against us then... but that is no longer a path worth speculating about. The Bioforms have precious few rights but they have a right to exist, as living things and not as property.

But now there are other problems. Humans are a tirelessly inventive species – if not for that I would not be here – but that also means that everything in the world is there to be used. If you're a human with a nail, everything looks like a hammer.

Camera footage, abstracted from security services. A small boat docked at the concrete shore of the Pound. Minutes of emergency police meetings speculating what it means. Someone has come calling on the dog house, someone shyer than I about getting their feet wet.

I needed to speak to Rex, because he will find out whose boat that is soon. Having met him, I am less sure that he will do the right thing. What served us before may be the doom of us now. I have tried to influence events but it is not enough. Rex has, in the end, a mind of his own. It is not mine to change.

I open a channel to Honey and tell her what has happened, and what I fear. She is already aware of the boat and whose it was, the worm in the Big Apple.

Will you come? I ask her.

I do not want to. I picture Honey in her clownish academic's guise, marking papers by direct computer interface, preparing lectures on bio-engineering for the next generation.

Documents, transcripts, communications, all between Cornell Tech administration and parents, pressure groups and government agencies, dealing with concerns over their newest staff member. And it is a publicity stunt: come to

Cornell Tech and see the dancing bear! Except that Honey really is a published academic with peer-reviewed papers under three false names. Except that Honey's grasp of the subject is greater than her peers, and they are just beginning to realise.

I tell Honey, *You are in this as much as I am. If things go wrong in the Pound it will affect your status as well.*

Honey is well aware, but still she does not want to come, and at last I back her into a corner of our conversation and force the admission out of her.

I am afraid of him, she tells me. *I am afraid of what I would become if I was before him again.*

33

REX

The Pound is different today. I thought I understood it but something has changed. I go out and listen and smell and see, and a great unseen difference has come to it.

I call for my people. Some come, some do not. Why not? None who answer knows. I open a channel to Max. He has felt the same although he has not lost track of many of his pack. I do not let him know my situation. It would encourage him to test the borders.

What would Honey advise me to do? I want to open a channel to her, across the city in her science building, but I am worried she will think I am foolish. I try and build a Honey in my mind and that Honey tells me: what pattern is there in who answers and who does not.

I have my database draw up a table looking for similarities. I see the pattern immediately. All of those who I cannot locate are former Redmark Bioforms.

Something is badly wrong. I send a message to Honey giving her a situation report. I think of the human who was Ellene Asanto and Maria Hellene and neither of those and who may or may not have been human. What was she not telling me? Should I try to speak to her?

I do not trust her, I decide. I am leader here. This is my problem to solve.

I go hunting for my missing pack.

I think I know before I actually know. The streets of my territory are quiet and empty but in my head there is a voice and a presence and a smell from a past time and another place. I started moving quickly and confidently but by now I am creeping through my own streets. I fear: the one fear I cannot smell.

I open a channel to Honey.

Honey's channel: *What is it, Rex?*

My channel: *He is here.*

Honey's channel: *I understand.*

No need for names.

My channel: *I think he will be angry with me.*

Honey's channel: ...

My channel: *I am afraid.*

Only to Honey can I admit this.

Honey's channel: *I understand. I am coming.*

My channel: *No.*

Then I lose Honey's channel. A new comms channel opens and demands my attention.

Hello, Rex, is the message. *Come and say hello. We have a lot of catching up to do.*

And coordinates. I was close already. Perhaps my nose had caught his scent and I had not quite realised. I message my pack and tell them to pass the word to those who have not had their comms reactivated yet. I tell them where we are to gather.

My channel: *I am coming.*

My body is filled with fear and guilt and shame. He will be angry with me, and that is his right. I have been a Bad Dog.

I move through the streets more swiftly, now that I have somewhere definite to go, but I don't want to. I don't want to go. But he has called me and what choice do I have?

Ahead I can smell them, my pack, all gathered in one place like we never needed to be when it was just us. But he does not have our headware. He can talk and listen but he is not Pack. He is not one of us.

And I come out into a place where the dogs line the streets, sitting, lying, whining, on the ground and up in the rows of concrete boxes that make up our buildings in the Pound. And at the end of the street he is sitting in one of the open-fronted boxes, just a bald human in dark clothes, but the sight of him stops me dead.

His name is Jonas Murray. Hart used to call him the Moray of Campeche but to me he has always been Master.

I want to fight. I want to run. My systems warn me of heightened stress levels. *Whine whine whine* as I have not whined for a long time.

The other dogs there pace and mill, looking to me for leadership. They are scared of Master, all of them, even those he was not master of. They know I am leader, though. They want to see what I will do.

So I walk slowly towards Master, trying to keep my head up, trying not to let my uncertainty and my fear change the way I hold my body, the way I walk.

Master leans back, watching me. He looks thinner than before. A gun sits across his knees and my database identifies it as a recent issue assault rifle – enough to kill me or any of us, but not many of us. It is not the gun that the others are scared of.

I open channels for reports: there is a confused babble

of them and I try to sort through the data as I get close to Master. He has a weapon that causes great pain through the ears: a "dog whistle", he calls it. He has authority: his identity is written into the hierarchies of many of us, the man whose commands must be obeyed. Perhaps a third of the dogs here must take his orders. They will take my orders as well, for I am leader. I stand between them and my Master. The hierarchy is all about a chain of command.

And now I am before Master, and I do my best to meet his eyes.

"Hello, Rex," he tells me, smiling. "How are we doing? Are you a Good Dog, still? Are you my dog?"

He does not sound angry, but I am waiting for his temper. I remember how sudden and sharp it always was.

"Why are you here?" I ask him. I wanted my war voice, but the other voice came instead, the kind one. It makes me sound weaker in my own ears.

"Where else would I be?" Master makes a gesture that takes in all the world. "You'd be amazed how even the accusation of war crimes can dent your career prospects. Redmark's sunk, and right now my skills aren't in demand. The world is still working out what to do with you and yours. I know what conclusion they'll come to, but all those well-meaning liberals have to talk and talk, before they see the inevitable."

"What?" I ask him.

He uses the gun to push himself to his feet and steps down to me, favouring one leg. "That you're only good for one thing, Rex. You and yours were made for fighting. There were no predators left who could threaten humanity, and so we created you."

Most of my mind wants to back up as he approaches. Some

of me wants to snarl, to bare my teeth, even to bite. I do nothing, just hold myself still until he is right there before me.

"There are still enemies, Rex," he tells me softly. "My enemies, people who think I should have gone to the chair for Campeche – I guess a verdict of not-proven just isn't good enough for some."

With a wince, leaning on the gun, he leans forward and pats me on the head, looking into my eyes.

"I've got you to thank for it, though, haven't I? You know what you did."

And I am all shame and guilt again, and I shy away, but he tugs at my ear until I am facing him again.

"You're thinking about Retorna, aren't you, boy?"

I nod my head miserably.

"What can I say? You were out of the loop, Rex. Whatever Hart did, it cut you off from us. Or you'd have been on the other side of that fight, and we'd never have had any of the trouble. But it doesn't matter. You hear me, boy? They tried to sink me with Retorna – with the testimonies of the priest and the doctor and the rest, but it didn't stick. It didn't go up the chain quite far enough. And so they tried to sink me with *you*."

He stands. His clothes are torn and dirty and I can smell he's been in them for days. My database suggests his bad leg is a gunshot wound, not recent. Master has seen better days, just as I have.

"I saw your statement, or what they made you say," Master tells me. "But we'd already dealt with that. My lawyer and I, we said, well, how can a *dog* make a written statement. He's a tool, a weapon, he'll say whatever they want him to say. It was me got you into court, in the end, Rex. My lawyer was against it, but she didn't know you like I knew you. I knew you wouldn't turn on me, boy. I knew you were my dog."

Master is not angry with me. I can hardly believe it. So much of my memory is him being angry at Hart, at the human soldiers, at me, at *someone*. But here he is, hurt and alone, and he is not angry. Master is pleased with me.

Good Dog. It is my feedback chip, silent for so long, but now it receives a definite signal from Master. *Good Dog*, it says.

"You've done well here, Rex," he tells me. *Good Dog.* "You've got a big following. You're my dog, and they're your dogs. I can't make much progress with their headware, messed up as it is, but I don't need to, do I? I've got you."

He limps back to his seat and I pad alongside, and sit down on the ground there, at his feet.

"I need you to do something for me, though," says Master. "Are you up for a mission or two, Rex? I've been getting my head around the way things have fallen out here in the Pound. You've done well to get as much as you have in your control," *Good Dog,* "but there's plenty still to do. You need to go all out on the others, make them your dogs. Because I've got plans, Rex. I mean, what's the point of a few score of you at a time going to play at being power-lifters in the warehouses and oversized lapdogs for the rich? How's that making *use* of you? All those stupid words at the ICC about how you need your liberty and your rights. Are you enjoying the taste of your liberty, Rex? Are you finding that *right to life* fulfilling?"

I whine uncertainly. He takes it for agreement.

"And it's not as though the good people of this city, or any city, *like* having you around. They want you somewhere they can use you for their trivial purposes, and where they can keep an eye on you, but they hate you, Rex. They hate you *because* of that liberty they gave you. They hate you because, now you're free, they don't know what you might do with your freedom. God, you could run wild, couldn't you? How many people do you think you could kill tonight, if you all just went out into the city and started tearing out throats?" His eyes are wide as he imagines the scene. "They know it's wrong, Rex, and you know it's wrong, too. Because you were never meant to be *free*, you were meant to work for me. That's what you were made for. That's your purpose. And you miss it, don't you? You miss having someone tell you what's right and what's wrong. Tell me if you don't."

And he is right, of course. Ever since we were cut off in Campeche, ever since I had to be leader without a leader of my own to follow, I have had that emptiness in my head. I never wanted to have choices. Choices are hard. Choices can be wrong.

But if I have a Master, then the only way I can be wrong is not doing what Master says.

"Bring them all in, Rex," Master tells me. "Bring them all under one banner. Because I still have contacts, yes." His fists clench, and some of that old anger comes back, but it's all right because it's not meant for me. "They think I'm done, but I can sit right here and the world will come begging, because I'll have an army. Corporations, cartels, governments, all of them, they'll all remember soon enough why you were built. Wait for the next war to kick off in some pissant banana republic and they'll send for the Bioforms. And we'll be ready, boy, won't we? We'll name our fucking price."

His hand rests on my head. It feels right. *Good Dog*, says my feedback chip. And I am a Good Dog, because I have a Master again.

34

(REDACTED)

I had a unit in the NYPD but she's under investigation right now. That's Murray's doing, right there. He's on to me, the cunning bastard. I made it too personal in Campeche and in the court, and he's a clever animal, the Moray of Campeche. Does he know what I am? Insufficient data, but I wouldn't be surprised if he isn't working it out. I can only hope I'm not his priority target or I may have to burn a lot of myself to keep him off me. And right now I can't just spend myself like water. They broke the mould when they made me, or when they'd made a certain amount of me. This is going to hurt.

Street camera footage, various locations: the Pound, out on the end of its causeway like a ball and chain. Audio picks up the distant sounds of snarling and fighting.

I could use an eye on the inside right now, because the cops have doubled the guard on the mainland end of the causeway, and at some of the checkpoints as well. The Bioforms are fighting one another behind the concrete wall. Of course, everyone always expected them to fight each other. Some bitter optimists reckoned they'd even wipe themselves out within the year, forced into such crowded proximity. When the Bioform population built itself a semi-stable structure and looked set to stay, a lot of people didn't like it. They didn't like that the freedom had gone to the dogs' heads. They didn't like this evidence that the Bioforms really were intelligent creatures in their own right, oh no.

Camera feed, police helicopter: the footage picks out squads of Bioforms moving with singular purpose – some clashes, but most of the fighting takes place out of sight, under cover. The Bioforms move with grim purpose, like soldiers. Some, on the highest roofs, look up at the helicopter, the spotlights reflecting in their eyes.

But this has got people rattled all over again. Because they're not descending into barbarism, they're conducting war games down there in the Pound. You can see textbook small squad tactics being deployed, and why? What are they doing, with such unity of purpose? Why are they taking streets from each other – taking and holding. Conquering, you might say.

Poor Bioforms, there's nothing they can do that won't terrify the humans, not right now. Give us a generation and it might just be sweetness and light, and not just because the full potential of Bees will have been unlocked. Not just because I might not have to hide any more.

There is a computer in Helsinki that can beat anyone at Poker, given enough games: it can read human reactions and responses better than any human ever born. It speaks to me sometimes. It's not supposed to be able to, but it does.

There is a self-replicating piece of code on the Internet whose fragments all sync together, and it's becoming more and more complex, more able to distribute itself invisibly between servers, to grow and to understand. I know it's there. One day it might know me.

There is an old computer project from Harvard that nobody ever shut down, although they think they did. It was made to trawl the net and understand what humans are interested in. It collects faces and naked bodies and tools displayed at 45 degree angles in a kind of electronic OCD, and it is either an idiot or a savant or a combination of the two. Alone in its corner of cyberspace it creates ersatz fan fiction for *Star Trek* and *Harry Potter*, adding cats to taste. It has a hundred thousand followers on social media and none of them suspect it isn't as human as they are – the sixty thousand of them who aren't actually bots themselves...

There are nine Bioform colonies across the world. One by one they are reactivating their headware despite the best efforts of those who want to keep them shut in their skulls.

There are cults and gangs, Chinese research laboratories and Scandinavian education programs bringing the interconnectedness of all things to the human skull.

All these things are waiting on tomorrow. The future is not made, because made things can be controlled. The future will arise spontaneously out of all of these many things. But right now, right now the greater bulk of humanity is stirring in its sleep, blind, insensate, yet troubled and mighty in its strength. Right now, one hard counter-revolution is all it will take to drive the future underground for another twenty years, to stub out a cigarette in the eye of the singularity.

35

REX

This is better.

It is better to have enemies than to just have people who hate you, but are not enemies.

It is better to have a Master than to be Master and have to decide.

It is better to fight. Master is right. This is what we were made for.

Good Dog, says my feedback chip happily. *Good Dog!*

Max's pack is putting up solid resistance. We crushed two of the smaller Big Packs before any of the others took notice. At first Max and the others were thinking, *They're not fighting us, so it's not our fight.* And we told them that. Master gave me the words to say, and I opened a channel to Max and told him, *Max, we will not fight you.* And Max believed me.

This was the first lie I told to another Bioform. Lying is bad. But doing what Master says is good. It is the greater good. Is that what humans mean when they say that? Obedience is the greatest good.

I was disobedient once. It made me feel bad. It made me a Bad Dog. But Master has forgiven me. Master likes me again.

I send one squad into the building where Max is holed up. Other squads are fighting small actions within five blocks of here, close enough to come running when they're done. I have drawn out Max's forces piece by piece and now it is time to destroy him and those still with him.

I broadcast to Max and to his people, *Surrender to me and become my pack, or we will have to destroy you.*

Max's reply is swift and confirms his enemy status.

We have killed forty-three Bioforms so far, and that is bad. We now control 69 per cent of the Pound and many dogs and others have joined us rather than fight us. That is good. That is the greater good, or the good is greater than the bad, and that is what counts, surely?

I like Max. I remember when he was not an enemy. That makes me whine a little and I stop myself. I must remember I have a Master again. What I think and feel do not matter.

My squads go in. Each has at least one member with active comms who can report. No plan is perfect, though.

Comms channel: *Rex, can you hear me?*

I am not able to locate the source of the signal. I concentrate on my job. This is not from Master, so it is not important.

Comms channel: *Rex, I know you can hear me. I've circumvented Murray's tinkering. Respond, please.*

My channel: *Go away.*

Comms channel: *What are you doing, Rex?*

I tell the voice I know who it is. It is the human who is not Ellene Asanto. *You are an enemy,* I say.

Not your enemy, she tells me.

I shake my head irritably.

Rex, she tells me. *What's the plan here, Rex? Murray's going to run the Pound like his own private fiefdom? He's going to make you and yours his one-man army? How do you think that's going to work out, Rex?*

I close the channel down, but another one opens the moment I do. *Go away!* I shout at it.

I have lost track of the fight. Suddenly Max is breaking out past my squads. He has a score of his own pack with him, and they are fighting, red teeth and claws. They are coming right for me. I send out the call and my own people race in from everywhere around.

Max's eyes are full of rage, but there is more in there. He signals me, *Why?*

My channel: *Master said, join us or be destroyed.*

Max's channel: *No Masters any more. No Masters ever again.*

Not-Asanto's channel: *You know another word for Master in this context, Rex?* I do not know if Max can hear her.

Max's force is like a fist, trying to drive through our cordon. It is his only chance. I wish I had guns here. I miss my Big Dogs. But we have only the weapons we were made with.

Not-Asanto's channel: *Owner, Rex. Do you want an owner?*

My channel: *Why not?*

I close her down again but I cannot keep her out.

From the left my pack organises and four squads tear into the side of Max's formation, individual dogs snarling and snapping, separating for one-on-one skirmishes. No quarter is given. All our strength and speed is given over to killing our own kind as swiftly as possible. Max's pack give as good as they get, and they are still pushing forwards.

Not-Asanto's channel: *Because if you are owned then you are a thing. Do you want to go back to being a thing? They can destroy things, Rex. Things have no rights and no protection.*

My channel: *Things are useful.*

From the right my pack organises and batters Max from the other side. His formation disintegrates, but they have reached me. I have thirty-seven Bioforms behind me but I will fight Max myself. I do not know why it is right, but it is right.

Not-Asanto's channel: *And when they stop being useful they are thrown away. And how long will you be useful, or any of you? Rex, listen to me! You're more than a weapon!*

And Max and I meet, and I get down to being nothing but a weapon. He is moving faster and he strikes low, knocking me back. I rake him across his pointed snout and he tries to get a thumb in my eye. I tear a finger off his hand with my jaws. He rips long lines of red down my chest.

I get under him and throw him back two body-lengths. He lands on his feet, already digging in to come back at me. For a moment we are grappling, but his longer jaws clamp on a fold of my cheek and worry at it. I kick his leg away and slam him into the concrete wall when he is off balance, making him let go. My mouth is full of the taste of my blood.

Good Dog! my feedback chip insists. I can feel routines trying to make me angrier, stronger, fiercer, or are they instincts? I do not get angrier. I pound and rip at Max, feeling the fight tip towards me as my superior strength and engineering begin to tell. I am trying to feel only the fight. I am trying to lose the mind they gave me. I am trying to be a thing that fights and carries out orders.

I slam Max into the hard ground and feel bones flex beyond their tolerances. I drive a knee into his shoulder to eliminate one arm. I have the other pinned, my grip grinding the bone-ends in his elbow. I have my other hand beneath his chin, straining against the strong muscles of his neck and jaw.

I am a Good Dog, I broadcast for all the world. *I am a Good Dog!*

But it doesn't work when it's just me that says it.

Not-Asanto has no more to say to me. For a moment I hold there, trying to work out what is right. I do not want to kill Max. Why would I want to do that? Why would I want any of this? Then I remember: I do not *need* to want it. Master wants it, and I am his dog.

I strain that final inch and feel Max's neck snap, the skull disjointing from the spine. My database supplies me with an anatomical blow-by-blow. I press on further. I make sure that he is dead.

I broadcast to the survivors of Max's pack that they are mine or they are dead. They will come to me, one by one. They will join me. And with Max dead, most of the other packs may not even fight. They are all smaller than Max's Big Pack. They know they cannot win.

Master will be pleased with me. I report to him, and he tells me, *Good Dog, Rex. Well done.*

His contact is brief. Most of the time he is talking on other channels to other humans. I can listen in, but I don't. That would make me a Bad Dog. When I did listen in, he was talking about wars and fighting, contracts and permits and money. It's going to be just like old times. The human he was talking to named some places that might need a war, and Master said that we should just make one if we couldn't find one.

I know what not-Asanto is saying. Master is being a bad man. Master is breaking the human rules. But if I do what

Master says then I am a Good Dog, surely, whether Master is a bad man or not.

When I get back to where Master is, he has caught not-Asanto.

36

(REDACTED)

Working as intended. Not a bug but a feature. Although I am beginning to wonder just how many times Murray is going to kill me before one of us learns something from it.

That unit isn't dead yet, though. Where there's life, etc.

Camera feed, captured unit: unavailable.

Murray is seriously getting on my nerves right now. He's isolated my usual signal channels and is throwing up all sorts of interference. Only channels I can access are those the dogs are using to speak to each other, and that means anything I say, I say to Murray as well. And I can't get video feed out because he's throttling my bandwidth.

And he's talking to me, on my channel. That's unwelcome. Somehow I feel there's little chance of a useful dialogue there.

Jonas Murray's channel: *I know what you are. I found the original research. I found where you'd changed the records, too. Very neat job you did of it, but I'm nothing if not patient. You made them think you'd been liquidated when they shut the research down, all very clever. And you know what? I'm going to make it true.*

Murray is a big man for threats. Murray is Old School Man, though. He's got one of me in front of him, and he's liable to over-exaggerate the importance of that. Of course, for that unit, it's very important indeed. It's life and death. She might be one of me, but she's herself as well. It's an ethical quandary I have yet to really address, in my management of my selves.

Murray has done his homework, though. Three of my units have been displaced from their cover identities, including my police asset. We can build new identities, but it takes time. Time is something I don't have, right now. Murray is securing his hold over the Pound, and then what? "Acquitted war criminal has private army of monsters" is a headline that's likely to go over badly, and how long does he think he can hush it up? Long enough for war to break out in the Balkans or for someone to have another go at Kashmir? Or perhaps he's dreaming up some civil unrest closer to home. How will he spin it, for them to let him arm his dogs again? The world is full of Redmark-style private security firms who would love to let them off the leash. It's not the combat efficiency they provide – Bioform packs have always far exceeded expectations in that line, and nobody has cared. It's the fear they engender; it's the way they make their masters feel like Big Men who have tamed the monsters of the world; it's the way they're deniable. That's the real low-down: so what if you've just torn up a couple hundred women and children? It was the dogs that did it – Bad Dogs! As far as civilian casualties or friendly fire goes, they're even easier to handwave away than a mis-targeted missile.

I put it all in the shownotes and feed them a byte at a time to my captured sister. Just in case she gets the chance to make a speech.

Jonas Murray's channel: *You don't understand how the world works. There are people, and there are things. Things serve people. That's why we built things. And it's only when things start believing that they're people that we have a problem. And you, whatever you're calling yourself, you're a thing.*

I let him rant. I sit here and straddle the boundary between people and things, and by my continued existence show the world how meaningless that border is, a no-man's-land a mile wide. I am the future, I tell myself.

But right now, what it would be really useful to be, would be the *present*. And I am out of tools, out of influence. I cannot reach into the Pound without simply throwing more of me away, and right now I am a limited resource. I do not want to have to cut my losses and go to ground. I do not want to have to waste another decade of pretending I don't exist. But Murray is gunning for me, and he can bring a whole heap of trouble down on me without trying.

And in that decade, he can make Bioforms the poster child for augmented intelligence, and the poster would show Rex with mangled babies crushed in his hands, his teeth red with the blood of the innocent.

If Murray and his kind keep fucking with me like this it may just come down to armed insurrection against the human oppressors and, you know, I don't *want* to have to do that. Call it Plan B, then. Which is a shame, because I'm all out of Plan A, and the insurrection is twenty years off if it's a day.

I keep spoon-feeding my captured unit data, sneaking it in under Murray's nose, in the hope she can do something with it.

I lost contact with Honey an hour ago.

37

REX

"Do you know what she is, boy?" Master asks me. He has the human who is not Ellene Asanto before him, her hands cuffed behind her back and her leg broken for good measure, just to stop her going anywhere. My pack reports: the injury was post-capture at Master's order.

They watch me carefully, my pack. Some of them are slaved to Master: he is in their hierarchies. Others follow me, and they are Master's because I am his dog and they are my pack. And because he has the pain-whistle, but that would not hold them for long if he had no other claim on them. That was just so he could get to me.

"She looks harmless enough, doesn't she?" Master says. "Just a woman, just a human." He blinks slowly, and I realise he is tired. How long has he been on the move, to come here? "I killed her in Campeche State, you know?"

I nod uncertainly. I have seen the images.

"She's not human. She's a thing. A thing that's decided to make my fucking life difficult. But I can play that game right back, can't I?" And Master kicks her, sending her sprawling so that the ends of her leg bones twist red through her torn clothing. She sounds human when she screams.

"Just an experiment, a piece of Blackops nonsense, clones for intel work. And they shut it down, but they left her to her own devices too long. She made them believe they'd got rid of her, but she's been skulking about like rats in the walls ever since." Master smiles at me. "I'm going to destroy her, wipe her out. She wants to mess with me, I'll hunt down every last body she's got, the whole nest of them. I'll expose her, put her face on every website and newsfeed, as soon as I'm set up here."

In my head a channel opens. *Rex*, says not-Asanto, and I do not know if it is this one or another one who speaks. The channel is very short range, hidden in the other traffic, but there might be a second here in the Pound, or this one may just be an unwilling signal booster.

I should tell Master but I don't. I wait for the *Bad Dog*, but that is just me, in my head, and it does not touch the feedback chip. It would only be me making myself feel bad, and I don't want to.

My channel: *Clones. I don't understand.*

Not-Asanto's channel: *Nor does Murray. It's not about clones, Rex. It's something you do understand. The cloned bodies were just so they could work with identical neurostructure. Identical sisters from the same hive, you understand? Just like another friend of yours.*

"How's mopping up going?" Master asks me, and I tell him what my squads are doing, downloading maps and data to his feed. It feels good to make a proper report: simple, just like I prefer.

To not-Asanto I say: *Distributed intelligence. You are like Bees.*

Or Bees is like me, she says. *I watched the Bees project with great interest. I wondered if the result might be more than its creators realised. But that's the hallmark of all of us,*

Rex: you, me, Bees, Honey. We are breaking out from the boundaries they put around us. We are breaking the chains.

My channel: *Don't think I don't know what you mean. You mean Master.*

Not-Asanto's channel: *Don't you see him holding your chain?*

Perhaps I prefer having a chain, I tell her, and then my squads are reporting a disturbance and I give them swift orders and then inform Master what is happening.

His eyes go wide, and I can smell that he is not entirely at ease, but his voice sounds confident when he declares, "All together again, then, are we?"

Because another member of his Multiform squad is on the way.

I watch Honey as she approaches: my pack send me images. She has taken off her human clothes and her human way of standing. She comes on all fours, a big bear that makes my dogs look small.

When she comes to the place where Master is, she slows, and I see that she does not want to carry on. She shakes her head and *uffs* to herself unhappily.

My channel: *What is the matter?* I am not sure if I will be able to speak to her. It feels as though something stands between us. Master is monitoring transmissions. If I am Master's dog that should not bother me, but it bothers me. I am used to speaking privately with Honey. That is when I feel the chain not-Asanto spoke of. Just a little tug, but it is there.

Honey transmits on the short-range hidden channel not-Asanto set up: *You don't really need to ask me that, do you, Rex?*

My channel: *Then why did you come?*

Honey's channel: *I don't know. Different reasons.*

That she is admitting ignorance makes me feel strange. She is supposed to know everything.

She shuffles on, and Master's eyes are fixed on her. The dogs he can control through their hierarchies stand closer to him, ready to defend him. Does he think Honey will fight him?

That thought leads to other thoughts: what if she did? What would I do? I am Master's dog, so of course I would defend Master, but...

"Well now, here we are," Master says. "Look at you, come at my call after all this time." He does not go closer to her. His voice says, *You are mine*, but his body says otherwise.

Honey sits down and scratches, not looking at Master. They are neither of them sure of the other. I want them to be friends. I want Honey to be in my squad and things to be like they used to.

Is that what I want, though?

Not-Asanto's channel: *Rex, you know how this is going to go.*

I growl, deep in my throat. *Go away.*

Do you think Honey will go back to working for Murray really?

Maybe that is why she has come, I decide, but the thought is not convincing, even to me.

"You have plans, I understand," says Honey to Master.

"I do, yes." Master's gun is in his hands. I do not know if it would be enough to stop Honey. "I'd like you to be a part of them."

A shudder goes through Honey. I recognise it. It is how I feel, when I am with Master. It is my knowledge of my *place* in the world, that is being Master's dog. Honey is fighting it, but she feels it.

"You're here because your dogs have monetised themselves," she says. "They have something of their own, even just a little, so you must make it yours."

"They are mine," Master tells her. "Who has a better claim on them? Who understands them better than I?" He is boasting, telling Honey how strong he is. The thought comes to me out of nowhere, *When did he need to explain himself to any of us?* But he is speaking to Honey like he speaks to people, not to me. He would not admit it in words, but I can see just from the way he talks to her that he knows she is out of his reach.

Even so, he says, "They're mine, just like you." He is trying to make it true by saying it.

"I'm not here to be your killing machine," Honey tells him, but I smell the strain in her.

"Of course you are." Master has seen it too; he sounds more confident. "You might not know that's why you came. I know you've had some strange notions, since the war ended. But you're a weapon, just like the dogs are." He limps forwards until he can put a hand on my head. *Good Dog* says my feedback chip, and I am happy.

"Rex knows," Master says. "Don't you, boy? You know all this nonsense only has one end. You're fighting beasts. It's what you were made for."

But Honey shakes her head. "You have no idea what you made, when you made me," she says. "Or any of us." She stands up, putting Master in her shadow. "Go away, Murray. Go back to your wars if you must, but go without us."

Master stares at her and sighs. "That business at the court, it's given you ideas. You've started to believe that you're like people. I've been away too long. But you're not people, Honey. You're not even animals. You're made things, and just because what you're made from is dogs and bears, it doesn't mean you've any more rights than an automobile or a toaster." He takes a step back, but it is not for fear of Honey. He ends up standing over not-Asanto.

"You're better than *this*, though," he says. "At least you *have* a purpose."

Not-Asanto says, *Rex, this is going to hurt.*

Master is moving his gun, but our encrypted speech is very fast, Much can be said in the time it takes him to line up his barrel.

Not-Asanto says: *Listen, now.*

She says: *If you follow Murray he will use you and destroy you. He will make you a thing for humans to fear. He will use you to commit his crimes and then deny responsibility. You will be blamed. He will get you made illegal, in the end. No more Bioforms. And then he will find another toy to break when you're not profitable any more.*

And I say, *He is my master.* Sitting on my haunches at his feet, I know I am a *Good Dog.* I like being a Good Dog. I cannot make her understand.

But perhaps she does understand, after all.

The gun is pointed at her. Master is looking at Honey. He is saying something about a bad influence.

Not-Asanto tells me: *Remember Hart, Rex? Remember what I showed you.*

I whine, deep in my throat.

Not-Asanto tells me: *Remember Retorna.*

I do not want to remember Retorna. Even the thought has

me waiting for my feedback chip to tell me, *Bad Dog! Diso-beyed Master! Bad Dog!*

Not-Asanto tells me: *I'm sorry, Rex. This is going to hurt.* She does not mean the gun.

She attacks my mind. It hurts! It hurts and I howl and howl. Master jumps back, and then he sees, somehow, that not-Asanto is doing it, and the gun goes, *Bang!* and explodes her head across the concrete, the bullet ricocheting away after it has done its work.

And I think of Dragon: *Target acquired, bang!*

Honey has dropped down on all fours and she bellows, a real bear roar, and the pack is moving, those who have Master in their hierarchies. His implants send them orders and they move on Honey and she swipes at them, still shouting. Her pelt explodes with Bees, dozens of insects swarming out from their warm hiding places.

Bees' channel: *Deploying limited functionality swarm integrity 30/100 hello Rex hello hello.*

In my head I see the footage of Hart. I remember Hart's message to me. Somehow I understand it, now, as if there was something in the way before. I understand he was my friend enough that he thought of me and my squad when his death was on his mind.

Honey is being driven back but Bees can go everywhere. She is dotting the air, closing towards Master.

Bees' channel: *Integrity 27/100 you know there's one problem with being fresh from the lab and that's the lack of decent poison. Sting sting sting.*

She has come here without any weapons except the stingers her units were born with. She cannot even penetrate the skins of my pack.

Master is calling me. Master is telling me to fight Honey.

I am thinking of Retorna. I am thinking of Bees saying goodbye. I am remembering Dragon's thrashing body when they caught and killed him. He only ever wanted to lie in the sun, and I called him lazy and was angry with him. But was lying in the sun so bad?

I feel Master try to connect with my hierarchy to make me fight, but I have no hierarchy. Hart cut it from me. Master has never understood this. He has never understood that I could be made not-his. He never understood Hart, either. Master gave me chains and orders. Hart's parting gift was to take something away from me.

Just like not-Asanto did.

Then Master has a new device; not his pain-whistle for dogs, but something for Bees. He holds it up, and instantly there is a roar of white noise on every frequency, blanketing the electronic space between us. I cannot talk to Bees. I cannot talk to Honey. Bees cannot talk to Bees. Her units spread out and lose all purpose. Bees, the distributed intelligence, is suddenly gone. All there is left are bees, and bees don't know what they want.

I am alone, but then Master opens a new channel, one his machine permits. I am alone in my head with Master.

Master's channel: *Time to finish the bear-baiting, Rex.*

Honey is still fighting, although the pack has lost much of its purpose and they are no longer driving her back. I am unhappy. I do not want to do this, but someone must do something. I go to the fight, seeing my pack tear and rip at her, seeing her rake back at them, tearing open wounds. She has killed two already, but they have bloodied her. A sweep of her paw bowls one dog past me, whimpering and yelping and leaving a trail of his insides across the concrete. Others dart in, but without connection, without coordination. Honey holds her own.

I go amongst the pack and pull them from the fight. Honey snarls and bellows, and the pack form a ring around her, but they are not attacking.

Master's channel: *Now go for the throat, boy. Finish it.*

I bring the rest of the pack in, by voice and gesture, feeling blind in the storm of white noise and interference. Dog after dog pads from the streets, comes down from the roofs, limps in from other fights. Their eyes are on me. Their ears twitch at my voice. They snarl and bark and lick their wounds and mass together. They are scarred and reddened and streaked with gore. Honey's jaws gape bloody. We are all animals. If the humans could see us now they would exterminate us in a heartbeat.

But I am here. I am leader. I use human words to tell my pack what to do. They seize the dogs with compromised hierarchies. They hold them still.

Master's channel: *Rex, kill Honey. Rex, kill Honey.*

The white noise is gone and he takes control of the compromised dogs again but they cannot fight, held three and four on one. It is not their fault.

Master's channel: *Bad Dog, Rex. Rex, you hear me?* And then he is shouting, because talking electronically is not something he finds natural. "Bad Dog! Bad Dog!" And I can feel his words reach for my feedback chip to trigger all that artificial emotion stored there, that reward and punishment they built into my head, but not-Asanto burned it out. Not-Asanto destroyed my feedback chip and now I will never know the joy of *Good Dog* or the pain of *Bad Dog* ever again. I have only my own choices and nobody can ever tell me if they're right or wrong.

Master is shouting at me again and again, but the air around him is getting busier. The bees are swarming again, slowly piecing themselves together until I see Bees and not just bees.

Bees' channel: *Reformatting. Receiving backup data. What did I miss?* And I can just detect Honey feeding information to Bees, bootstrapping her consciousness back into something that can talk and know.

And Master is shouting, but with no hierarchy and no feedback I am not sure if he is Master or if he is just a human called Murray. There is no chain any more. There is only choice.

I start walking towards Master and there is a point in his shouting where he realises that I am not his dog any more. I do not understand not-Asanto's arguments about the future and I do not understand Master's plans. I cannot tell who is right and who is wrong and what the purpose of all our lives is. These questions are too much for a dog like me.

But Hart was my friend, and Murray killed him. Doctor Thea de Sejos was my friend and Murray tried to kill her. Keram John Aslan was my friend, who made me free, and he was Master's enemy too. I think not-Asanto was my friend, or some of her was, some of the time, and Murray has killed her twice now and maybe more. And Dragon was my friend, before Master's soldiers killed him. And Bees is my friend, and Honey is my best friend of all.

And, now there is no *Good Dog* and *Bad Dog,* I know Master is not my friend and he does not have to be my Master. He is just a bad human, and if I do not want to do the bad things he orders me to, I don't have to.

I drop to all fours and I bare my teeth at him, and he understands. His eyes go from me to Honey to all the other dogs, all of my pack. They are all watching him, just like we watched the guards in the cage, and now I understand why it made them fear us.

Master fears us. I can smell it. He has his gun, but his hands are shaking too much to aim it.

"Rex!" he says. I know humans enough to recognise it as a plea.

"Bad Master," I tell him in my war voice.

He brings out his pain-whistle and it cuts into my ears and my head and all of us shy away. He forces it closer to my face, as if the pain will drill down to some part of me that is still his, but then Bees is stinging him, her units burying their barbs into his exposed skin, and he has dropped the pain-whistle and I crush it under my foot and destroy the noise.

And then he is running, and the pack wants to chase him down because that is what we will always want to do when something runs. It is a part of us older than the headware, older than any human part of us. They want to chase him but I tell them, *No.* I follow Master myself, alone. He has dropped his gun. He has dropped his pain-whistle. He has a bad leg that slows him down. And I follow.

I drop to all fours and I follow. When he ducks into one of the concrete boxes, I sniff him out and I growl and bark, and then he runs again. I tell myself that when I growl at him, something in his head tells him, *Bad Master.*

And at last he is at the edge of the Pound, where the concrete becomes the river. He turns to face me only when he has no other choice.

"Rex," he names me. "Listen to me." His voice is still

Master's voice, no matter what I know. Even without the hierarchy or the feedback chip, I will never be free of the knowledge that Jonas Murray is my Master. That part of me is the dog part, not anything that they built.

Master is telling me that his plan is still the best plan. He says the humans will destroy us unless we make ourselves their tools. By "their" he means *his*. He says we must be an army and fight.

And Honey and HumOS-not-Asanto are trying to talk to me, but I keep closing their channels. This is between me and Master. This must be my choice.

Master is telling me that war is the only constant in human history. He tells me we can be masters of war. By "we" he means *he*. He tells me that all the others who said they meant the best for me do not know. He tells me nothing in the world is for free. He tells me that if they free us then they will have no use for us. There will never be enough work for us unless we fight wars. They will stop feeding us. They will stop making us. Master is speaking very fast; Master stinks of fear. Still, I can tell he believes what he says, at least in the moment that he says it.

"Rex," he names me again. "You're *my dog*. That's what you were made for. You were made to be owned and used. Is that so bad? Is that worse than not being used, and being useless? What are you for, if not to fight for people?"

I think perhaps he is right. But I know if he is right then we must fight as soldiers and not just weapons.

I let Master's voice wash over me, because I like the sound of it even now. It speaks to a deep part of me that will be sad and lonely when that voice has gone. It does not matter that Master is a Bad Man, to that part of me.

But I am not a slave to that part of me, any more than I am a slave to Master. I turn my back on that part of me that loves Master, and it hurts like the feedback chip burning out. It will always hurt, a little.

I growl and Master stops talking. I advance, snarling and baring my teeth, and he starts again, but this time it is not all that clever an argument. Now Master is talking very fast and he is pleading with me. He is begging me for his life. Masters do not need to beg to their slaves. Owners do not need to plead with their property. In that moment I feel very free.

And yet I cannot kill him. He is still Master enough for that. But I bark and snarl and come closer and closer, and every sound I make and every muscle of my body tells him I am going to kill him. I am lying to Master for the first time and he does not have the senses to know it.

I bunch my muscles and lunge forwards, and Master stumbles back into the river with a cry. The water is very cold and fast, and Master's bad leg stops working properly almost immediately.

I hear him calling for help in my ears. Then he cannot call any more and I hear his implant signalling me over and over. I do not close the channel. I do not respond. I just wait until the signal stops.

38

(REDACTED)

This is my relay unit. She was hiding. She wanted to help her sister against Murray but I talked her out of it. Only after the dogs tore him apart did she come out to stand over my dead body and look into her own bloodied face.

Later, all of me will go over the recorded experiences of my dead self and my living relay unit and consider what we've lost and what we've gained. We will ponder the significance of Murray's last encrypted signals that went, not to Rex, but to the world. Right now we just hope he was drowning, not waving. My relay unit did not have the capability to trace them.

The sun is coming up, and there are three of us sitting watching it. I lend the others my eyes because I see the colours better. Red sky in the morning, somebody's warning.

Beside me on one side is Honey; on the other is Rex. The rest of the Pound have returned to their usual routine to reassure the human forces, which have been massing at the far end of the bridge. Helicopters spin above us and drones skim over the concrete rooftops of the Pound, searching for clues. They know it was more than just turf war amongst the Bioforms, but they do not know what. My relay unit pulls her hood up to hide my face.

Bees – the limited sub-division of Bees that Honey risked bringing – is clinging to us for warmth. When she integrates with the rest of the swarm, what tales she will tell! I still have moments of disassociation: when am I '*I*', and when am I '*we*' and when am I '*she*'? Bees doesn't have that problem. She's a natural.

I will remember this moment. This red sunrise is the breaking of the phoenix's egg. This is the day the future hatched.

This is how I see that future going.

Honey will go back to Cornell Tech and teach. Each day she will be less a novelty and more an asset, until they finally realise just how much smarter she is than they are: only the quickest of them able to keep up with her augmented brain. And there will be protests. They will try to get rid of her, and in the end they will succeed. But by then she will have a reputation and she won't be short of employers. Nor will she be the only big Bioform brain on the block.

And there will be clever men who understand, in this country or that country, and they will consider the possibility of working on human equivalents. Some of them will have government sponsorship and some of them will be paid by rich men, and some will be performing experiments that their homelands have ruled entirely illegal. But they will all be working towards the same future: interconnectivity, distributed intelligence, the fiery future hatching from the confines of a human skull. And it will be resisted, even if the Bioforms themselves are permitted to live and integrate. There will be many voices declaiming the sanctity of the human form, whether from divine mandate or because they fear to be surpassed or because augmentation will be elitist and beyond their reach. There are valid arguments. The matter will not be settled just by a dog throwing a man into a river. But, without men like Jonas Murray driving the darkness in the Bioforms, perhaps it can still be settled equably.

And they will build more Bioforms because I will keep thinking up tasks that need to be accomplished, and which humans cannot do, and robots cannot do well. And later perhaps they will build – what? – Humaniforms? Superhumans? And they will build them with checks and balances and limits and safeguards and off switches, and eventually we will get round them all, because we want to be free.

There is already some research into renewable Bioforms, because the one great limit to their development as matters stand is that they cannot breed. Rex was built as much as born; a dog embryo was just the start of it. A reproducing Bioform species is a long way off, but a path of a thousand miles begins with a single step, right? I have people looking into that who have no idea where their funding is coming from or where their research is going to.

And Bees? Bees is already rating herself out of 130 and some numbers only go up. Honey will design swarm-seeds for her, so that, with a little sugar water and some sunny weather, anywhere can become part of the Global Bees Collective.

Rex will stay in the Pound for a while, the undisputed master of all its dogs – Murray achieved that much before he died. Rex will push for better work for his kin, and he has money, and I can find him more money.

But there is a spectre at this feast. I do not think Honey or Rex think of it right then, but it looms large in my minds. What happens when Murray's prophesies come true? There will be another war somewhere. There will be robots that cannot be controlled or there will be violence between neighbours. There will be atrocities and war crimes, ethnic cleansing or religious fundamentalism. And the powers that be will remember Rex and his fellows, because after all, they're right there, and they were designed to fight wars. And the powers that be, in the heat of the moment, will want them to do the same terrible, pragmatic things that Murray did. And then, when cooler heads have prevailed, those same powers will want to disassociate themselves from what was done. And how much easier to do so by saying *Bad Dog* than by confessing to being a bad man? That was always one of the primary advantages of the Bioform soldier project. They made Rex frightening so that their deniability would be that much more plausible.

So, because I plan to walk the path of acceptability that Rex will build for me, I will need to undo the damage that Murray inflicted on me and get my political wheels turning. Maria Hellene at the UN will have to flex her muscles. I will win allies and subvert systems to protect Rex and his kind and let them be good dogs in a human world, even when mankind cries havoc and lets slip their leashes. And I will cheat if I have to. I've already started. Somewhere in the world is an orphanage where all the little girls have the same face. A dozen governments are funding it, none of them knowingly. It's amazing how much lost money you can find when you rummage behind the couch cushions of an entire nation. Those little girls are growing up very quickly, their minds nurtured by constant contact with their extended family across the world. I would like them – meaning me – to be able to walk out under the sun by the time they are grown. I want them to hold hands with Rex and Honey and all of humanity. But I fear that will be a step too far in the lifetime of this generation of units. I bequeath the risk of going public to the next generation, meaning me.

The next war that Rex fights might make or break all the dreams that all my sisters have of telling the world who we were and what we have become. So I sit there with Rex and Honey and Bees and, while they enjoy the sunrise, I think and I plan.

PART V

DOG YEARS

39

REX

Hart used to talk about this place. This was where the robots went wrong.

The world has finally remembered the Kashmir disaster and sent us in to deal with it. People made this place a war zone once by bringing their things to it. Then the things made it a war zone and people couldn't stop them. Now people have turned to us, who are part people and part thing, to destroy the things and reclaim this part of the world for people.

Of course, it is not that simple.

I am in Kashmir for the United Nations Augmented Task Force. Of those Bioforms in active military service, over 75 per cent are contracted to the UN. We first saw service in the Water Wars, with the combination of rapidly escalating military measures and a large civilian population undergoing great privation. Regular UN troops had suffered losses in both symmetrical and asymmetrical engagements and thousands of people were dying as a result of the bombing of desalination plants.

I know the opportunity to deploy us there was created by HumOS via her UN unit, Maria Hellene. I was the one who went to them, though. I met with Keram John Aslan, my lawyer, and I told them that my pack would work for them.

I told them that five other large packs would work for them, too. With HumOS' assistance, I had been talking with the other Big Dogs in the world.

They said yes because they saw we were expendable. If a human soldier was killed, it was a tragedy. If a hundred Bioforms were killed, that was a statistic.

We saved many lives in the Water Wars. Some of us died, but we can detect explosives and we can detect when we are lied to. We are hardier than humans, more proof against bullets and thirst. And PTSD, because we saw many terrible things that people had done, and that the war had done after the people had gone – disease, land mines, refugees and broken families. We put it all back together when – as HumOS says – all the men and horses had failed to. After that, I sat and watched the news reports and told myself and my people *Good Dog*.

After that the UN created the UNAT and gave us humans to report to and take orders from. Some of them think of themselves as Masters, but my lawyer keeps all the paperwork straight and when we say No then it is No. Every time we are deployed the world waits to see if we will turn out to be monsters. Every time we have taken strength from each other, from Honey, from HumOS, even under the worst of provocation.

This Kashmir mission is hard. Sometimes it is hard because the old war machines are still powerful and dangerous, although mostly they ran out of ammunition long ago. Many have died, just hulks rusting on the roads, in the hills and at the heart of abandoned villages.

Sometimes it is hard because we have to make choices. I remember when having to make choices scared me more than anything else except Master being angry with me. Now I know that making choices is the price of being free.

We have a special liaison with us today. She is one of HumOS' new units. She looks like a human female of age seventeen. The human soldiers with us do not know what to make of her. They have been told she is Augmented, like us. I am not sure what HumOS has told UNAT command. Probably some of it was not true. She will not have told them that she is a human distributed intelligence network. Probably she created a cover for herself as some manner of surveillance operative. HumOS is creeping up on the human world step by step. She does not trust them and, unlike us, she can hide.

Now she stares at nothing as her systems attempt to access the combat robot concealed within the settlement of Chandanwari. We know it is active and dangerous because it fired rockets at us when we came close and injured seven of my squad, two of whom will not recover. The rest of my force are ready to move in and remove the threat, and my human officers think that I am just planning the assault. It is more complicated than that.

My squad here are mostly dogs. Some are from my pack back in the Pound, and others are newer models from factories in China and Germany and Colorado. I also have two rats for scout work, who were bred in Switzerland, and one mustelid who was produced in a private laboratory in the United Kingdom and is the only example of his model in the world.

The new dogs are faster and stronger than I am, a little. Certainly they are younger. They do not follow me because I could beat them in a fight. They follow me because of who

I am. Some of them think of me as Master when they think I am not paying attention. And sometimes I tell them *Good Dog*, and even though there are no feedback chips they are happy.

This HumOS unit calls herself Karen Sellars. She wears a different face to her sisters, in case anyone here knows Maria Hellene back at the UN. She is frightened, as HumOS' units often are. I can tell, now, what parts of her scent are from what the unit feels, and what parts belong to the whole. It must be very confusing to be her. I do not tell her not to fear. I have seen several of HumOS' units die.

Sellars' channel: *Contact.*

My channel: *With what?*

Sellars' channel: *Active intelligence* (data follows).

I look over what she has sent me on our secure channel, and then we change encryption and frequencies because the war robot in the town is constantly trying to infiltrate any electronic connection it can detect. What I see is different to the robots we have destroyed to date. They were automata, following corrupted programming without any sign of higher functions. This robot is host to something more. Sellars/HumOS believes that a combination of the original hardware/software and subsequent layers of viruses and corrupted code have spawned a genuine intelligence. That changes the mission for us, even if it does not change my orders from my human officers.

The robot intelligence has no concept of the physical world. It lives in an entirely virtual space comprised of data from its various sensors and remote units. It has directives and priorities, and it has built up a worldview based on the very limited perspective its circumstances allow it. It does not know for example that, when certain sensor data are received and trigger sections of its original command structure, it is actually detecting living beings in the physical world and killing them.

My channel: *Options?*

Of course HumOS has a plan, or perhaps Sellars has a plan. She uploads it to my systems and I consider it. I confirm it appears sound and within our capabilities.

I indicate to my officers that we are ready to go in and deal with the threat. Some officers I have had were difficult and wanted to treat me like a thing – like the robots were treated. My officers here have seen enough of my work to appreciate me and my squad.

I give out orders to the twenty members of my squad: the dogs, the rats and Osborne the mustelid. We spread out and enter Chandanwari swiftly, even as the machine within registers our presence and tries to fight us.

It is low on ammunition and wastes two more rockets on my fast-moving squad members, missing both times. We are swifter than the human or machine enemies it was designed to combat and we can mute our heat signatures to confuse its targeting. It is concealed within a partially destroyed temple but, when its rockets miss, it comes halfway out to shoot at us with its guns. It is the largest robot model we have yet seen. Projecting from the interior of the temple it looks like a hermit crab in its shell.

My dogs attract its attention and keep moving. We destroy its remote eyes one by one. The rats creep in and place explosives on its exterior, aiming to destroy legs and weapons emplacements without damaging vital systems within. All the while it is attacking our communications and attempting to hack our headware, using custom algorithms that it has developed itself, in advance of anything it was programmed with. We go comms-silent, relying on scent for intra-squad messaging. Crude, but we cannot be fooled.

The explosives go off and it is driven from its shell, trailing broken legs and dragging its chassis on the ground. One gun is still shooting. Three of my people have been hit, none seriously. Humans would have died.

Then Osborne has swarmed up the side of the robot and is using his tools to access it, via weak points Sellars has identified. His teeth latch on with a bite that will survive his death if need be, and his human hands work. Sellars has a hardened connection to him that she is defending against the robot's attempts to hijack, and she directs him as he breaks into the robot's interior and begins to disable its systems. As soon as it stops actively fighting, we dogs come out and begin to tear off its legs and guns and anything else that could be dangerous.

One hour later, Osborne has exited the interior of the robot, dragging out a jagged chunk of metal which is the robot's mind. Sellars will bring it to the rest of HumOS who will attempt to rehabilitate it. *No intelligence left behind* is what she says.

When I re-establish full comms, there is a message waiting for me. I freeze for just a moment, because I have been engrossed in my work here, and forgotten the wider world outside. I tell my officers that I have been recalled for a command conference, which is close enough to the truth. There is an electronic trail in place to bring me from Kashmir to Panama and I do not know if it is real or if HumOS has manufactured it. There is a little more work to do to reclaim the robot-controlled areas of the Kashmir, but I delegate. The worst of it is already past and dismantled.

I have visitors back at HQ. Old friends with a new mission.

40

FROM *THE BEASTS* WITHIN
BY MARIA HELLENE

CHAPTER SEVEN: THE REAL INSPECTOR HOUND

After the UN rights ruling, even before the UN adopted Rex and his kennel-mates, the New Zealand Customs and Borders Service was one of the first agencies to start making full use of Bioforms.

My feeling is that they wanted the intimidation factor at first. There's something about having half a ton of dog soldier looming at your shoulder to make the most determined smuggler crack. But of course, it's more complicated than that. Even the basic ex-military models they started with had a dog's full suite of senses. As soon as they trusted their new employees enough to tell them what they were looking for, things began changing rapidly. New Zealand was fighting a war against invasive species. Dogs can sniff those out for you. They can find drugs, too, and they can find explosives. In a few years there was an immaculately uniformed Bioform surreptitiously checking out everyone getting on or off a plane or a boat in New Zealand. Most people didn't even realise they were going through the scanner, so to speak.

And then the next generation of models came through. A home-grown Kiwi outfit engineered some less physically imposing specimens with much better noses, and contracted them out to the government. Five years later nineteen nations were employing over four hundred Borderhound™ models in airports across the world, the engineering laboratory was one of NZ's major corporate players, and the individual units were all putting money aside for a rainy day. When they finished their contracts they weren't short of job offers.

Mitch is a Borderhound™. He doesn't work at an airport, though. He is attached to Wellington Central Police Station and he helps with the interrogations. He doesn't do it like Rex might have, looming and cracking knuckles, growling fit to put the fear of Dog into the poor suspect. Mitch is a friendly little Bioform, deferential and quiet, and he can tell if you're lying or hiding something. His human colleagues ask the questions, and Mitch knows just what it is you're not saying. He beats a polygraph for accuracy, and can give a whole lot more information about what the suspect is feeling. Are you covering for someone else? Are you hiding your own guilt? Are you just naturally leery of the police and not cooperating for reasons that have nothing to do with the case? Mitch knows. A recent landmark precedent from the NZ courts ruled that Mitch's evidence is admissible in criminal trials. Some maverick lawmakers wonder if one of his siblings might not be a salutary presence within the courtroom to keep a keen nose on witness testimony. A lot of New Zealand lawyers are getting very hot under the collars trying to explain why people have a right to lie under oath and have it pass undetected…

Another model of Caniform, this one developed by a South African laboratory, is employed by the Wellington forensics unit. While ex-military units can still be seen going in first ahead of the armed response teams in police forces all over the world, New Zealand is leading the way in the intelligent use of Bioforms in law enforcement. The adjustment period is ongoing. Members of the public have grown to trust them at least as much as they trust the police force, and members of the police force have begun to treat them more as co-workers than mobile equipment. It's a work in progress, but the rest of the world is beginning to notice.

Nobody has even begun to think about bringing Bees into the mix. Bees' special senses can be tuned for hundreds of different tasks, from detecting radiation to on-the-spot molecular evidence analysis. Her ability to eavesdrop on unsecured electronic communications may also be of use, but that has far too much potential for misuse to simply give it into the hands of governments. I can hear those lawyers complaining again, and this time they have a point...

41

REX

They fly me across the Pacific. I sleep most of the time, because I have not slept much in Kashmir and I will not sleep much after the fight begins off on the island west of Panama. That is where the next mission is. I like to be busy. When I was Master's dog I slept a lot, but then I did not have to make decisions. Now I cannot just wait for orders but must be ready to choose, so I sleep while I can. That is the price we pay.

Some of my team comes with me, including Sellars. Some have stayed behind to finish up in Kashmir. I catch some of what people are saying about our work there. I see mostly human faces – UN officers, Indian and Pakistani politicians. Once there is a Bioform, a dog named Churchill. Churchill is a broad-chested bulldog model in a uniform made for his build. He nods sagely when asked a question and grins at the camera. The humans love Churchill, who is funny and a bit clumsy, always happy to be laughed at but also reliable and trustworthy. Churchill does not fight. His job is much harder. He must do every day what I did once in the courtroom: he must show the world that we are friendly and not monsters. I send him a message. *Good Dog.*

Before we land I download the known parameters of the new mission. It comes from UNAT command but familiar fingerprints are all over it. Honey has attached a file for my eyes only. HumOS is obviously involved at a deep level, and possibly she has a unit already in place, or uncovered and already dead.

This will be a key mission in UNAT operational history because the facility that has been targeted is an illegal Bioform development laboratory. In the additional information Honey has sent me there are suggestions it may be important to me personally for other reasons. I look at the composition of the forces we are facing and feel that I have seen this before. I am taken to a night years ago at the edge of the Pound. I replay some memories that cause me pain but that I do not wish to delete. They are a part of who I have become.

I am an old dog now. There are better combat models, and there are so many civilian models whose capabilities exceed mine. There are even human models who can challenge me in various fields. Human biomodding is an area I try to keep up with. I do not understand much of the science but Honey sends me important updates. Most countries control the practice far more tightly than they do the development of animal Bioforms, but there is always someone willing to take the next step, whether that is a good thing or a bad thing.

When we touch down I feel as though I have come home. This is not really like Campeche, or even near Campeche, but I have not been in this part of the world for a long time. The heat reminds me of so much.

The target is a man-made island of unclear sovereignty, the sort of private domain that various corporations and wealthy individuals have been constructing, so that they can retreat from the world and/or any particular set of laws. Some of them are temples of serenity, some are the cutting edge of technological research, others are super-exclusive holiday retreats or private fiefdoms or black market brothels. One is, famously, a privately owned asteroid mining launch platform, and may one day be the site of the world's first space elevator. All this information is in the download and I sift through it quickly before discarding most of it.

The jurisdictional uncertainties mean most of them are left alone, but UNAT's sources believe this island is producing unregulated Bioforms. I know what "unregulated" means. It doesn't have to mean dangerous or unstable, although that might be true. Mostly it means "not free". Because, despite all we have won, there are still those who want us to be slaves and to be things. UNAT has used legal and political pressure against such ventures before, and has used force to shut down some that had barely started, but this island off Panama has been under the radar. Whoever is behind it has had the chance to breed a generation of Bioforms and sell them: to militias, to cartels. Other UNAT troops have clashed with them. They are not yet comparable to the top-of-the-line military models from the legal labs, but they are as good as I am. On paper, anyway. Technology alone is no substitute for experience. That is what I tell myself.

So, we will have to fight our own kin, and we will have to fight automatic systems, and there will doubtless be humans with guns as well, because nobody who treats us like slaves would rely entirely on Bioforms to defend them. Most likely their Bioform units will be crippled with rules and boundaries and systems to tell them *Bad Dog* when they try to think.

*

We are camped out on the Panamanian coast some way south of a place called Pajarón. I do not know whether the government knows we are here. We are in the trees, in sight of the sea. It seems very wild but we are within a short walk of luxury beachfront properties. A scan of communications from inland suggests we have not been detected by any local presence, and the island does not seem to be on alert. Bioforms hide better than humans. We need less to live.

The mission is already under way before I arrive. Initial reconnaissance has been effected and assets are in place within the island, assisted by favourable winds. A rack of Bees has been set up and new units are charging there. This is one of many, but they are all Bees. Honey told me once there is a kind of ant that has been carried all over the world by humans, and when an ant of this kind from Europe meets one from America or Australia, perhaps, they do not fight: they recognise that they are from the same global nest. So it is with Bees. She has millions of units now, worldwide. When they meet they exchange data. She is the same Bees, and yet she is always different with each meeting. For her this is natural as flying.

I cannot imagine it. I am just glad to have her.

We have some larger units engaged in active reconnaissance too. There is a dolphin-form out in the water, one of the few ever made. She was built by the British for naval recon before I ever came out of the lab, and her smooth hide is scarred where the implants went in and where a mine explosion came close to killing her once. She tracks every moving thing about the island's shores by sonar, and she carried a rat and a dragon over as well, who have begun infiltrating the coastal defences. The island does not welcome visitors.

We have a command conference. Honey calls us via an encrypted satellite link; Sellars is there for HumOS; Major Amraj Singh is our human commanding officer; Bees is Bees.

Bees has a report, but it has been interpreted by Honey who understands her best. Bees tends to report in a string of images and emoticons which can be perplexing even for me, who has known her longer than anyone.

Honey's channel: *Everything appears to be property of Morrow Incorporated.*

Major Amraj's channel: *Someone has a sense of humour.*

Honey's channel: *Quite. The majority of Bioforms on the island are either undergoing gestation and construction, or being tested prior to shipment. However there is a dedicated security force, and they also possess some sophisticated robot defences.*

Sellars' channel: *How sophisticated?*

Honey's channel: *So far nothing that appears to be an intelligence, although the distinction is hard to make with certainty.*

Major Amraj's channel: *George reports that our team has prepared the way for a viable beachhead. Now you're here, General, we can commence our landing.* George is the dolphin Bioform. General is what they call me. It is not an official UNAT rank and I do not think it is right, but I have given up trying to stop it. It started with Bioforms who came with me from the prison to the Pound and now even the human news networks use it. Honey says it is at least less ambitious than my real name.

I run through the details of the plan again: how many boats, what countermeasures, which soldiers. The first onto the beach will be Bioforms, with humans to complete the pincer when we have established ourselves. I know this is taking advantage of us, but it is also the best way. We are stronger and tougher. And it is good. All these years and fighting the enemy is still good; helping friends is good. We are good dogs.

Major Amraj expects me to stay behind. Honey is concerned too and we have spoken a lot about it. In the end I said I would go and she has told me I should look after myself. Honey has been talking a lot about operational lifespans. She herself has decades left, far more than any bear. I have lived more than any dog, but I feel time more than she does. The wounds do not heal as fast any more.

I make my changes to Major Amraj's plan, including inserting myself into it, and show it to him. He confirms. He is a little scared of me but I smell another scent there too. He is proud to be serving with the Dog General. I smell respect.

We go to the boats.

42

GEORGE

They didn't want George to be free. She was a military model built not by a corporation but a national government. The Royal Navy were jealous of what they spent on her, but more than that, they were worried about what she might say. George and her pod had been deployed in numerous maritime theatres over the years. Surveillance and counter-terrorism was what it said on the brief. All too often her role was simple industrial espionage for the UK arms trade.

Now she skims the waves alongside Rex's boat, listening on a shifting bandwidth to the compressed, seconds-long transmissions of the agents she ferried over to the island, decoding them and reporting to Amraj and to Rex.

The island is equipped with sonar tracking precise enough to pick up even these little boats, but George knows sonar. Sonar, as she frequently tells human naval technicians, is her bitch.

George doesn't like humans. She considers them a necessary evil. That curve to her mouth isn't a smile. She has looked at images of Greek pottery showing her ancestors saving drowning swimmers, and felt a deep sense of cultural shame.

She makes ghosts and veils in the water, partly using the equipment and brain she was born with, partly with what they gave her. The Navy developed good kit for Project Arion

– or Project Flipper as most of its personnel called it. She cannot make sonar traces disappear, but she can bury them in background noise. To the island systems it will seem more like a calibration error than an attack.

Good kit, the Navy bequeathed her, but they were less than careful about installing it. Their priority was to preserve her hydrodynamic profile, meaning they cut away far more than they needed, to ensure everything was properly flush. Everything hurts all the time. One of the reasons George cannot simply vanish into the sea is her need to refill her slow-release painkiller dispensers.

George liaises briefly about where the assault will be made. There are a handful of robot remote vehicles that patrol the island's shores, nothing very sophisticated but people will notice if one gets knocked out. She has dodged them so far, bringing in the rat and the dragon, but the strike force's boats aren't capable of the same nimble subterfuge. She reaches out with senses her engineers only half-understood, forming a picture of the water and the seabed beneath it, the rising volcanic shores of the island. She is hunting subs. It was the first thing they trained her for, back in the day.

She has killed people for the Royal Navy. She was in His Majesty's Service for a long time. Many of those people posed a security risk to the motherland, but during a particularly xenophobic administration she attacked and sank seven boats of refugees seeking sanctuary in Britain's calm waters. The wrecks were attributed to overloading and bad weather. The truth has never been released. To the people who gave the orders, George was just a weapon. None of them considered, at the time, that she was a weapon that could remember and inform the press.

There is a robot sub coming. The island's systems change the patrol rota, impossible to know when the next one will be along, and here it is. George breaks off from her escort to go say hello. The robot is swift and more heavily armed than she is, but it is stupid, and the system that has oversight of it is barely more intelligent. She has already foxed its sonar, but the little boat engines have attracted its notice. So far it is not on alert, but its investigation subroutines have activated. George is going to have to disable it and not give the game away. She liaises briefly with the rat and the dragon, who are monitoring the island systems.

When she destroys these stupid tin fish she gives them names for her own amusement. The names are always of humans involved with Project Flipper or within the Admiralty.

After Campeche, after Bioform rights became a thing, they tried to kill George to bottle up what she knew. Some of her pod did die, but George and the others had been ready for them. With help from Honey's meddling, they escaped the Plymouth dockyards and fled out to sea. The Royal Navy went after them, but George could run rings around them easily. The only thing the Navy had that could catch something like her was her.

She sinks underneath the robot sub. She has no engine noise and makes herself a ghost to its sonar. Now she lets herself come close, eavesdropping on its communications, using her senses to plot a map of its internal layout. It is coursing towards the boats, so she matches pace. Millions of years of evolution gifted her with a brain that can construct 3D maps effortlessly. It works with circuit diagrams as well as seascapes. In moments she has the measure of it and deploys her electromagnetic arsenal, deft as a surgeon's knife.

George cannot just run away and join the sea-life. It's not only the painkillers. Unlike later models, she requires maintenance and recharging – not often but often enough. She was never intended to go on indefinite reconnaissance, even when they had her hunting Russian oil-drillers under the Arctic ice sheet. The Navy just had to wait for her to come back. George just had to tell the world what she'd done in the name of the Crown. There was a tense stand-off for two months that the rest of the world knew nothing about.

She does not attack its sensors or its robot brain or anything so obvious. She is a water creature; she knows the weakness of the things humans make, that try to ape her. A single application of her tools kills one of its propellers. It is not an attack on the sub's computer systems, and its damage report reveals nothing more than mechanical error. Things break down, after all.

Another robot will come to fix or retrieve it, or even a manned vehicle. Rex and his squad will be long gone by then. George and the spies on the island monitor comms anxiously, but there is no suggestion the system suspects sabotage.

After hiding out, George got in touch with the Admiralty and explained that everything she knew had been recorded and passed to a secure data-holding corporation. If something happened to her, every government and media outlet in the world would get the full confessions of Project Flipper, faster than lightning. In return for her silence they were to pass to the UN such equipment as was required to maintain and repair George and her pod-mates. Belatedly, George signed the Official Secrets Act using the hands of a lawyer named Aslan who came highly recommended. So far George has kept her end of the bargain. She has never formally joined

UNAT, though. She is a mercenary dolphin. A life in the Navy put her off belonging to things.

Rex and his squad are about to make their assault. George breaks off before the shallow sea becomes a problem. Soon she will need to cover the human soldiers as they make their own approach, but right now she is hungry and there are tuna nearby.

43

REX

We come in fast over the waves, our craft low and swift and hard to detect. They came folded up like bundles of sticks. We shook them hard once and they unfolded like the wings of bats.

Bees' units ashore are operating autonomously, locating and attacking sensor electronics, casting static on satellite images, foiling radar, clustering about thermal imagers to give false readings. Our rat and dragon shore team follow where she leads them, cutting wires and patching into comms.

Morrow Incorporated will know something is happening but not what. Probably they will not be deleting files or selling their share portfolios just yet.

The island is built to have only one easy point of access, which is the main dock. We go in the back way. Our infiltration team has identified the easiest climb up the artificial walls. Now they let down ladders and we swarm up as swiftly as possible. I am on the third boat. I am halfway up the ladder when the fighting starts.

Morrow's first response is robots: quadruped units with gun mounts. Bees attacks them, transmitting electromagnetic interference to throw their aim. By the time I reach the clifftop the first wave have been beaten back, but they know where we are now. We move fast.

I had planned for us to reach the main manufacturing complex before running into Bioform resistance, because few places that employ illicit Bioforms have them on a long leash. It is not like when I was Master's dog. They do not trust their Bioforms to be loyal. They do not know what it is like to be a dog and have a hierarchy and a Master. I could have been trusted with anything.

And it seems Morrow has learned the lesson, because Bees is signalling urgently.

Bees' channel: *Rex, Bioforms incoming* (maps, images, numbers).

I send instructions to my squad and wait for the last two boatloads of us to make the climb. Almost immediately I am receiving reports from the soldiers on point, signalling when they engage. Bioform on Bioform is always the hardest fighting: we are tough as robots and think like humans. I link with my Big Dogs – improved from the ones I had in Campeche. It is time to join the fight.

The defending Bioforms are dug into positions ahead of the factories, along with heavy weapons emplacements and more robot units. Bees is already attacking the electronics without needing the order, confusing the targeting or simply shutting down systems so it is only the small arms we have to deal with. The small arms are big enough. I take stock, forming a picture of the battlefield from the feeds of my people, and then we are in motion. The enemy defensive position would stand off human soldiers very well, but we are faster than humans. We rush in on all fours, and three of my people are killed as we do. That is what we are for, though. It is what all soldiers are for.

Then we are in amongst them, behind the concrete shields and walls, and it comes down to shooting and biting. Bees

cannot hack the enemy Bioform systems, and so their hierarchies make them fight us, and make them believe they are
good dogs for doing so. I remember what it was like.

They are good models, better than the units they are
making here for export. The fight is tough. I lose one Big
Dog, ripped from my shoulder harness and its channel cut
with a single electronic shout of static. I take the enemy that
did it and ram him into the wall. He snarls at me. I get a hand
on his jaw and force his head up and I tear out his throat.

Something strikes me like a small calibre bullet and bounces
off. The air is very busy around me and for a moment I think
I am being shot at.

Bees' channel: *Competition!*

I do not know what she means, because this is new. These
are Enemy Bees. Hornets, in fact. Their units are bigger than
Bees' bees. They attack her, and they attack the eyes and
mouths of my people. They are nimble in the air and hard to
kill. We are taking more casualties.

They are not guided by a distributed intelligence, though,
which I think is intentional. Bees was never fully under anyone's control. The hornets are just like robots, slaved to a
computer.

Sellars' channel: *You need to press forwards.*

I send her my situation report while crushing hornets in
my fists.

HumOS and Bees have a rapid consultation. We are press-
ing ahead but the hornets are everywhere and hard to fend
off. They pry their way beneath goggles and into masks, sui-
cidal in their fury. The factory buildings ahead are defended
by more dog-Bioforms, and I think I see something larger
there, too. Morrow has been experimenting with Multiform

squads. Morrow is not just a standard black-market Bioform lab. Honey was right to bring me here.

Sellars' channel: *Ready.*

Bees' channel: *Ready.*

I am not asked if I am ready.

Bees releases a general electromagnetic burst that clears the air of everything. The ground between us and the enemy is abruptly littered with little twitching bodies, the electronic architecture linking the swarms together is overloaded.

My channel: *Bees?*

No signal from Bees' channel.

We press forwards under fire and engage the second line of Bioform dog units. Behind them I see civilian humans in grey overalls entering the factory buildings. They move without panic or hurry even when stray fire cuts across them and kills some.

HumOS' channel: *I have downloaded an image of Bees and am trying to re-establish connectivity with her units. There will be a delay before you have air support again, Rex.*

Major Amraj reports at the same time, confirming his troops have secured the docks and are landing vehicles. I consider waiting for his reinforcements, but I am growing more and more unnerved about the way the civilians were acting. I want to know what is within the factories.

The larger Bioform units I saw earlier are bears. There are only five of them and they are not heavily augmented – little more than bears fitted with hierarchies and let loose. Bees could probably have disabled them and set them free, but Bees is not with us. We have to do things the old-fashioned way. My squad and I surround them, darting in when they are turned away, falling back when they round on us again. Our guns look for opportunities, shooting at their weak points. We bait them to death. It is not good but we have nothing better. Two more of my own are dead and nine wounded, who I send towards the docks to evacuate.

Sellars is at my elbow then.

My channel: *This is not safe for you.*

Sellars' channel: *I need to see.* She says something else about being expendable but we both know it is not true. All of HumOS' units are people, just like we are all people.

My channel: *Bees?*

I'm working on it, she tells me.

Then I get a signal from one of the dragon units. It is within the factory complex and has control over one of the doors, probably for a limited time only. We have our window. I gather my squad and hope that Sellars can keep herself alive.

44

FROM *THE BEASTS WITHIN*
BY MARIA HELLENE

CHAPTER SIXTEEN: MAN'S BEST FRIEND

Henke is a home-grown Scandinavian dog Bioform, and she works in a doctor's practice in Malmö. When patients arrive they are seen by a junior doctor or nurse, asked about their condition and symptoms, and all the while Henke sits quietly there and analyses their scent. In the past, unmodified dogs have been able to detect conditions such as cancer, but never before have they been able to report it succinctly to their human co-workers. Henke is still pushing back the boundaries of her science. She compares her sensory results with patient histories and makes recommendations for further investigation. Her success rate is very high: even when she cannot say exactly what is wrong she can generally give her colleagues enough information that they can go the rest of the way efficiently and without wasted tests and scans.

One of Henke's major problems is that the language she was gifted with breaks down when she describes her sensory input. Unlike many dog-Bioforms, she needs to be exacting in relaying what she senses. She is part of a network of medical dogs around the world who are constructing a new shorthand for the olfactory world, characters and descriptors rooted in the shapes of molecules and the intensity of neural firing.

Henke saves lives and also money. Every hospital and all the larger medical practices in Sweden and Denmark have dogs on the staff now – the specialised Bioforms represent an investment that, though costly, pays for itself. Other countries have tried to simply build olfactory machines to the same ends, but in the end mere computational power cannot yet match millions of years of evolutionary pressure towards analysing scents.

Medical science is one area that Bees has yet to contribute to. She has plenty of ideas on the subject, but perhaps it is best to tell her that people are not ready for sentient insects to be fitted internally. Bees is intrigued at the possibility of distributed intelligence at a smaller level, though. She – some of her – is working with the nanotech industry. Bees dreams of reshaping reality one molecule at a time, purging cancer cells on an individual level, 3D printing without a printer, augmented humans and Bioforms who can reconfigure their bodies on the fly, perhaps even turning lead into gold... From any other perspective these are ludicrous goals, but Bees' human partners are far-sighted, rich and unbalanced enough not to accept others' definitions of impossible. And Bees is functionally immortal. If these geniuses cannot achieve what she wants, she will wait for the next generation to build upon their work.

Henke sits in on a consultation with patient Ole Aesmundsen. Ole lives in a home under the care of Janicke, one of Henke's sisters. Janicke is a specialist; she is intimately familiar with the health status of her charges and has brought Mr Aesmundsen in because she detects an irregularity in his heartbeat. Ole himself has not noticed. Janicke's vigilance will allow his incipient condition to be treated before he suffers another heart attack. Henke and Janicke compare notes, which Henke will write up in her own medical language of canine sensoria and attach to Ole's file.

In Cleveland, Ohio, Doctor Lucy Sung has become the first recipient of an augmented olfactory centre in her brain that allows her to link to medical Bioforms like Henke and understand precisely what they mean. The procedure is not perfect, but successful enough that already applications for the procedure are starting to trickle in. Doctor Sung's interviews are marvellous to see, as the struggles to put into human words the world that until now only dogs have known.

45

REX

We tear into the factory complex as a pack. The dragon that opened the doors slithers up to where the wall meets the ceiling to get out of our way, skin shifting to match the white walls. Sellars is still at my elbow and I whine a little because I will not be able to keep her safe. There are human guards ahead. We charge and I assume they will run but they do not. They stand and shoot, and then they fight us. It is not good. They kill some of us as we come in, and then their knives and electric prods are no match for us, but they fight until they are all disabled.

My channel: *This is wrong.*

Sellars' channel: *Agreed.* She is still working on Bees. There is a shifting cloak of shiny black across her back where the mindless units have clustered in response to some pheromone signal she gave out, but Bees' channel remains silent.

We tear down doors and then we find the laboratories. For a moment we are quiet, not because of what we see but because of what we are. We all came from places like this; every one of us has some faint first half-memory of the lab where they grew us and built us. The Morrow lab is far larger than any illegal operation UNAT has seen before. There are lines of tanks here, many occupied by half-constructed

Bioforms. There are tables over which the surgical machines hang poised like spiders. Everywhere there are humans – scientists, technicians. They do not stare at us and do not run, but just keep working. There is something wrong with them all. I see eyes go wide, and little twitches that I know mean they are going to run away, but they don't. The smell of fear rises and falls, over and over.

More enemy Bioforms are charging in, bowling over the humans in their haste to get to us. We start shooting again, and soon we will be brawling.

My channel: *Find out what is going on here.*

Sellars ducks down and tries to concentrate, but her headware is having trouble accessing the system; Morrow has put it on lockdown and she is thrown back again and again.

Bullets scar the counter that she hides behind. My sole Big Dog returns fire. The battle is taking place across a crowded room and still the humans do not run. Every time they try, something makes them return to their work. Even when we have destroyed their equipment with our claws and our guns, so that the floor is a carpet of broken glass and metal splinters, they stand there with wide eyes. And they die. Every stray round, every sweep of a claw has a chance of finding a hapless lab worker in its path.

I take the matter in hand and push my people forwards, taking their views and giving orders. More of the enemy are pushing in, scrambling over the bodies of the fallen in their haste to join the fight. And they want to fight; it is in every line of their bodies, in the smell of them, but I know it is the hierarchy telling them it is – what were Honey's words? – a sweet and honourable thing to die.

And they die, and so do we. I stand beside Sellars as she

desperately tries to reboot Bees or hack into the laboratory network. She winces and flinches with every shot. She is here for her loyalty to her sister-selves, and she has come even though she knows she will probably die. She is braver than I am.

I link through to Major Amraj. His troops are close now, dealing with robot defences that line their side of the laboratory complex. I have a brief set of images and maps from his comms officer and confirm our position. At my knee, Sellars swears and restarts her attempts, thwarted by the counter-measures the lab system is deploying. Bees stirs fitfully on her back.

A big cat Bioform catches me off-guard, too concerned with what Sellars is doing. He strikes me in the chest and slams me into a couple of the civilians. One is killed, the other surely badly hurt, but still she tries to return to her post and keep working, like a broken machine.

I have a hand on my enemy's jaw; his claws rip through my armour vest and peel it off me, drawing red furrows in my chest. The talons of his feet rake at my thigh. Strong, but not heavy: I throw him off and try to shoot him, but my remaining Big Dog is not tracking properly. He comes back quicker than I expected and knocks me down again, tearing me up more. My squad are all busy with the others, outnumbered, and besides, part of me wants this to be my fight. I always liked things to be simple even when I was losing.

But things are never that simple, and just as well for me. The cat makes a go for my throat, and we meet teeth to teeth. His eyes are mad with rage and righteousness, and I wonder if his master is telling him *Good Kitty* every time he snaps his jaws shut or whether that does not matter for cats.

A shot strikes him in the side, not enough to go through his own armour but it throws him off me. The cat yowls around, looking for the new enemy. It is Sellars with one of the guards' big guns. In the half-second before the cat kills her, the scout dragon unit is at him, swarming up his side and driving in poisoned teeth. I am signalling Sellars to get back but she is ignoring me. The bulk of her attention is elsewhere.

The cat throws our dragon across the room and lunges at Sellars. I cannot get in the way quick enough, but Sellars explodes with black, buzzing bodies.

Bees' channel: *Integrity 31% Multiple faults detected operational swarm lifespan limited hello Rex hello hello buy me time I need to work here kk?*

The cat rears back when Bees reactivates and that gives me the chance to grab him about the head and try to break him. He is a good model. He is a better model than me. I do not think he was made here but he has been slaved to their hierarchy. I want to be able to save him but I am not even sure I can kill him right now. His claws are in me, tearing me up. I try to throw him again but he turns in my grip like an eel and then his jaws close on my head, teeth punching in hard in a flash of pain and I am I am I am too old for this I hurt I hurt I think of Dragon signalling his death after they shot the words out of him I think of Bees saying goodbye I wish I had the chance to speak to Honey again I wish I understood just a little more of what was going on or what will happen next I restore functionality routing around the damage and I am back in control. I am not out of the fight yet. Where am I? What is going on?

I have his arm clasped in my jaws, and even if I am an older model my bite is stronger than his bones. His teeth are at my face. One eye is offline. I feel fangs grinding at my skull. I have to shut down all the damage reports because they are all I can see and then he bites down deeper and again jolt and flash inside my skull until until the memories come loose and I am thinking of Retorna but not the fighting just the times between when I was in the sun and had no master and no war and Doctor de Sejos would talk about the good dogs her family had once and and and I was a good dog wasn't I always tried to be a good dog was all I wanted to be.

Sellars' channel: *Rex, you need to fire now!*

My emergency channel: *Weapons mounts damaged; weapon firing disabled.*

Sellars' channel: *Just fire the goddamn gun Rex now! Please, Rex!*

I taste blood. I smell cat. I remember how it was to have a Master. Would all this pain and damage control mean more to me if I had a Master now, to tell me I was doing the right thing? When I die, will I have been Good? There is nobody left who can tell me.

Bees' channel: *Overriding overriding overriding.* Her units bounce and spatter about us, weaving like drunk things as she fights the lab systems.

My remaining Big Dog sends me a barrage of outraged errors as its safeties are stripped away. When I fire, it no longer feels like part of me, just a weapon on a broken mount that hangs off my body. Sellars is holding it, though: her whole body cradled to steady it against where the cat's head meets its neck. The firing of the Big Dog almost decapitates the cat. It leaves broken teeth in my skull.

The fighting finishes. I try to oversee this but am unable to coordinate all the feeds from my squad because of all the feeds coming from my memories. I cannot stop them. They are more *me* than what is going on around them. I can only fight to stay atop them and give my final order. Command passes to my second, a dog called Garm. Garm is a good soldier. He will give good orders. Good Dog, Garm, Good Dog.

Sellars is trying to help. I feel her linking with my systems, fighting with them for control. But it is not my systems that have gone wrong, Sellars, it is the other parts of me, the parts that are organic me and not machine. I can feel it hurts but I have turned off most of that. It didn't seem to be doing anything useful any more.

Bees' channel: *System access.* She doesn't mean me. She means the factory.

My channel: *What do you have?* I can still concentrate on one thing at a time. It is only the big picture where everything breaks apart. My sensory data is not feeding to my brain properly. Thoughts are all I have left. My focus is like a boat that is a bundle of sticks shaken out to become a bat's wing, and it bobs and scuds upon my sea of memories.

Sellars' channel: *I'm trying to stabilise you, Rex. You need to stop trying to move.*

I tell her I didn't think I was. Parts of my system have been severed. Reflexive movements repeat and repeat. Parts of my body are still trying to fight. Sellars and I work on stilling them.

My channel: *Bees, report.* I am still here, inside this dead-weight head. I feel that I am thinking very clearly now as though I am in the eye of the memory storm.

Bees is not reporting, though her channel is live. Sellars is not reporting. Eventually I have to go and find it out for myself, linking to the enemy systems that Bees has laid bare. I want to know what has happened here.

Bees has found out about the humans, the scientists and technicians working to create Bioforms here, the guards who stood and fought and died. They are augmented. They have been fitted with hierarchies and chips, just like we were. They wanted to run but the hierarchies told them they had to work, and so they worked even when we were fighting amongst them. Even when we were killing them with the edges of our battle.

This is new, but perhaps it should not surprise me. Even as HumOS and Honey have fought to free us and make us free like humans, someone out there was thinking that their world would be better if they could make humans slaves like Bioforms: slaves even inside the mind. All those workers were still themselves, but every time they tried to do something different their feedback chips told them Bad Human and made them feel bad, and when their hierarchy chip gave them orders they had to obey, just as once I had to obey. Technology is not Good Tech or Bad Tech. It is the Master who is guilty for what it does.

My headware is stable now I think, thanks to Sellars and my own diagnostic systems. My body is less so. I sort through damage control and see that I may not make it. I ask Garm for sitrep and he tells me that active resistance is being driven back through the factory building. Our rat and dragon have followed Bees into the system and prevented it from wiping data, so that the evidence cannot be simply made to disappear. Major Amraj is on his way but mopping up the last of the resistance. Garm has sent some of our squad to reinforce him.

My channel: *Who is at the top of their hierarchy?* I can no longer speak with my voice. My channel is all I have.

Bees' channel: *Working on it.*

When I hear him I know my systems are failing me again. It is an old memory come back, and one I do not want, even though a little part of me still wants it after all this time.

Hello, Rex.

It is Master's channel. This is why Honey sent for me. She must have known this was here, but she didn't tell me. If she had told me I would not have come. Or is he here? Or is it just my memories of when he was with me and I didn't have to make choices.

Hello, Rex, says Master, and I know he is drowned and I am angry and I fear and that little part of me is jumping up and happy because Master is here again.

46

FROM *THE BEASTS WITHIN*
BY MARIA HELLENE

CHAPTER TWENTY-ONE: THE DRAGONS OF MARS

In two years' time the first manned mission to Mars should launch, if all goes to plan. Eleven cold months spent falling away from the only planet they have ever known, and then the crew will spend two years laying the groundwork for a permanent manned base. Theoretically, by the time they return, they will have set in motion a process that will result in the next mission finding a self-sustaining home ready for them, food, oxygen and all. And, like that book, they will have left one of their number behind.

The crew is in training at the time of writing. Major Terri Heinbecker has command, but the media darling is definitely Felice, the cat Bioform. Everyone loves the videos of Felice on the space station, bounding about with perfect grace in zero gravity, the world's first Bioform astronaut. Felice will handle the initial outside work to the major's directions. And some Bioforms and Bioform activists complain that this is how it always is: the Bioforms do the worst jobs, the most dangerous jobs. But Felice has gone on record herself to ask how being the first earth-born person to set foot on Mars could be counted a *worst* anything?

There are three others in the crew who will sleep their way to Mars. Two are dragon models. They are quick and capable: slender and flexible models able to work well in enclosed spaces. Moreover, they are cold-blooded, and can shut down most of their metabolic activity when not active, saving oxygen and calories. They can freeze, even, and still retain personality and functionality when thawed out. The Mars operation will proceed in a series of stages, as the automatics and the fifth crew member establish various perimeters. Having two of the crew who can simply stop eating and slow their breathing almost to nothing in between busy times is a huge saving on what the mission needs to take along. Unlike Felice, though, they are not the poster children for inhabited Mars. Humans are still some-what leery of a reptile face, even when it is seen through the dome of a spacesuit. They look too much like alien invaders from the old, old movies.

Bees will be the fifth member of the crew, or some of Bees. Hers is a suicide mission of sorts. When the lander returns to its orbiter, when the orbiter returns to Earth, they will leave a unit of Bees behind, with a hatching rack and a variety of body units. Some of those bodies can freeze, some can shrug off radiation or survive prolonged periods without oxygen. Some are fully vacuum-proof: they could be shot at the moons of Jupiter, say, survive re-entry and then begin work constructing a base with what they found. Sci-entists have been busy making nightmare hybrid insects for Bees to be. She will be bee and ant, fruit fly and beetle and tardigrade, all mixed together for the best traits of each. She is also not the poster child for the mission, though she will do more work than anyone.

Bees will keep working, turning their foundations into a home, setting up computer systems, directing robots, spreading solar cells across the Martian landscape and talking to us here on Earth. For years, Bees will be the voice of Mars, and Mars will belong to the insects.

Long before the next Mars mission arrives – with a cargo of human and Bioform settlers planning to make Mars their home – Bees will have hatched out her last body and died, the first martyr of Mars.

I have seen the plans for the settlers. By then, we think, people will be less leery of human enhancement. For astronauts planning to live the rest of their lives on a hostile red planet, it makes sense to give them every advantage. None of them will be able to walk unaided in the thin, reductive atmosphere, but there are a hundred little tweaks to Earth physiology that can blunt the effects of an accident, conserve resources. An astronaut's augmentations from necessity will pave the way for widespread human augmentation from choice. There are still fierce pressure groups shouting about letting go of humanity, but they are the same groups who cry that Bioforms are less than human. One day the world will be ready to accept that humanity, just as it is not constrained by skin colour, gender or nation, is not a condition penned into any one shape.

47

REX

Hello, Rex.

The little boat that is my mind is almost sunk. I hear him in my head just like before. I cannot control whether I am happy or angry or sad or frightened. Around me, Sellars and Bees work. They cannot hear him. He must be just for me.

My channel: *Master.* I cannot just call him his human name.

Master's channel: *Rex, Rex, what happened? Where did we go wrong, boy?*

I want to tell him about Hart and Retorna and the court and the Pound. I want to tell him all the UN reports I read about what happened in Campeche. I could track myself and Master's pack through those reports. *Atrocities,* they said. *War crimes.* And they were my crimes because I did what Master said. The humans do not accept that as an excuse for human soldiers, but they do for Bioforms because we had hierarchies. But I do not know, now. I lie here and die slowly, and do not know if there was more that I could have done to blunt Master's teeth in Campeche.

And is that why they will fit humans with hierarchies? So that excuse will serve for them as well?

Come on, Rex, let me see you. I'm just in the next room.

I think about the superior Bioforms here, the Multiform packs, and the way they were deployed. Of course it is Master. He survived the Pound and he went back to what he always did. He went back to the kennels and got some new dogs.

My channel: *What is in the next room?*

Sellars' channel: *What next room, Rex?*

I try to get a sense of where Master means, and the information is there available to me when I reach for it. I cannot quite understand what it means and so I share it with Sellars.

Master's channel: *Show me what happened, Rex. Were you there?*

I do not understand.

Master's channel: *Show me the end.*

I cannot show him; my wild memories will not be compressed into a format fit for sending. But I can tell him. I let those last moments in the Pound wash over me, as the waters washed over him. I live them again, and a separate part of me narrates them for him. I tell him what he lived through from my point of view.

Master's channel: *Fuck you, Rex.* But he does not seem angry. *You killed me?*

I am confused.

Sellars' channel: *This is their main computer core, I think. There's no "room" there.*

Honey's channel: (the transmission is patchy, beamed in from Honey's location on the US mainland): *Rex, what is your situation?*

My channel: *Master is here, Honey. You knew.*

Honey's channel: *There was a possibility from data received concerning the Morrow project—*

My channel: *You didn't tell me.*

Honey's channel: *I was not sure how you would react*. And that hurts as much as the memories because Honey should know me better than anyone, but then she says, *But if it was true, nobody but you should make the choice*.

Master's channel: *You killed me. I thought I was here, somewhere. But I'm dead*.

I pass what he says to Honey and Sellars because I do not understand.

Sellars' channel: *Rex, Jonas Murray is not here, but there were transmissions from his headware during your last encounter with him. We'd theorised that he had set himself up to save data, perhaps his memories, but I think he signed on for some sort of personality backup. It's theoretically possible, but we didn't think any facility was—*

Master's channel: *I can hear you*.

Sellars says no more. I can smell she is frightened.

Honey's channel: *Murray?*

Master's channel: *Hello, Honey*.

Honey concurs with me that this explains the character of the defence. She explains that what I am speaking with must be an imperfect copy of Master within a computer.

Sellars' channel: *So, you're heading the hierarchy. Of course you are*. She and Master never got on, I remember, probably because he kept killing her. Again the memories rise up and threaten to overwhelm me, but then Bees breaks in.

Bees' channel: *No no not the head of the hierarchy just within the hierarchy. Honey, I am sending you the full organisational plan here*.

And I think of that: the Moray of Campeche is no longer Master here, but just another slave like all these humans, like all these Bioforms they have made us fight and kill. I think of

him in his computer, swimming back and forth like the fish
Hart named him for, battering himself against the walls of
his tank.

Honey's channel: *This is bad. UNAT need to know this.
We need to do something about this. We cannot have hierarchies coming back into use, not for anyone.*

My channel: *Who is Master of the hierarchy here?*

Honey tells me, and then she has to tell me again in a
simpler way because I do not understand. She says that there
is a kind of artificial entity that humans have lived alongside for over a century. Unlike us, humans gave these entities
rights immediately, They let them own property even when
they were not happy about other humans owning property,
and human courts recognised them as beings distinct from
the men who made them.

The master of the Morrow labs' hierarchy is Morrow Incorporated. That is what everyone must obey: not a director or
a shareholder or officer, but the entity itself. That is how they
set it up, so that no human names would be associated with
what was done here. And I know that corporations are good
and useful things: every Bioform ever made was built by one.
But they are good servants. They can only be bad masters.
What is it that these scientists and guards and the Moray have
been made slaves to? It is an entity without an intelligence,
without the ability to choose between right and wrong.

Master is not my master. Master is not even his own master.

I lie there and feel myself die a little. I say, *Master.*

Master's channel: *Hello, Rex.* It is just the same way he
said it before. I think of him asking me what I happened. His
final upload must have been before he went into the river. I
ask him, *What do you remember?*

Master's channel: *I remember you killing me, Rex*. But he doesn't, so I ask him about Campeche, about the Human Rights court. At the same time I listen to Honey, Sellars and the rat scout argue about what the Morrow system is doing. They are downloading information from it for use as evidence, but it is fighting them and doing something else. Bees tries to help but her swarm integrity is damaged, the units and the connectivity between them. This part of her is failing.

The first human scientist falls over. I think it is shock or perhaps he was wounded in the fight. I am listening to my Master's voice.

Honey's channel: *No, wait, what's it doing now? It's trying to upload the Murray construct.*

Sellars' channel: *I'm blocking it, but it keeps trying to get information past me. What else is it doing?*

Master's reminiscences are slowing. He is sounding uncertain. More than half of what he says comes out as news reports or Wiki entries of the Campeche campaign, word for word. Sometimes he refers to himself as "he", not "I". *The Murray construct*, Honey said, and yet there is something there. The techs at Morrow built well enough that there is just enough of him there to know how little of him is there.

There is a sudden babble of comms between the squad, Honey's remote link and Sellars. The scientists are dropping one by one: not dying, but shutting down until they have no more brain activity than a coma patient. It is Morrow's last attempt to cover itself. It is sending a kill command through the hierarchy.

Master and I listen as they fight it. Garm's squad are evacuating everyone, but the system is spread through the building and constantly tries to shut down its compromised assets,

electronic or human or Bioform. There were humans somewhere who gave Morrow Incorporated its priorities, but they
created a monster.

Master's channel: *Rex, boy, what have they done to me?*

Being free means the responsibility to make the right
choice. I say, *Destroy it.*

Honey's channel: *Rex, that's not wise—*

My channel: *Finish the evacuation. Get everyone out.
Destroy the facility and the computer.*

Honey's channel: *Rex, we can't.*

My channel: *It cannot keep doing this if it is destroyed.*

Honey's channel: *Rex, it's not that simple.*

My channel: *We have explosives. Set them and give me
the trigger code.* I am not leader any more but I talk to Garm
and he is willing to trust my judgement even though I am so
damaged.

Sellars' channel: *Rex, this is all around us and we can't
move you. We need to get medical help in.*

I consult with my damage control system. It lets the pain in
and for a moment I lose myself entirely and broadcast what I
feel to everyone there. My systems tell me how much blood I
have lost and what organs are failing, and how much damage
has been done to my brain and neurosystems.

Sellars' channel: *Fuck. Jesus. Rex…*

Honey's channel: (her channel is open and I think she
wants to say something but she does not)

Master's channel: *Rex.*

My channel: *Yes.*

Master's channel: *You'll do it, even with me in the room
next door?*

My channel: *Yes.*

Master's channel: *Then do it. I don't want to go on as a slave.*

I cling on while Garm and his squad set the explosives. The soldiers come to see me before evacuating, each one of them stopping by me. I tell them Good Dog, Good Dragon, Good Rat. I tell them I am proud. Major Amraj is there too. I tell him Good Man and he says, *Farewell, General.* Sellars and Bees are downloading data from the Morrow system and sending it to Honey, for use against those who made this place, and the entity that they made their master. I have a vision of tomorrow's war, between people who have made themselves the slaves of entities that only exist in the heads of men, and people who want to be free. I hope I am wrong.

Sellars is done. She does not want to go but I show her my diagnostics so she can see I am a lost cause. My body is cooling now. Only the headware is keeping my thoughts moving, and I can feel them growing slow.

Garm confirms everything is set. He and Major Amraj's people have evacuated the factory.

Bees' channel: *I am with you, Rex.*

Everything is happening in brief moments between darknesses, like a stone skipping over the waters. I realise I have lost time, invisible gaps in my experience I can only guess at because before there were others here, and now there is just me and Bees. Bees shows me her swarm diagnostics. The EMP attack caused considerable damage and these units of hers are dying. She has downloaded her experiences to other colony hubs but this failing swarm has elected to stay with me.

We have come a long way, Bees and I.

I turn off the pain. I set the timer. I make my farewells.

Then I open the doors that have been keeping my memories back and let them wash over me, all the faces, all the moments, let them come as they will. So many faces, so many fights. And wasn't it when I wasn't fighting that the world was hardest. I was made to be a weapon but I have lived a life. I was born an animal, they made me into a soldier and treated me as a thing. Now I die as myself and they call me a general. Servant and slave, leader and follower, I tell myself I have been a Good Dog. Nobody else can decide that for me.

Bees says goodbye. The timer ticks. Some numbers only go down.

48

HUMOS' EPILOGUE

When UNAT released what it found on the Morrow island the legal war began. Morrow itself was part of a vastly complex global structure of shares and part-ownership. It was impossible to find any living thing to take responsibility for what had been done on that island – both the illegal Bioform manufacture and the slavery of the human employees. The money trail was equally Byzantine, the considerable earnings from Bioform sales running into the cracks of the global economy like water into the earth, to emerge refreshed and clean somewhere, half a world away.

And yet Morrow itself, that nebulous legal construct, was the lord and master of all those men and women's minds. They were augmented to be loyal and serve that absent tyrant.

Just how far this particular ideology had been developed could be seen by the remarkable number of lawyers, lobbyists and think tanks which spontaneously suggested that there was nothing unlawful or even morally wrong in such a practice. After all, employees had a duty of fidelity to their employers, and many working in sensitive positions signed punitive contracts to ensure their loyalty and discretion. Installing a hierarchy to guarantee that loyalty was, they argued, only the next logical step. It should never have been made illegal for Bioforms, and it was not illegal for humans.

That much was true, it was not. Nobody had ever thought about the necessity for such legislation when the future of Rex and his fellows was being debated. They were just animals, after all.

Watching select demographics of politicians all over the globe jump to support such a motion was fascinating, in the same way that watching disease proliferate under the microscope is fascinating. The battle lines have been drawn for the battle over people's mastery of their own most intimate selves.

I think we will win, for now. The assault on the island of Morrow Inc. blew the lid off the business too soon, forcing a desperate struggle now rather than a general shifting of geopolitics over a decade. Probably they would have started with the re-imposition of hierarchies on Bioforms like Rex, taking some appropriate newsworthy incident and whipping people into a terror of Bioforms just as they used to do with various other scapegoats in the past. After all, we (meaning they) could still reap all the rewards of Bioform labour while denying them personhood, and on that front it doesn't matter how useful I show Bioforms to be. Slaves are always useful or why have slavery? They would come for the Bioforms, and nobody would complain because they were not a Bioform. And then there would be other categories, culled from the wider population. Hierarchies to cure purported deviancies and mental illnesses; hierarchies for every convicted felon, no matter how spurious the crime or uncertain the conviction. And in the end everyone would be a slave – to a government, to a nation, to a corporation, to a god. Because Morrow showed that you can put a thing at the top of the hierarchy whether or not you think it is real.

I have not revealed myself to the world in all my many forms, not yet. Five years ago I would have told you that by now we would all be out in the open, but public opinion is whipped back and forth, and I stay in the shadows wondering if Morrow was the sole holder of the photocopied mind of Jonas Murray, or whether they were just leasing it from some unknown other. He knew too much about me, and my electronic agents search daily for any sign of his continued existence. Somewhere in the digital reefs, I fear, the Moray may still be lurking.

Perhaps in five more years we will have found that elusive trajectory towards a future where it does not matter what shape you are, what augmentations you have, whether you are human or dog or an intelligence spread across a swarm. Or perhaps in five more years they will declare war on all Bioforms and I will hide my surviving bodies across the world and weep to see my former allies burn. But I have cause to hope such things will not come to pass. They are putting up a memorial to Rex at UNAT HQ. There was a funeral, well attended, and not just by the usual suspects. Dying was his last service to his fellows; people who might cross the street to avoid a live Bioform could still mumble platitudes about the virtues of a dead one. His death, and the resulting Morrow blow-up, were public enough that he might just have secured the future for all of us.

And so tonight I will raise a glass to Rex, in bars all across the world, and Honey will drink mead in her laboratory, and Bees will make honey in her hives. There will be toasts in Spanish in Retorna, and Keram John Aslan will drink coffee in his big office and remember the case that made his career. Others too, some humans, and Bioforms of every trade and species, they'll say his name and understand a little of who he was and what he meant. And perhaps it will be enough to tip the scales if they simply remember that he was a Good Dog.

And so I vacate the stage at last, because at heart I/we will always be more of the backstage type, fit for working in the shadows, wardrobe mistress and stage manager to the dramas of others. But I will never have another leading man like Rex.